Mission

Paul Forrester-O'Neill

Hookline Books, Bookline & Thinker Ltd.

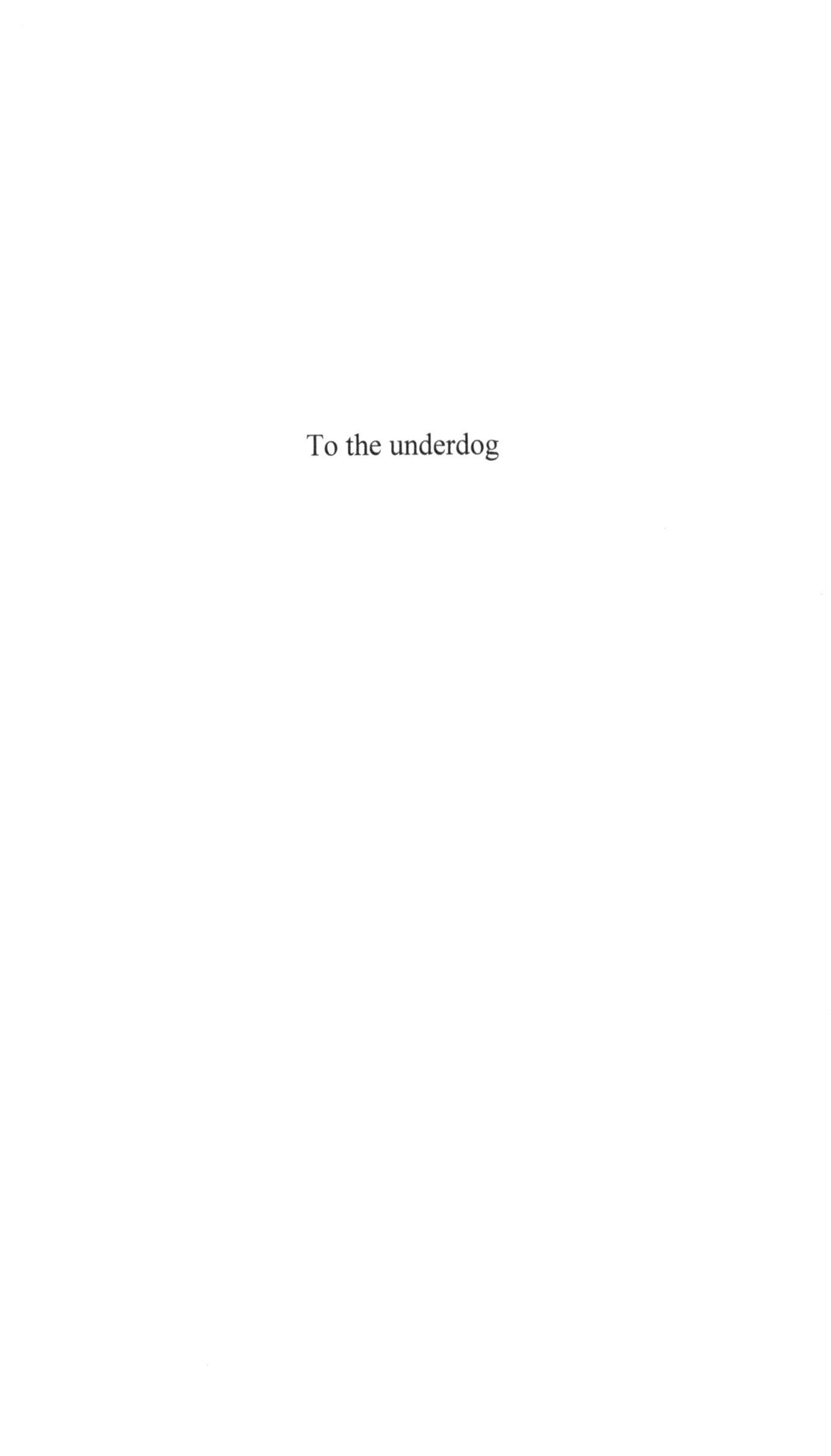

To the underdog

Copyright © 2021 by Paul Forrester-O'Neill

All rights reserved. No part of this publication may be reproduced, distributed or transmitted in any form or by any means, without prior written permission.

Hookline Books, Bookline & Thinker
www.hooklinebooks.com

Publisher's Note: This is a work of fiction. Names, characters, places, and incidents are a product of the author's imagination. Locales and public names are sometimes used for atmospheric purposes. Any resemblance to actual people, living or dead, or to businesses, companies, events, institutions, or locales is completely coincidental.

Mission by Paul Forrester-O'Neill. -- 1st ed.
Cover Design: More Visual Ltd
ISBN 9781838057930

Part One

It began on that Saturday morning in early February when John Cassidy sat in his room, his bag packed, his winter boots on, and waited for his father. Every once in a while, he'd stand up and walk over to the window and look out, not because his father was the best father a child could ever wish for, not because he was heroic or even ever-present, but because, in spite of the absence, he *was* still his father. Now, John, at five and a half years old, didn't know what that meant. He couldn't find words to describe it, but it was there all the same.

His mother, Margaret, and Dwayne, the usurper, stood in the kitchen downstairs. They looked up at the clock. They made drinks. They watched the snow begin to gather on the neighbours' rooftops. And, as time went on and one cup of coffee melded into the next, Margaret began to plot. At first, it was just a reaction to the lateness. It was plain and ordinary bile, a vent of frustration only. But then, stoked by the disdain that'd started in courtship and grown through pregnancy, childbirth and the few half-hearted years of rearing, it twisted. And, by the time Jack arrived two hours late, at 12.30, with no better excuse than he'd risen late, Margaret's plan had hardened into something altogether more brutal. She stood on the sidewalk; a coat draped around her shoulders. From somewhere close by came the sound of a wood-saw piercing the frosted air. The car window was halfway down.

"Where is he?"

"He's upstairs."

"Is he ready?"

"He doesn't want to go," she said.

"Because I'm late?"

"No," she said, the snowflakes starting to fall around her, "… ever. He doesn't want to see you anymore, Jack. He's had enough.

And he's got Dwayne now. Why would he want to suffer you for a day every few weeks when he's got a real man here?"

The wood-saw wheezed to a stop and, in the sudden, white silence, Jack didn't know what to say. He was tired. He was hungover. He'd had a week of fruitless travelling from one town to the next where one person after another had shaken their heads at his shirt boxes and now the situation that he dreaded the most, the crushing monthly exchange of his only child, had just got a thousand times worse.

"Can I speak to him?"

"There's no point. You'd make him feel uncomfortable. Just go and don't come back. Let him get on with his life. That's what he wants. That's what he said."

"He told you that?"

"Yes, he did."

"He said that?"

"Yes. Now go."

The neighbourhood was turning white. Driveways and roofs, lawns and sidewalks, the hoods and trunks of cars. Jack sat there for half an hour at least, the layers of snow forming on the windshield. The window stayed halfway down even though Margaret had turned and walked away after she'd said her piece. The side of his face was cold, his gloveless hands whitening on the wheel. Sometimes he looked over towards the house hoping to see his boy run out, across the snowy path and into the car, but he didn't. He saw no-one and nothing, because the three inhabitants of the Cassidy household, Margaret, John and new kid, Dwayne, were upstairs.

"I don't know the whole reason, honey," she said, kneeling in front of him as he sat on the bed, "he just said he didn't want to see you anymore. He said it wasn't working. He was going away and it would be a whole lot easier for him if you weren't around. That's what he said. He didn't explain."

John felt like he'd been punched hard in the stomach. He looked down at the winter boots, at his packed bag next to them on the floor. At just before one o'clock his father drove away from the house for the last time and two hours later, with the snow still falling, his bag still packed and his boots still on, he went downstairs.

*

By the time he'd reached his mid-teens John, his mother and Dwayne had moved house no less than four times. The theme of the moves was always hope. Hope for something better, something more solid, whether it was a job for Dwayne, a good neighbourhood or an increased quality of life. And why so many? Because the difference between their version of hope and their reality, in every single case, was always greater than they imagined.

Firstly, they moved out of the house where John'd grown up because, for his mother, it reminded her of Jack. And she didn't want that. She wanted somewhere she couldn't see or feel the presence of her shirt-salesman mistake, no matter that John looked like him, walked like him, and even ate like him. So, based on a job opportunity for Dwayne as an instructor in a fitness centre, they moved. But Margaret didn't like it. Margaret didn't like the morning birdsong, or the church bells, or the way the quiet seeped into the house. Margaret got bored and when Margaret got bored, she drank. And when Margaret drank it was to escape whatever reality she found herself in. So, they moved again, to a neighbourhood thirty miles away which meant that Dwayne had to get up an hour earlier just to get to work and where, in the larger bedroom that got the sun in the morning but the glue factory at night, they tried for a child of their own. But it didn't work out, and when they went to find out why it was, they discovered that Dwayne, for all his fitness regimes, was firing blanks. The news changed them. Margaret started to drink again and Dwayne's toned façade began to creak under the strain of his impotence. So, they moved again. And then again. And when John was just short of his sixteenth birthday, they were living in a small suburban house on the edge of an industrial city out east.

For Dwayne, with too many hours to fill and not enough things to fill them with, John was only ever Jack's son and until that day in the doctor's surgery, he treated him as if he was an attachment only, a piece of machinery that served little to no purpose. But that afternoon changed everything. From then on, instead of ignoring the boy the way he had, Dwayne started to drag him into the wake of his own resentment. He criticised him. For everything. The way he looked, the way he spoke, the friends he had, all kinds. By the time they'd been in that small suburban house for a year, baiting John was a sport.

On John's sixteenth birthday, there was a party in the house. As it was August, it was hot and so the party spilled out into the garden. There were a good thirty guests, including a handful of school friends, neighbours and some of Dwayne's work colleagues. After the first gifts had been handed out, the fake-marble chess set, the local history book, the T-shirts, it was Dwayne's turn.

He walked slowly towards John, a thin pall of barbecue smoke behind him and, with a smile that to everyone else there spoke of kindness and the selfless nurturing of another man's child, handed him a box. Inside the box, wrapped in tissue paper and smelling deliciously of every gym he'd ever walked into, was a pair of nut-brown boxing gloves. Dwayne undid the laces, squeezed the leather into his fingers and suggested there was little point in having a pair of man-sized gloves unless they were tried out, properly. John knew what was coming.

A makeshift ring was set up. Towels were fetched, stools brought out from the kitchen and one of Margaret's garish gold belts was offered up as the prize. The MC, a car salesman neighbour, announced the two contestants who nodded they understood the rules, removed their bathrobes and stood face to face in the middle of the garden in shorts. Now, even though Dwayne was at least seventy pounds heavier, though he was bedecked with ranges of body-hair and he himself had a visible rib cage that looked like one of his collected fossil prints on a chalk-white surface, John was prepared.

The first round he ran. His guard held abnormally high, he watched through the gap between his forearms and gloves as Dwayne pursued him, shoulders hunched, and as the glass was chinked for the end of the first round of three and the crowd laughed and cheered; not one punch had been landed and John's gloves were as shiny and as squeaky as the day they were bought. He sat on the stool and drank water. His coach, a bespectacled chemistry student called Kyle, dabbed the beads of sweat from his face with one of the towels and offered what he considered to be sound, logical advice into John's ear: "You can run, buddy, but you can't hide."

The second round was the same. John ducked and dodged and Dwayne's pursuit was reduced to a turning of the upper body to whichever direction the boy was running in. He got close to him once, just as the timekeeper was checking his watch. He moved forward and, at the very point that he was about to penetrate the guard, John closed his eyes and threw himself forward onto his chest and held on as tight as he could. The timekeeper picked up the glass in one hand and the fork in the other, Kyle grabbed the towel and the onlookers smiled. This was, wasn't it, the stepson holding onto the man who'd stepped up to the plate? This was a big thank you, not only for the birthday present that he quite patently didn't want to sully, but for the party, for the whole day, for everything. They cheered at the end of the round as both man and boy separated themselves with an audible click of sweat and they cheered again as the two fighters emerged for the third and final round with not a single mark on the judges' scorecard.

After a minute of the third, though, with a calmness that belied the fact that he'd been running around his garden half-naked for the last seven minutes, John stopped. His guard dropped. He looked at Dwayne, Dwayne looked back, and for that moment, they understood each other clearly. They understood the dislike, the disdain and the monumental lack of connection between them. John moved a step closer. He took a breath in and, with the audience keening in and the sunlight beating down, he began to pummel into his opponent.

He pounded into the terrain of his chest and the paunch of his belly for what seemed like a whole minute until that point where he felt Dwayne ease himself away. He was ready.

The blow hurt less than he imagined. Yes, his head did rock back with a jolt that made the back of his neck jar up into his skull. And his nose, both flesh and bone, did feel like it had been sliced and spread like a banana split. But he knew it would happen. And it *was* only pain.

As he lay there on the ground looking up at the sky, he could sense the blood sliding across his cheeks and down into his mouth. He could feel his hands ringing inside the casing of the gloves and, as faces loomed goofily over him, partially blocking out the sunlight, as his mother never moved from the door of the house, cradling a tumbler of something clear in both hands and Kyle the corner-man draped a dampened towel over his nose and mouth, his frontal lobe, that storage area of so many of his better chess moves, began to pound like a piston. But he was calm. And, through the pain, through the sense of jagged bone somewhere below his eyes and above his mouth, the invaluable lesson was slowly seeping and trickling into him; that expectant pain can do more damage than actual pain, so that at just sixteen years of age he learned something that would stay with him – the ability to detach himself.

*

They moved again after the fight. There were patterns by then. From the house where they'd tried and failed to have their own children onwards, they'd gone gradually smaller. They'd also gone further east, more industrial, and Dwayne's working hours had got fewer and fewer. This time he worked weekends only as a doorman in a downtown bar. The rest of the time he either spent drifting through the TV noise of the house looking for projects or down at the gym. When he was home, he checked out the mechanics of the car, or the aerial on the roof, the guttering, the tiling, or the masonry. And when he was doing the twisting and the tapping and the tweaking, he was thinking about anything that existed outside of Margaret and the old sofa he'd find her in when he got home from the bar, head at an angle, the skin on her sallow face as though dragged by gravity and pinned.

One of the first things John did after they'd moved was to make peace with Dwayne. He apologised. He was contrite. It'd been hard, he said, to accept another man into his life. He hadn't given Dwayne enough of a chance. He'd judged him. He would speak to him more respectfully. He asked if he could go with him to the gym, to help him fix things around the house and to eat with him when his mother was passed out on Prozac and peppermint gin.

Over those first few weeks his connection with Dwayne seemed to blossom. In fact, John told him one morning, as they ran through those neighbourhood streets tinged with the russets and golds of fall, that he'd actually helped him; that, in life, he realised, you get what you deserve, and that that short, counter-attacking uppercut that'd disfigure his nose for the rest of his life had shown him a way of becoming a young man who could deal with things. It'd taught him a lesson, he said. And for that, he was grateful.

They had similar regimes; running and rowing machines, followed by weights, upper body work, and punch-bag. An hour-and-a-half altogether. Then the warm-down, the energy drinks from the vending machine and the mile run home. In a move suggested by John and picked up readily enough by Dwayne, they got into the world of proteins and supplements, some purchased by recognised suppliers, some not, some with listed ingredients, others not so much. Each day, morning and evening, they'd sit at the breakfast table and open up those packages of powders and pills that'd come in the mailbox. Dwayne'd sort out the tablets and John'd make up the drinks. And then, with Margaret either asleep or blue-lit from the TV, they'd put those cocktails away.

By early November, John had bulked up by almost twenty pounds. He looked like a different kid from the one who'd celebrated his sixteenth birthday with a broken nose and a visible rib cage.

Mainly it was the upper body, but the arms and legs too had grown more muscular and, if you looked closely enough and weren't distracted by the general adornment of bulk, you'd notice the eyes: where once was that adolescent lack of conviction, that teenage roam that went nowhere, there was purpose and direction and, in a matter of weeks, he began to walk those neighbourhood streets not like the freshman he was, but as if he'd lived there all his life. Some nights he just walked. Some nights he stood on the bridge and watched the traffic. And, on those weekend nights, he hung around the line of downtown bars. He found a street corner where he could stand and watch without being seen. And watch he did.

He watched the neon signs splash the sidewalks, the cigarette smoke, the steam of the hydrants, the whole thrum and buzz of the place. But essentially, he watched Dwayne. He watched him rooted to his spot by the door, chewing gum, cling-filmed in black. He watched his assertion, his decisiveness quick and economic when it came, and how some nights when the bar had closed, he walked over the disused lot to his car with one of those many sleek girls clinging to him like a mollusc to a rock. He'd see the back door open and close, his hands clawing at the curve of the shells. Then he'd see no more.

John could, at any point, have done a number of things. He could've just told his mother about the girls, for one. He could've taken photographs, shown them to her and watched as her face melted even more than it had already. That would've been easy. It would've been chicken-feed. Or, he could've hit him, an eye for an eye, a tooth for a tooth, a nose for a nose. He could've stolen from him, cut up his clothes, sabotaged his car, his ladders, his weights. He could've found anything from the boxing match onwards. But he didn't. Instead, he chose something that used that frontal lobe of his, something subtle and nuanced and that fucked up Dwayne in a way he could get to see, every day.

Buying the amphetamine sulphate was easy. You take some money from your neglectful, forgetful mother's purse and stand on one of those street corners long enough someone'll come along and find you. The painstaking part, the part that needed the most care and attention, that took place in those early hours when Dwayne wasn't there, was getting it into the individual supplement drinks, lining up Dwayne's containers next to his own and making sure they didn't get mixed up. Then, when the morning came and the evening came and Dwayne had set out the protein pills on the table, they took their drinks together, as was their routine, and Dwayne and his chemical descent was none the wiser.

Around Thanksgiving things started to get a little different. Or, should that be that Dwayne started to get a little different. For one thing, when they got to the gym he would concentrate almost entirely on the punch-bag, beating into it, his teeth bared, his eyes tight shut, an occasional deep growl coming from somewhere inside of him. The run home, too, was faster, the words between them fewer. There was a violent incident outside the bar and a rumour that one snowy night in early December a young woman was seen running and screaming from his car on the lot.

He got edgy. He couldn't take a walk down the street or drive his car or go to the corner store without being edgy. He couldn't stay home without something, whether it was Margaret, the TV noise, the untidiness, making him unable to sit still and do regular things. The only time he found solace was at the gym, so he went more often, sometimes with John, but usually without, so that by mid-December he was there every day. He knew something was going on but he didn't know what. He couldn't explain it, not the edginess, not the surges of violence. He couldn't say why by seven o'clock on Christmas morning he had, with his bare hands alone, been the first in the neighbourhood to build a snowman; man-sized, hard-packed, carrots and coal. Then, at the request of some of the kids, built three more just the same in less than an hour. Or why on New Year's Day, while Margaret lay on the sofa, he'd ripped every sheet of wallpaper from the upstairs of the house. When he mentioned it to people, they suggested all kinds: too many pills, too much protein, not enough sex or fresh air, no father figure, no son, no best buddy, no therapist, no love. And some of them may've contained grains of truth in them somewhere. But none of them were the real reason.

By the time John left on that January night, with his packed bag and his winter boots, Dwayne was pacing the sidewalk outside the bar non-stop. His mouth was dry, his shoulders jerked and the first onset of chest pains were pressing down on his sternum like an anvil. He couldn't think straight. He'd lost weight. His heart rate had boosted, so too his blood pressure. He wanted sex all the time. Any kind, blowjobs, hand-jobs, anything. And still he couldn't figure any of it, even if he could've sat down long enough to try.

At eight o'clock the following morning, with the snow having coated most of the neighbourhood, Dwayne would walk downstairs and sit at the breakfast table. After less than five hours' sleep, his eyes would appear small and bloodshot and he would rub them incessantly. In the quiet of the day, he would listen out for John to come down so that they could take their proteins and drinks together. After almost an hour of waiting, with his teeth beginning to grind, he would stand, shuffle over to the refrigerator and the small kitchen cupboard and take his own pills and supplements. He would go upstairs then. He would wait outside the young man's room and, with his pupils dilating with the passing of each second, he'd look inside. The bed would be slept in but no longer warm, the pillow lacking indentation. The wardrobe door would be slightly ajar, with some things missing, some things moved. Dwayne didn't know. He couldn't think. Close to the window with the drapes still drawn, the boxing gloves hung on the wall, almost as shiny as the day they arrived.

*

To begin with, John drifted. He rode the freight trains. He slept wherever he found himself, in the rackety cars themselves, in barns, outbuildings or beach houses he broke into if they were empty. Sometimes he found work; mostly outdoors, fruit picking, or farm labour, mostly for money to live on alongside what he'd stolen from his mother's purse, but in those places where something to eat and somewhere to sleep was part of the payment, it was as much to fill the hours of the day, and for those days to fill his week, and the weeks to fill his months. And so on.

Sometimes he found somewhere and stayed longer. He found rooms in run-down neighbourhoods, or small, cheap apartments he shared often with vermin and bugs. He lived simply. He practised his chess moves, got to know most constellations and where and when to find them. He could remember the periodic table, the presidents, the states and, on a good day, the capitals, alphabetically. He could distinguish a male rat from a female, delineate birdsong, chronicle rust. He could, with his crooked snout, ascertain foodstuffs to a high level of precision. He collected an assortment of objects that might someday be of use to him, usually those small enough to keep in a pocket or a shoe. And he read, often for hours at a stretch, often through the night with the sounds of chaos all around him, gorging on one encyclopaedic page after another.

He was almost wordless, like an animal.

He headed south to the Florida sun, got work cleaning cars on beachfront forecourts, making them spotless inside and out. His hands smelled of cherry wax and damp leather, his clothes of industrial soap. He was, also, over a period of time, an assistant lifeguard, a croupier, an Everglades guide and, for a short time only, at a number of Disney or quasi-Disney locations whose noise, colour and show he grew to quietly despise, he was a hot, large-headed, roly-poly bundle of Mouse-, Duck-, or Dwarf-like jollity.

Until he moved again. This time across country, to California where work and places to stay were easy to find. He spent an entire winter in one empty beach house after another, never for longer than a week at a time and always leaving them as he found them, even down to washing the towels and sheets. He waited tables, tended a string of bars and clubs along the strips, and then one night, a quieter than usual Monday in one of the downtown places, he was offered permanent, if unusual, work from a silver-haired man in a black suit who sat at the counter.

"You don't give anything away, do you?" the man said, leaning in.

John looked at him, and raised, minutely, a single eyebrow.

"I've seen you," he said. "I've seen you work. Nothing you have is shown, nothing slips out. If there is anything there, and I'm assuming there is, then none of it is for public consumption, not what you think, not what you feel, not what you know. And I like that." He checked no-one was listening, lowered his voice to a purr. "How would you like to come and work for me? I've just got rid of someone for smiling too much. I need a Buster Keaton. Do you know Buster Keaton? Are you familiar with his modus operandi?"

John nodded, once, remembered the encyclopaedia page. He served another customer, then went back to the man whose long, slender fingers drummed on the counter.

"What's the work?" he said.

"My name is Mario. I'm a magician. And I need an assistant."

For John Cassidy and his lizard-like stillness, it was second nature. He became, comfortably, that unflappable, stony-faced assistant that Mario was looking for. After a probationary month of practice and rehearsal, the performances began, weekly certainly, sometimes daily and occasionally twice daily during which time, black-suited, white-shirted, bow-tied and wordless, he was, amongst other things, pinned by knives, spun on a wheel, mesmerised, and sawn in half.

They played up and down the strip mostly; bars, private gatherings, weddings and birthdays. He was the silent figure from whom Mario would remove a host of watches and coins, of necklaces, bracelets and keys and a myriad of other audience valuables. He was the storer of rabbits, doves and mice, the cache of floribundas, real or otherwise. And he didn't smile, didn't break. He never once gave anything away, not even the deep and quiet relish for the blindfold as it chicaned over his crooked nose with a slide of warm cloth.

After a couple of months, he moved into an annexe of Mario's house up in the hills. He ran errands for him, drove him around. He fixed things. He answered any fan mail, slipping the signed photographs inside the envelopes. He cooked for him, using his crooked snout for his mixtures and blends. Sometimes they'd have days together, they'd spend whole evenings in the house watching silent, black-and-white movies to see how people moved, how they communicated without speaking, how the audience knew what was happening without a word being spoken. They worked on moves, on stagecraft and blocking, on the perfectly executed mimes where meanings were gauged by gestures the other understood, like a language they had between them. They spent two Christmases together, New Year, Thanksgiving Days, and the four birthdays. *But* there was a stipulation. They were not to become friends. They were not to get to know each other, and on those Christmases and birthdays, they were not to give presents. Mario was insistent. "The act," he said, "will suffer. You are my assistant. That is what the audience believes. The spell is lost if they don't. It's called persuasion."

And that was how it worked, for two years. A professional relationship. They were not noticeably elder and junior, nor master and servant. They were neither companions nor confederates. But there was something John felt in the buzz of the magician's presence, in the sensation of trust he had as the knives flew towards him, that took him back to the feelings he had when his father was there, when he reached up for his hand or scampered alongside him, those feelings he could never put into words as a child of five years old.

That was until, one late summer day, without any word of warning, Mario perfected the ultimate act and disappeared, without trace. As if in a puff of clear, white smoke, he was gone. Gone from the house in the hills. Gone from the strips and the bars. Gone from the city itself. There was no letter, no explanation. The house was left the way it was. Nothing had been taken. The car was still in the garage. And the wheel and the knives and the menagerie of rabbits and doves and mice were untouched.

There were rumours of tax evasion, of sex scandals, Mafia links, illness, wagers, rivals, magic itself and even suicide, but whatever it was, John Cassidy, stony-faced and whey-toned, standing outside the annexe with some of its contents stuffed into his pockets, felt abandoned, again, felt that same punch to the gut he'd felt all those years ago.

He moved out of the annexe as soon as the place had been searched and foul-play discounted. He bummed around the city awhile. On the day he left he had the words *Restless* and *Fearless* tattooed on each shoulder blade and, without the stability that being rotated, dismembered and put back together again brought, he became random again.

His hearing was out, his sense of smell scrambled. Breaking into those beach houses got beyond him, in spite of the hatpins he'd acquired. The barns and outbuildings he slept in were riddled with animals he caught only glances of. Most of the time, day or night, he was a just a figure in the landscape, a shambling, shuffling shape with old boots, a packed bag and a peacoat, making his way from one place to the next against skies bellied daylong with snow and rain. The money he had, saved or stolen, he rarely used. He stitched it into the bag he carried, as if it was there for something other than living with.

As the months passed, so, given the long days and nights and the absence of Mario to wordlessly guide him, given the ache of that abandonment, he began increasingly to think of his father. Actually, he didn't *think* about his father. It was more that the thoughts that started to *happen* around the misty, half-remembered image of him, like where he was, where he'd been to, what he looked like and why did he leave him behind so easily, wouldn't go away. And neither would that curdle in his gut.

*

One evening in the mid-March of his twenty-fourth year, he was on the empty parking lot of an industrial park somewhere on the edge of a mid-eastern town. His face, arms and back were bruised where he'd been half-beaten and his own knuckles and fists were cut and skinned where he'd fought back. His pockets felt laden with watches and coins, with lockets and keys that rattled with each step he took. A light, brick-dusted rain started to fall. There was a phone booth on a street corner and he shuffled towards it. He gathered his coins. Outside a scrawny, three-legged dog sniffed at a dumpster. As he stood there, he wanted only for the blindfold to be pulled down over his eyes and for the world to go soft and dark and quiet.

"Mom," he said, "I need help."

His mother wheezed, and then spoke as if seamlessly trailing a conversation from somewhere beyond that seven-year absence.

"What the hell do I care?" she said. "What do I care what you need? I don't. And that's the truth. You put me where I am. You steal from me. You make my life a misery. You put a spoke in it the day you came out, you little bastard."

A car drove past the phone booth, slowed up a little.

"And what did you do to Dwayne? You fucked him up, that's what you did. I don't know how, but you did, and now they give him all kinds of names and lock him away and won't let him out because they say he's got too much shit in his system. I know Dwayne, and Dwayne never had too much shit in his system. So, whatever it is that you want, you won't get it from me. I don't have it. And if I did, you would be the last person I'd give it to. So why don't you try that old, dying father of yours? Why don't you try him? Did you know he'd got land up in the north-west? He never told me once he'd got land. And if he's got land, he's got money, so try him for whatever it is you want. Go and ask that fucking shirt-seller I wish I'd never met for it," she said, and wheezed again like a spent balloon.

John closed his eyes. He went back to that same winter's day when he was five years old. He got the snow and the swollen glisten of the sky. He got the winter boots, the packed bag at his feet. He got his hands on his knees and the sore, drying saltiness of his face and the crunch of the tyres through the padded whiteness. He got the faint smell of the coffee and the thought, loose-formed, but intact enough, that from those moments on, his life would never be the same.

*

He hung around the town for a few days, walking the neighbourhoods with the randomness of a dice-roll, not because he liked the place, or because of all the people he'd come across, worked with, slept with, shaken large, bloated hands with or been sawn in half by, the people of this town were kinder and showed him more understanding than anywhere else, but because he didn't know what else to do.

He tried to figure how such a young life had been cast into a wilderness from which he struggled to return, to figure why it was he didn't have enough warmth in his heart or how he'd driven Dwayne into that world of derangement with such calculation. And he tried, more than anything, with the haul of his packed bag and the rattle of chains and pins, to figure how he could even think of seeing, never mind speak to or share time with or be in the same room as, the man who'd left him behind, who'd walked out of his life on that winter's day almost twenty years before and left him to rot. And no, he didn't know he'd got land.

On the fourth day, when the reasons to stay had become as threadbare as his old, frayed laces, he started to walk out. And if the direction happened to be towards the north-west of the country, towards the foothills of the Cascade Mountains and the town of Mission, if that was where he was drawn, like a moth to a flame, then so be it.

*

Heading west across the north of the country you'd start to leave the towns and the cities behind. You'd forego the power plants and the car factories, the acreage of business parks, the urban and suburban neighbourhoods, the relentless noise and movement you might only notice had gone in the hush of dusk somewhere. You might start to notice that all the goods and the freight, the people and the cars were all going in the opposite direction and you'd sense, in the slow curve north, the lengthening hours of light and the broadening of sky and the starlit bowl of night so vast and open you felt like you were right there in it.

You'd catch the great patchworks of earth then, the squares of rich-red soil stitched next to those smaller shapes of Indian land upon which little had ever grown. And, strung onto those rough-edged sections of land, like velvet next to sackcloth, would be the miles and miles of prairie that would stretch as far as you could see. You'd make out the start of the low-lying hills, like lions' paws lounged across the land so that the single highway that the network of roads from the east had become, would move a long arc around them, sometimes rising, sometimes as flat as a pan base.

Sometimes the rains would come, blown in on stronger winds. The clouds would move in over the land like mobsters, smothering it suddenly in predatory shade. Hours of rain would be deposited, heavy to begin with, hardly visible through, veiling the corn and wheat-fields like the trawling of stained lace, hammering the land, pounding like fists on any fluted rooftop of any outbuilding, holding or barn. The old, dried riverbeds and creeks would start to run again, coursing clear or clay-brown under rook-black skies, scuttling in rivulets, loosening scree and wood until those hours would pass and the squalls of rain would ease and lighten and stop.

And when those hours had stopped, whether it was day-break, noon or dusk, or whether milky stars were blinking out in the darkness, you'd be further out. You'd be in places it was rare to travel to, places you wouldn't go to just for the sake of it. And the further out you were, towards the sandstone and granite foothills of the Cascades that stood between land and eventual sea, you'd have to have reasons to be there, you'd have a particular purpose in mind.

After three days of cars and trucks and station wagons, next to workmen in overalls and caps, to college kids, salesmen, off-duty firemen, medics and dogs, in no particular order, and to whom, if they ever asked him where he was heading and why, he said little in terms of direction and nothing in terms of reason, he took the last hundred miles by train. The closer he got to the town of Mission, the more his heart rate began to increase. The moisture lessened in his mouth and gathered instead on the palms of his hands. His synapses began to zing, the serotonin levels, the endorphins, the dopamine, all thrown into a mounting chaos. His gut swam and his vision blurred. By the time he got there, hungry, thirsty and tired, in the early evening of light rain, his system had more or less closed down. He became a heap, a sack, a bag of bones retching up little but strings of acid bile. He couldn't walk out of the station, which is how come he was on the floor of the waiting room when they found him, the packed bag as a pillow, the old coat not worn, but draped over him.

*

The old hatchback bumped its way over the unmade track that skewed from the end of the homesteads to the highway, its headlights jerking through the dusk. It took a right then, heading clockwise on the half-circle of road, running along the base of Rupture Hill and arcing south past the tended spread of the Mallender estate, the wooded girth of Blessings Point and the Indian burial grounds until it sidled up to the rail-tracks that made the same symmetrical curve from the prairies to the east.

It made the turn into the rutted side-road, the rove of its lights picking out diners in Sizzlin' Steve's steak-house, including, on that spring evening, amongst others, Ted Mallender, head of the Land Management Agency and the most influential man in Mission, his considerably younger wife, Lily, Ned Scarratt, Chief of Police, and Rita Mahoonie who sat in the corner with her friend Delilah with one eye on her rare to bleeding steak and the other on the two young law enforcement officers sitting with Ned.

The shacks of the migrant houses were single storey with asbestos roofs and walls no thicker than Rita's 8oz steak. Built as part of a scheme to attract extra workers to the town over fifty years ago, they had scarcely been touched since and so had the perennial look of temporary shelters for people made homeless by an elemental force rather than places to be proud of, to house decent furniture that could stand the test of winter and electrical goods that didn't zap the fuse-box at least twice a day.

Not only that but the shacks were but a frisbee's throw from the timber mill which buzzed and boomed and whose siren twice a day was louder than an air-raid warning and shook most things in the shacks that weren't pinned down. So, decades then of broken glass, smashed plates and ornamental keepsakes sent tumbling, not to mention tinnitus, fractured sleep and anything that could be damaged by the constant inhalations of dust. But, for Sophie Li, driver of the old hatchback with its backseat full of cleaning fluids, mop-heads and brushes, it was home. Inherited from her Oriental great-grandmother who, once upon a time, had worked at the laundry, she kept it as neat as she could on cleaners' wages and with a cleaner's eye for the enemies; dirt, dust and wayward food.

She unloaded the mop-heads and detergents, shook loose her jet-black hair with its hint of goose fat and bed linen and sat on the striped deckchair of her living room as the smell of steaming, root vegetables and rice drifted around the shacks. She lit a cigarette, closed her eyes and thought once again of the old man sitting at his kitchen table, fingering his deeds.

*

The timber mill siren had sounded already and a cluster of the workforce, including the new boy Jake Massey, had gone straight into Harry's bar across the bridge from the mill and five hours later the young Massey man with the short and chequered biography had talked himself into a night in the town's cooler. Not for the first time.

Born of a sizzled Vietnam vet and a slave of crystal meth who could no more hold onto him than they could a dutiful dog, he'd not had the best of starts. And, raised on the outskirts of Mission by a single aunt with a propensity for the tremors, he'd also received little in the form of guidance, giving him a radically short attention span, a desperation to please and a general absence of judgement. What he also had was a dogged persistence that made him difficult to refuse, so that even though he'd worked and fucked up on a regular basis from the age of sixteen, he would always appear like a tongue-wagging spaniel knocking on someone's door for work and that someone, knowing they were being foolish and sentimental, would always offer him something.

At the end of his first working week at the timber mill, he'd overstayed his welcome in Harry's bar again. He'd got bumptious and loud and instead of leaving when the other mill workers did, to fill those empty stomachs, he'd decided to stay and that lack of judgement had careened into a loss of self-control. It wasn't that he was a danger to others. He wasn't. No, those nights in the cooler were there to protect him, to prevent him from going home, drinking himself into a hazardous oblivion or falling out of a window he'd opened to smoke. And even though it happened four or five times a year at least, he was never charged, only told with that mixture of warning, advice and a hint of resignation by whichever Desk Sergeant was on duty, not to be so damned repetitive.

That Friday was no different. He was informed of his situation by the two young law enforcement officers smelling of aftershave and relish. His belongings were transferred into a transparent zipper bag and he was led down the stone steps into the cool vaults of the cells that had barely changed since the days of the panhandlers.

Within a minute, he was asleep, as per usual in his three-by-four-yard suite with the springy mattress and the blanket the colour of maize. And, within another minute, he was snoring like a piglet trapped in a squeeze-box. Back upstairs, the two officers played pinochle and talked about Rita and her friend Delilah while the Desk Sergeant, Frank Bellow, ironically a cousin of Jake's single aunt, studiously wrote up the night's events, including Jake and his 'exuberance', and, on the sheet next to him, the appearance of the ragged young man with the old peacoat down at the rail station, incapable of giving his own name and with no word to say on why he was there.

*

The following morning of a bright, spring day, with the crags of Rupture Hill veiled in mist, the town of Mission with its fifteen hundred souls, tucked neat into the crook of the flat lands and the granite bluffs, began to busy itself: The baker shovelled his breads, while Ike, the barber, sharpened his cutthroats. The chandler laid out his wares on the corner of the covered boardwalk and, over in Sylvie Buckle's Beautician's, Mrs Lily Mallender was having her weekly treatments and talking, with a curled, but beautifully shorn lip, about her husband's gastric entrapments to Rita Mahoonie whose eyebrows were being plucked to near extinction.

Jake, meantime, rearranged his belongings at the desk, trying both to lick moisture back into his lips and to manage the eyes that strained to open and whose lids felt like they'd been sandpapered by a bored child.

"So, listen," Frank was saying to him, leaning forward to deliver his periodic and pointless sermon. "Give yourself a break. Get your head down. Keep off the booze. Go home when the others go. Find yourself an interest. You get my point?"

"Who's the guy downstairs?"

"He's none of your business."

"He said my snoring was a fucking noise. Who is he?"

"No, Jake."

"I want to apologise."

"He's a guy they found asleep down at the railway station, turns up here with nothing to say as to why. No I.D. Vagrant. He's on the midday train back east. Or at least he'd better be."

Jake looked down into the last few dregs of the zipper bag.

"Where's the pool chalk?"

"There was no pool chalk."

"Is that all the money there was?"

"That's it."

The zipper bag lay empty on the desk.

"You got any spare cash, Frank? I'm clean out of milk."

"No, I haven't. Now go home."

"What kind of day is it?"

"Bright."

"Fuck." Jake blew on the bones on the backs of his hands.

"How old are you, Jake?"

"Twenty-two."

"Don't let's see you for a while, huh. Let's see if we can have ourselves a summer of love."

"Where's his zipper? The guy downstairs. He's got a zipper, right?"

"Leave. Go home. Learn some lessons."

"What's he got?"

"Jake."

"Few bits and bobs…Uncle Frank?"

"He's got a packed bag."

"How packed?"

"Packed."

"And he's new to town?"

"As far as I know. Now go. And watch yourself. He shakes, he sniffs. I don't know, Jake, there's something."

Jake sat and waited on a low stucco wall, the brightness making him squint, ironically, like a man in the throes of concentration. He'd gone across to Parker's general store and bought gum, keeping his slitted eyes on the doors of the Police Department building and the three stone steps that led to the sidewalk. But, while he spent his sticks of peppermint gum, chewing hard and trying with all his might to keep watching that door, to wait for those vagrants' shoes to walk down the steps and to see just how packed the packed bag was, he missed him. Snared both by Rita Mahoonie crossing the street in a dress too thin and summery and the sudden, excitable whir of the key-cutting machine next to Parker's, he never saw the doors of the building open those first few inches, or the man stand in the doorway, drop his packed bag to the floor and stoop to tie the laces of his worn winter boots.

*

At 11.45 John Cassidy was in the small, square waiting room at the railway station, the packed bag down at his feet, the coat unfastened and the efforts to restart his same failed system seen in the rapid blinking, the movements of the mouth and the jerks of the fingers and feet.

Sometimes he lifted his head to look at the woman and the young boy who sat close to the opened door. Sometimes he stole glances at the boy, at the excitement when his mother looked his way, and the uncertainty and tension when she didn't. He caught how she tidied him up; the way her mayfly fingers adjusted his collar or pushed the flick of hair away from his face. Sometimes, in his half-listening to them, he got snippets, pieces of the puzzle: The boy was going to see his father. His father had been away for most of his life. The boy's memories of him were so isolated and brief they hardly made sense and in spite of his mother's insistence, in spite of her attempts to generate something upbeat, he remembered little that moved of his father. John could see in the way his face played its animations like piano keys that he was working the scale between hope and disappointment and back, between a good day and a bad day, between what he might resent and what he might forgive.

"Washington, Adams, Jefferson, Madison," he whispered to himself. "Monroe, Adams, John Quincy, Jackson." He stopped. His crooked nose took an inhalation, his head tilted a few degrees to the right. "Are you checking on me?" he said.

The woman and the boy glanced up. They looked first at John and then towards the doorway which, from where they were sitting, framed nothing but the prairie land beyond the tracks.

"I said are you checking on me?"

Slowly, and in incremental shuffles, Jake presented himself in the frame of the waiting-room door. "How did you see me?"

"I have a nose and a pair of ears."

The young boy looked quickly from one to the other, and his mother, fearing the imminence of bloodshed, whispered for him to stop.

"I came to apologise, for the snoring."

John stared at him a good ten seconds. "You want to make some money?" he said, still staring.

"How much?"

"Ten dollars."

"What for?"

"Information."

"What kind of information. Some might be ten dollars, some might be fifty."

John licked his lips. "Where are the homesteads?" he said.

"That's fifty."

John narrowed his eyes, heard the soft implosions around his mouth, "Van Buren, Harrison, Tyler, Polk." He unzipped the packed bag, took out and counted the fifty dollars, held it between his fingers.

"You first," Jake said.

John handed over the money.

Jake looked down at the bag. "Over the rickety bridge, beyond Coronation Point. Why do you want to know?"

"That's my business."

"You looking for the Cassidy man? That's where he lives. They say he has land. And money."

The woman brushed at the young boy's coat, at the collar and sleeve.

"You want to make some more?" John said. "Five hundred dollars."

He stood then, his worn winter boots squeaking as he did so. "Do you know these people?" he said, nodding towards the woman and the boy.

"No. Do you?"

"No, I don't. So, here's the wager. We'll guess the boy's birthday," he said. "What's your name?"

"Ben," the boy said, tapping his polished tan shoes on the floor.

"We'll guess Ben's birthday. You can have one guess and I'll have two. Odds of two to one, right? Right?"

Jake nodded.

"Except…I'll give you odds of a hundred to one. If I get closest you give me five dollars, but if you do, I'll give you five hundred."

"Let's see it."

John crouched down again to reach into the bag and unpicked a small compartment at the side. Then, looking between Jake, the boy, and the five hundred dollars, he counted the notes out and held them rolled in his hand. The clock showed six minutes to twelve as the two men faced each other.

"Who goes first?" Jake said, slavering.

"You do."

Jake, a slight whisky sweat rising up on his skin, looked away from where the money was and over towards the boy, who glanced up at his mother, then back towards Jake. "He looks like a summer child. I'll say June…seventeenth."

"That's your guess?"

"That's it."

The boy and his mother switched their rapt attention to John. They got the old navy coat that hung from his shoulders, and they got the scuffed boots with soles as thin as ham slices. What neither of them got, though, as the train sounded in the distance and the station bell rang out, was that the young, dishevelled man with the dog-legged nose and the pale-yellow bruising around the eye, whose ear visibly twitched as the train sounds got closer, was getting his system back. He looked hard again at Jake and tried to weigh up more than his stab in the dark. He leant in towards the boy, took a ten-dollar bill from behind his ear and put it, folded as small as a stamp, in his hand.

"That's for your help, Ben," he said. Then he turned to Jake, picked up his bag and said, "June sixteenth, June eighteenth. Now give me the five dollars, I'm getting on the train."

*

Three days later, he was back. He'd got almost as far as the state-line and then stopped, climbing off the train in a place called Bethel that smelled of rapeseed and aluminium and where he'd found an old barn on the edge of the wheat-fields to sleep in. He'd stayed the rest of the day and the following day and night and then the morning after, in a light rain, after he'd gathered himself as best he could in a barn beset with snakes, he got on the train out west again, as far as the town of Serpentine twenty miles away and, with his damp, pea-coat, sometimes on and sometimes off, he'd walked the rest of the way.

He got to the edge of the town by mid-afternoon via tracks that skirted the burial grounds, and from there, over rough and untended land, to the rickety bridge in under an hour. The gauze of the morning had lifted from the crags of Rupture Hill and the dull-silver bluffs of its torso were sharper. He looked round, the head raised, the cochlea and snout prickled and pert. He got pintails and warblers, shovelers and hawks. He got the sudden, scooted flights of cinnamon teal and grey geese. He settled his bag down on the slats, draped the coat over the loosened rail. Ahead of him the soil and the grassland gave way to bushes of mesquite and juniper, to steeper ruts and rises and to the woodland beyond.

It wasn't just the boy and his story that turned him round. It wasn't just curiosity or hope or those feelings he could never put a name to. It wasn't to do with the money, or the land, or the heritage of the family name. It was that he couldn't leave it behind, that the thought of walking away, of leaving everything unknown, and unfinished, was not possible. He had to see him.

The further he went towards and into the woods, through creosote and prickly pear, on tracks that bevelled and dipped, he sensed the same twist in his gut come back, and by the time he got to Coronation Point where, so the story went, young Nathaniel Hansetter found his traces of gold, he had to drop to his knees and take the count. Sunlight sliced through the lattice of the trees, and he raised his head only to look out to a section of flatter land in the middle of which, like three leather buttons stitched into it, were the three homesteads, in the furthest of which lived his father, Jack.

*

The story of how the Cassidy land became the Cassidy land was one passed down like an unwashed heirloom through the various inhabitants of Mission for over a hundred years. And, no matter it may've gained a few spurious appendages here and there or that Patrick John Cassidy himself may have gone from the young, ragged panhandler who wandered into the Station Hotel on that rainy night in the dying embers of the mining days and asked to play cards, to the gold-toothed trickster who schmoozed his way past local businessmen and walked away with the deeds of the land, it acted as a reminder of the town's hubris and foolhardiness still.

You see, even though it was just a handful of wealthy and opportunistic men who saw in wild-haired Patrick and his request no less than meat served up on a platter, and one member of the group in particular, Edward Mallender, Snr, whose sense of his own invincibility led to the surrender of the land, still it was the complicity and silences of others who allowed it to happen. Of course, the town didn't see it that way and laid every ounce of blame at the grimy feet of the stranger.

What was worse was that not only did those men lose the land, not only was it ripe for the kind of development that would've made them all a healthy profit *and* boosted the economy of the town, but

Patrick John Cassidy, with his full house of threes and kings, left the land alone for forty years. And when he did return it was to build a home for his orphaned grandson, Jack, who, at just four years of age, had lost both his mother in childbirth and his father on the shores of Utah beach, and who, until just six years ago, had never once visited the town of Mission nor the house on the land won by his grandfather over a century before.

The land itself, stretching from the homesteads, along the track as far as the road and around in a mile-long arc of rough terrain was, when Jack got there, those sixty years of his life overgrown; a splay of tumours and growths, in places riddled with sot-weed and bunch-berry, in others tangled with devil's club and vine. There were sudden ridges of soil, powdered in summer, crusted in winter. There were gullies where the rain had collected and stayed and where snow and ice had bored into the land. There were places of deep shade, of leaves and branches bedecked with liverwort, places that drew in like purse strings so that only beads of sunlight ever got in.

Further out towards the curve of the road were patches of open land, either grazed upon or gnawed at, with prints of skunk and vole and strands of coyote fur. At its closest to the base of Rupture Hill there were the gnarled outcrops of granite and sandstone and, if you looked with a geologist's eye, you might find those mineral veins of copper and chalk.

On the other side of the track that led to the road were the two other homesteads. The story went that when Patrick returned to build the house that his grandson might one day live in, he leased the land not to the Land Management Agency in the town but to a private development company who sub-leased it for rental purposes. The story also went that whereas the two neighbouring homesteads were built with a noticeable economy of cost and looked indistinguishable one to the next, the Cassidy place, overseen by the near-septuagenar-ian Patrick, had adornments and flourishes of every shape and size in all of its rooms and on every one of its external walls from gar-goyles to guttering. Pity, then, that that single-storey home, from the very day of its completion, when the lone figure of Patrick John Cassidy stood resolute in the doorway smoking his cheroot, would stay empty for another sixty years. And pity, too, that those imported tiles, the ornate cornicing, the brass legs of the enamel bath and the veranda painted the most verdant of greens, all suffered from neglect so that by the time Jack eventually arrived one rainy fall afternoon those many years later the house was a rank shell of atrophy and decay.

He did what he could. Already stricken by his illness, he was physically limited. The cracks, rust and rot he could do little about, and so he was left only to restore it to the habitable. That was it. No adornments, no flourishes, just the bare bones, just a place to live in, for however long. The other thing was that, until Sophie, he had no help whatsoever. One of the homesteads was empty almost a decade and the other was lived in by Ruth and Elijah Anderson and their two pale-faced children, who went nowhere without clutching a Bible to their chests and for whom colour was a sign of Godlessness and frivolity, and who had an immediate mistrust of Jack, not only because he refused the offers of neighbourly prayers, but because the resentment had passed down through the town so seamlessly that there was a confederacy of spite towards any member of that godforsaken family.

And even though, in those first few weeks and months, he tried, he soon got to realise that part of that confederacy came out in the closing of doors in his face and the frosty silences and, on occasions, the slashed tyres of his Toyota. So, he hunkered down. He had no choice. He stopped going into the town and drove into neighbouring Serpentine instead, to places where the mention of the Cassidy name didn't trigger revulsion, to stores and garages and bars where he was treated like a human being. But, after a while, the hour-and-a-half round trip, plus the loading up and off of the goods, began to exhaust him. So too, the weekly hospital appointments, the upkeep of the land close to the house and even the simple maintenance of the rooms themselves.

The advertisement for help was prudent not to mention that surname of his, but everyone knew. It spread like an air-borne virus that the Cassidy bastard out on the stolen land was on his last legs, that his miserable days were numbered and that, finally, the town of Mission might get its land back. After a month there was one applicant, Sophie Li.

*

The hatchback pulled away from the migrant shacks where the previous day's rain had wetted the gravel to a muted crunch. The clean mop-heads were in the back, as well as the fresh bottles of detergents and bleach. At the end of the road Sophie, with her hair washed and tied up, took the left on to the road that ran by the rail-tracks, shaking the axle bearing twice as she did so.

It was a journey she'd made three times a week for the last three months. She'd gone from midwinter with its frosts and drifted snow to an early spring of rain squalls and nascent buds. Other days she cleaned and cooked in other places. Saturdays, she did a ten-hour shift at the hardware store, stocking the shelves and working the till. Sometimes she drove out sacks of cattle feed, or machinery bits or cuts of timber. And once, she'd taken a pot-bellied pig halfway out to Serpentine.

She got to Blessings Point with its girdle of fir and Ponderosa pine that stretched as far as the Mallender land and the house with its whitewashed walls and balustrades where Lily Mallender, some thirty years younger than her husband, sat with drying, crimson nails and waited for Jorge, the even younger Venezuelan gardener, to arrive in his tool-rattling jalopy.

By the time Sophie'd taken the long arc of road past the burial grounds and the sandstone bulk of Rupture Hill she was thinking of the hours to come, of how she'd open the door from the porch-way and see him sitting at the wooden table; that rag doll of a man, leaning on bare, gnarled elbows, his jawbone cupped in his hands, those rheumy eyes roaming the spaces of the room. She was thinking how the collars of the plaid shirts he wore were always open, and how little neck there was for them to contain. She stopped the car, as she had done from the first day, on the turn of the unmade track, rolled down the window and, come rain or shine, lit her first cigarette of the day.

She watched him as she slid the mop-head over the linoleum floor, as she hissed out the freshener or ran the faucets with broom-lined hands. She watched him as she went through the house, as tresses of hair sprang from the bandanna she wore and those dainty boots glided over the damp of the floor in a beginners' waltz. Each room she cornered and creviced for dust. Each room she picked something up to polish underneath and in each room, even after all the cleaning and the dusting and the polishing, still the smell of him wouldn't go away; skin, hair, breath, the rare-changed clothes he resisted to shed, all of it, as well as the leaks of piss and sweat, held in a fetid warmth that festered because he wouldn't open the windows, because in those last few weeks whatever will there might've been had puttered out to nothing.

And it was there, in those flickering still-lives, those tableaux of Jack Cassidy in his plaid shirt sitting at the table with reed-like fingers holding the deeds of the land while Sophie moved around him amidst the paltry allowance of light, that the knock on the door came.

Any noise of mop or broom halted. The dainty boots stilled. Sophie glanced over at Jack, who swallowed, narrowed his eyes and allowed the oval of his radish-red mouth to pucker. She wiped her hands on the skirt and moved towards the door. When she opened it, the light hit her like a slap so that it took her a few moments to make out the young man with the crooked snout. She smiled, faintly, stepped out and closed the door to a chink only behind her.

"Is Jack here?"

"Who wants to know?"

There was a pause, a gathering in of breath. "It's John."

"John who?"

"Cassidy," he said, with the tiniest of breaks in his voice, "I'm his son."

Sophie didn't know whether Jack had heard or not. She blinked, smiled faintly again, and looked down at the porch-way floor, picking out leaves of stray wisteria.

"You're not the first person to turn up here and claim to be related," she said. "There's been another son already. We've had a nephew, a niece, a second cousin. We've had them all. Why don't you leave the poor man alone?"

The voice that came from back inside the house was like the cough of an old motor. "Who's there?"

Sophie looked at John again and half-turned. "He says he's your son."

The pause fell around them, around the figures in the porch-way, around the house and every one of its contents. "Tell him I don't want to see him. Tell him that. Tell him he's twenty years too late."

*

Rain fell in the late afternoon as if sprinkled from old metal cans, pattering the dome of leaves above him like the steady drop of bearings into a pitcher's mitt. The soil responded. It got moist and scented. It got darker. It got softer. Over by the clearing of Coronation Point, it got richer red.

From where he was crouched on the wood's edge, he could see through the bracken to the slow descent of land. He could make out the homesteads beyond, could see a bonneted Ruth Anderson and the taller of the embalmed children pulling in the washing from the line as the rain moved steadily west and the tremors of trailing wind shivered skunk cabbage and salmonberry. He could see the figure of Sophie Li closing the door of the house behind her, hauling the bag of mop-heads and detergents over her skinny shoulder and walking away, down the track to where she'd left the car. He watched her sling the bag onto the back seat, light up a cigarette, and drive out towards the road.

Rupture Hill was coated in rain and a slow-rolling dusk that leeched the sandstone of its peachiness. And, as clouds with the sheen of industrial sinks began to drape around its crown, John Cassidy stayed on his haunches and bided his time. Still, he didn't know what it was, or what to call it. Still, it was just a wordless swathe around him, a smothering, just like it always had been. It was like an animal pulse, a twitch of the hindquarters.

He waited until the light was squeezed out, until the gibbous moon was swallowed up and the clean-living Anderson family had snuffed out their beatific candles and gone to sleep. Then he stirred, his feet shifting in the undergrowth and soil. For a moment, he stopped on Coronation Point and tried to map his way down to the flatter land, and then with his packed bag and his peacoat fastened in the chill, he headed for the house. And, in fifteen minutes through the darkness and hush, past the Anderson place with its crucifix hung in the porch-way and the long-empty shell of a house, he was there.

He took off his boots and left them by the veranda steps. From out across the land came a long coyote howl. His ear twitched, so too his snout. He crept towards the door in stockinged feet and whenever the boards gave out a creak he'd stop, his breath held tight against his chest. He tried the door. Nothing. Same with the windows at the side. He looked around, at the house and the gloom-bound land beyond. In the pocket of his coat he had an assortment of hatpins and hairpins. He took out a handful as he peered down at the lock. He tried each one and listened, sensing the tiniest of scratches and scrapes. He bent and twisted them, the beads of sweat running down his forehead, taking the chicane of his nose and dropping onto the boards. Finally, with the twitch of the last ridged and angled pin, the door clicked open. He put the pin back in his pocket and pushed at the door, creeping in in tiny steps. And, because there was so little light, because there was no sound but the faint whistle of the wind, the first thing that hit him was the smell. There might've been scents of cooked meats and refried beans, the smack of generic bleach and powders to clean the floor with, but the reek of a sick and dying man overrode every single one of them. Outside, there came a second coyote howl, like the mewl of a baby left out in the woods.

He stood still on the linoleum floor, made out the table in front of him, a handful of wooden chairs, one of which was pulled out at an angle. On the table was a half-empty glass of water and a large manila envelope. Next to the glass was a small droppered bottle and next to the envelope was a pencil stub the size of a child's thumb. His fingers jangled the pins. Behind him, a stronger gust of wind shook the frame of the door. His ear twitched again, his snout sieved the rainy night air and the netted kitchen drapes shivered like a spinster at a graveyard.

"You make one more step and I'll blow your fucking brains out, kid."

The door beyond the table's far edge inched open and gloom or no gloom, grizzled light or otherwise, the black, shiny barrel of a gun loomed out a good two feet ahead of the hidden face behind it.

"What do you want?"

John looked at the owl-eyed barrel and swallowed.

"I asked you a question. What do you want?"

A barely discernible schoolboy shrug.

"You come out here. You break into my house, and you don't know?"

He saw the bony hand, the ridge of knuckles.

"To see you."

"Oh, to see *me.* To see me what? To see me how?"

He heard the wheeze of his father's voice. And not a word even whispered in his own.

"What I wonder is this. How come it's now you're here?"

The door opened a few inches more. The figure edged forward, so too the gun.

"Now, I know people want the land. People have always wanted the land. And I know I'm despised because I have it and that people will cherish the day the Cassidy land is returned to the town. I know all that. So, you can see why it is I wonder why now a nephew comes to the door, why now there's a niece out of the blue and how come there are two sons, the first of which is bigger than a barn door and the second of which, *you*, breaks into my house like a coward and a thief. You see my point?"

He heard him breathless then, the gasps as if trawled and spat from the pit of his lungs to rattle down the barrel's sheen.

"I knew nothing of the land…My name is John, John Cassidy."

"So was the other son."

"Born August ninth."

"Yes."

"West Creek Hospital. Six pounds and six ounces. My mother's name is Margaret. Margaret DeMille."

"Yes, I know. Next. This is information any fool could know."

"She was the one told me you were dying, where you were."

He heard him sniff, clear his throat of phlegm.

"And she drinks. And she's fucked up. And she told me I put a spoke in her life the day I came out."

The barrel lowered slightly, and the face of his father as if cowled by the shade.

"You remember Dwayne?"

The face mumbled he did.

"Did the other son?"

"Yes, he did."

"Did he say where he was?"

"He said he was in an institution."

"Did he say how he got there?"

"No."

"I put him there. I sent him psychotic. I put amphetamine sulphate into his protein drinks until he didn't know what the fuck he was doing."

Jack fumbled around in the room, the gun propped between his knees. Then came the sudden torchlight, blasted in John's direction.

"How come?"

"Because he deserved it," he said, shielding his eyes with the sleeve of his coat.

The torchlight snapped off.

"What else?"

"What do you want?"

"The other son had places. The other son had the make of the car, the licence plates even. He had the river, the drive across town, the ice-cream store on the corner by the railroad tracks. He had the laurel trees, the turn off the road, the dusty track."

"I don't have those."

"He had the suitcase full of shirts. He had colours. He had candy stripes, button-down collars, long sleeves, short sleeves, pockets or no pockets. He had music on the stereo. He had songs he remembered, tunes he could sing along to, and did."

John took a long breath in. The hatpins pricked the ends of his fingers, drew baubles of blood.

"I have only a winter's day," he said, looking away from the barrel of the gun and the bony hand that held it, away from the half-hidden face and the opened door. He pulled one of the chairs away from the table and sat on it. The snout gave out a short twitch, so too the ear, "I have snowfall. I have a packed bag and winter boots. I have the sound of the tyres crunching across the snow…and I have the pain that I never found a name for. Not then, not now."

The coyote howled a third time.

*

They circled each other for almost a week, the days like long, attritional sparring sessions. They didn't know each other. Apart from the first five and a half years and even then only sporadically, there'd been no connection between them whatsoever. Nothing. And, aside from the absence, from the lack of contact of any kind, there was the weight they couldn't shake, the weight so heavy neither could drag it out into the open and leave it there for both to see, so that it clotted the air, so that Jack might shuffle back into his room and close the door behind him, or John might put his boots on and take a walk out just to breathe; that they both believed the other had abandoned them.

And yet, in spite of that weight, of neither knowing what to say or whether those words if, or when, they came, should be brutish or forgiving, an acceptance began to grow between them. On the third day, Jack invited John to stay at the house on a permanent basis. Perhaps invitation is too strong. It was more like a nod in the direction of the spare room during a meal of chicken and rice. A day later John helped his frail-boned father out of the house and into the old armchair on the veranda for the afternoon, and the following day, with that drift of pine on the westerly wind, they both climbed into the old Toyota, and went to see Dr Abraham Stone, a physician with a heart made up of his surname. Dr Stone who, at the designated time of two thirty, with a sheet of headed paper half-hiding that peach of a face of his, delivered his final diagnosis as if informing the man his Toyota needed brake fluid.

"Mr. Cassidy," he said, glancing up for but a moment, "you've got a month. Tops...Next."

Jack didn't take it well. He knew as much, felt as much, sensed the days were numbered at best, but to hear it so dismissively clipped was something that hit him hard. The doors of the house were closed, the lights put out, the drapes drawn. He wouldn't eat or drink and instead of sleep he ground his way through the dark hours. At times his nails dug at the sheets until the rips came and he burrowed his face so far down into the pillow he could hardly breathe. When he sat on the bedside chair his bones ached with the weight, his muscles tightened and then slumped and grew weak. His eyes, for the entire time, were tight shut.

Sophie didn't know what to say, and even her few practical words per day, more often than not domestic or food-related, became non-existent. Her manner of busying herself around the two men as if they were simply blocks of skin and bone stayed the same, but around Jack, she was more delicate. She brushed instead of hoovered. She ran the water slowly into the bucket to fill it and when she mopped those heads never rose more than an inch above the floor. In the evenings when she drove back to the migrant house she cried the whole way, quietly.

And what of John? Well, he knew that his father was dying. He'd known from the moment he'd called his mother. He'd known as he walked the neighbourhoods of the town and the ten miles to the highway west, as he made his way across country in those cars and trucks. He'd known as he lay on the floor of Mission station, on the mattress in the cell and in the barn beset with snakes. He'd known as he set out to find his father's homestead, as he'd knocked on his door and sat at his table. And yet, when Dr Stone had sat behind his desk and dealt his callous blow in one short sentence and a flippant addendum, when whatever colour was left in his father's face had drained to nothing, then all that knowing crumbled into no more than powder and dust.

Two days later, with his father showing no signs of emergence, he knocked on the bedroom door. It was 7.30 in the morning.

"What is it?"

"Get up. Come on."

"What?"

"We're not doing this?"

"Doing what?"

"It's over. Let's go."

"Just let me be."

"No, I won't. Come on. We're leaving."

The sound of bed springs and shuffling feet, of drapes swooshing back, of a light switch clicked on again, and the tiniest chink in the door that let out that warm, pungent air and a paper-thin voice that said, "Where are we going?"

"Back."

*

It was not exactly a regular father-son road trip. To begin with, the two men had nothing that drew them together. They had no memories, no shared experiences and so for the first couple of days they sat in the old Toyota with the landscape moving by them, like the same two magnetic poles trying, clumsily and without success, to make a connection.

Jack slept much of the time anyway, his head either back or slumped down on his plaid shirt, as John drove and chewed and stared ahead, heading randomly south and then cutting across to the east and the north-east. The land grew flatter, the roads straighter. They'd hit great stretches of pasture and farmland, fields of rapeseed and corn, acres of wilderness, of woodland and scrub and plain. Sometimes John listened to the radio. Sometimes he stopped at a roadside store, picked up a few provisions, put them in the well of the back seat and sat as his father wheezed next to him. Sometimes he'd sit by the side of the car and scrape at the rust. The sills were the worse. Looking at the cupric shading he could tell some of it had started at least five years ago and been ignored since. Then there were the pocks and crusts around the exhaust, which sputtered the faster he went. One of the wiper blades was broken. The screenwash was disconnected, the dipstick jammed. A couple of the hubcaps were chipped and split. Whenever Jack coughed, he had to slow down to listen.

From the homestead, he brought an array of blankets in degrees of thickness. He brought case-less pillows the colour of semolina, a brush-mat to put his father's feet on whenever he took his shoes off. He brought a kitchen bowl, six boxes of tissues, liquid soap. He brought a brush for the rust, a brush for the shoes and a brush for his father's hair. He brought a small portable stove, a cool box with ice, and pots and pans that shook in the trunk next to the frames of the collapsible chairs. He brought air freshener that smelled of fresh linen on a summer's day.

For the first two nights, he pulled over to the side of the road whenever he got tired, closed his eyes and got some rest. On the third, they found a motel and shared a mid-size room on the ground floor. They slept in single beds with the texture of watermelon flesh. A night lamp, hung at an angle on the wall, strained out light the colour of beeswax, the faucet dripped and hawked up something glutinous and brown and, throughout the night, waking them both every time, came the sound of restless, hirsute beasts from the land beyond.

They had breakfast of pancakes and coffee in a diner next to the motel, suffocatingly bright, with a jukebox that jumped. Jack got crumbs around the corner of his mouth and a syrup stain on his shirt. The coffee mug shook in his hand, rattled against his teeth. He took his medication by lining up the various tablets on the table top and taking them one by one, his throat lurching as he swallowed them, his eyes closing with each gulp. As they got up to go, John picked up a napkin, dampened it with spittle and rubbed at the stain, hearing the creaks of his father's breath as he did so, feeling with his steadying hand the scooped-out groove between the scrawny neck and the ridge of shoulder bone. Jack thanked him, apologised quietly, and thanked him again.

On the afternoon of the fourth day, they stopped by the side of a lake. John took the car as far across the pebbled shore as he could. He took out the chairs from the trunk and faced them towards the sun close to the water's edge. Then he guided his father over the stones, sat him down, took off his shoes and socks and, carrying the kitchen bowl back and forth to the lake, he bathed his feet, grooving the water between his toes with his thumb. He cut the nails, filed down the growth of hard skin on his heels. He unbuttoned the plaid shirt, slipped it back off his shoulders, wrapped the near-translucent torso in one of the softer blankets and washed the shirt in the lake, squeezing the water out tight and leaving it draped across the stones to dry. He then put a towel over the blanket and, with the sunlight trembling across the water and the bowl back on his father's lap, he shaved him, taking the blade up from throat to chin, pinching his nostrils shut, watching his father go from staring up at the sky to closing his eyes, like a child.

He used the towel to dry his face and a tissue to stem a small nick on the lobe of his ear. Then he took out the brush for his father's hair and softly swept it back, hardly touching the scalp of the frail and blanketed figure with the bare feet and the sunlight warm upon his face. He fetched one of the pillows from the car and settled it behind his head. "Close your eyes," he said, "listen to the birdsong."

He took a walk along the shoreline, gathered up kindling and armfuls of dry wood, and laid them down on a flatter stretch of sand and shale closer to the line of trees. When he got back and his father slept and the sun began to sink down below the western hills turned to burgundy felt, he poached eggs, cooked beans and made coffee on the stove.

They ate as the water lapped on the pebbles. The sky was rose-ate and lilac, the lake silvery-black. A fingernail of a jaundiced moon sloped above the trees behind them and by the time Jack had laid his empty plate down and sucked out the last few dregs of the coffee, by the time he'd been draped in the blankets; around the shoulders and the dried, plaid shirt, across the lap, and covering the swollen, stock-inged feet, John had finished up and a small fire was crackling away. He held a stick of driftwood like a monkey's forearm, poked at the fire with it.

"My aunt used to drag that comb across my skull until it bled."

*

The following morning the mist hung low over the lake. The two men sat around the embers of the fire and drank lukewarm, sugarless coffee and when it was time to go, John lifted his father from the chair and carried him back to the car, his arm cradled under his back, his father's head nestled inwards in the bowl of his shoulder.

They drove aimlessly east for the next few days. They needed a new tyre, an oil change, a makeshift fan belt. They had to stop every time it rained because of the buckled wiper. They lost one of the chairs to the wind and one of the blankets to an old man by the side of the road with a single tooth and a sick dog. The air freshener ran out, so too the tissues.

They began to speak more, in ways they hadn't before, about ordinary things, about the food they ate or the coffee they drank, about the landscape they passed or the weather that blessed them with sunlight, cloud or rain. Sometimes they spoke about other stuff; chess moves, card tricks, puzzles and conundrums, about those multifarious facts from the encyclopaedias that Jack used to sell and John used to read, about the best cotton of the shirts and the best leather of the shoes. They named the presidents together, ran off the states in alphabetical order and between them, a good majority of the capitals. But with all of those, and with every sideways look they made in the other's direction, every half-smile and nod, there was still no place for abandonment, no room for rejection, or for the cold winter's day almost twenty years back.

In the early evening of the second Saturday, with the promise of heavier rain, they pulled into the parking lot of a town's-edge motel. John got out, checked the rust, booked the room and took whatever belongings they might need while his father slept. He sat in the room as the rain started in from the east and the low bellies of the clouds glistened with gloom. From where John was, leaning forward on the edge of the bed, he could see out across the lot. He could see his father's face slanted towards the window, the narrowed mouth slightly open, the forehead resting on the pane, the knuckles up around the chin, and as soon as those eyes drew themselves open and there was the slightest movement in his spindled frame he was out, running across the lot in the driving rain and sitting in the car until it stopped.

The room stank of nicotine and crusted male sweat. The bed was a double with a quilt the colour of lemon rind. The two men ate take-away noodles in a carton, John quickly, his father slowly, dragging the pasta up to his mouth and sucking it gradually in or letting it dangle back down into the cardboard bucket, staining his chin as he did so. After he'd done, and John had propped him up against the head-board, cleaned him up, changed his shirt, washed the old and dirty one in the sink, brushed his teeth, taken off those shoes no longer of the best leather and listened to the whistle of his father's chest, he sat on the wicker chair in the corner of the room, and said, "So why did you go back to the Cassidy land?"

*

For a while his father couldn't, and didn't, answer. The truth was he didn't know where to start. Every time he thought he'd found somewhere he needed to explain how that point had been arrived at, and when he'd explained *that* and had another starting point, he had no option but to explain that one too. And so on, until he was all the way back to Patrick John Cassidy walking into the Station Hotel and winning the land in a card game.

His mouth moved several times as if to begin. His head nodded, his brow furrowed, his hands twitched. His story, when he started, was this: He was a fifty-five-year-old divorcee whose days of vigour and fizz were done. He drank. He gambled. He still moved around from place to place but it was less to do with the spontaneity of the younger man and more about the dulled pragmatism of the working salesman with no other choice. He tried to tell himself that his purpose was as strong as it ever had been, but everything else seemed to say otherwise; the low sales figures, the lost, chaotic weekends, the medication for the shakes. He tried to convince himself that, as with all salesmen, there were good days and bad days and you couldn't legislate for the vicissitudes of a life that hung almost entirely on the whims of other people. But then those good days were rare and those whims, instead of being unpredictable, started to become wholly predictable because those *other people* were not convinced enough. They didn't like the booze fumes. They didn't like the sweat. They didn't like being persuaded by a man who couldn't look after himself.

And so, one particular night, after another long and fruitless day dragging those encyclopaedic tomes door to door to people who no more needed the bee population of Venezuela than they did a slap in the face, he was sitting in a bar on the corner of a downtown street. He'd been living there a week, in a small apartment above a Chinese laundry close to the river, and was nursing a beer in one hand and a bourbon in the other when a well-dressed man walked in, sat next to him and, with a firm handshake, introduced himself as Vincent.

Now, when you're fighting an uphill battle with your dignity and your sense of purpose is on the wane then the sight of an obviously successful man could go one of two ways. Either you resent him, or, in Jack's case, the fact that he reminded him of himself as a younger man kindled something inside him. There was a silkiness, a grace of movement, a congruence. And the spiel was just like listening to his own effortless patter back in the halcyon days of real estate, cars, shirts and leather shoes. It was there. It was in the moment. The man was in his heyday.

Anyway, Vincent stays for maybe an hour and then excuses himself, saying he has to get home, he's new in the neighbourhood, and his wife would be waiting. In fact, just as he's leaving she calls and he makes one of those grimaces, man to man, designed to encapsulate that whole masculine experience of compromise in a matter of seconds. And then he's gone.

He's there again a week later. This time Jack is sharing the counter with a bulky forty-something who has cynicism coming out of his hairy ears already, about everything; his life, everybody else's life, the government, the tax system, you name it, he has a gripe about it and you'd hear about it whether you wanted to or not. Vincent's more casual this time. His wife is away on business for a few days, so he can relax, he can stay a while longer and have a beer with his buddies down at the bar and not have anyone tell him otherwise, right? The other guy is as cynical about Vincent as he is about everything and everyone else. "He's a shyster," he whispers, "Look at him. Look at his nails."

At the end of the night, they're onto sport, horse racing in particular, about which the cynic is a self-confessed aficionado. He knows the horses, he knows the tracks, he knows the trainers and the split-times, and he says anyone who places more than a single, one-off bet needs their heads examining. Why? Because they'll never win overall. Once, yes, twice, maybe, anything more than that, forget it. Vincent disagrees. He says he's got a system. It's not foolproof but it's as good as anything he's seen. Show me your ten bucks. I'll find a horse and I'll prove how good the system is, he says. The cynic scowls, mutters something under his breath and keeps his hand on the counter. Jack, on the other hand, whether it's the chance to piss the cynic off or it's that Vincent has that same barely restrained swagger that he used to have, doesn't.

The next week Vincent walks in, stands there in between Jack and the other guy. For you, my cynical friend, he says, nothing. But for you Jack, here's your one hundred bucks. What did I tell you about the system? And if either of you gentlemen are interested, I can make the same thing happen again. And again, the other guy doesn't move and Jack offers up another ten. A week later Vincent shuffles eighty bucks into Jack's hand and leaves.

The next time the cynical guy isn't there. Vincent and Jack bat the breeze about this and that, mainly Jack and his younger days, how much real estate or insurance he sold, how many cars, how many shirts, how many shoes and how, with a spring in his step, he was going to make those encyclopaedias fly again. After an hour, Vincent gets the call from his wife. He nods, pulls the grimace, then looks over at Jack and says into the phone, "Honey, put out an extra plate. I'm bringing a friend." So, they go back. Jack meets Vincent's wife, they eat, Vincent calls Jack his bar buddy and they spend a couple of pleasant hours together. The food is good. The apartment is warm-coloured and tasteful. There's music on from Jack's heyday and by the end of the night he's telling them all about his father and Utah beach, about his mother, his aunt and uncle, the way she used to drag the comb across his skull and how, at seventeen years of age, he jumped a train heading east with his packed bag and never went back. And then he parted with fifty bucks to Vincent's system.

The following week the other guy's back there next to Jack. Vincent comes in and without saying a word, as if handing out candy bars in kindergarten, counts out five hundred dollars into the palm of

Jack's hand. There is no third time, he says to the other guy. Every time is the first. Think about it. "It's just luck," the guy says. "There is no such thing as luck," says Vincent, "it's a system." "So what is it?" the guy says. At this point, Vincent smiles, slaps the guy on the shoulder and says: "I'm not going to sit here and tell you *my* system, now am I? Why don't you show me your ten bucks and we'll see what's what? Carpe diem, my man. Seize the goddamned day."

The other guy, with some hesitation, hands over his ten, and Jack, after a good week on the encyclopaedias, gives him a hundred without so much as a flinch. Then Vincent gets his call, does his grimace, and leaves.

This happens for the next three weeks. The other guy gives him ten and Jack a hundred, and every time Vincent walks in and pays them. Every time is the first, he says, it's like a new roll of the dice. For Jack, it was like being in his twenties again. It was summers on the coast, selling second homes with sea views. It was Cadillacs and Cuban heels. He felt good about himself. And there *was* a spring in his step when he walked those neighbourhood streets and if people did start to get a little more curious about those Venezuelan bees and their numbers, then Vincent and his system was playing no small part in it.

By this time, the other guy is converted and the ten bucks gets quickly upgraded to twenty then fifty then a hundred until one particular night he comes in with a thousand dollars and gives it to Vincent. And the following week Vincent comes in and hands the guy an envelope- "Ten thousand dollars, my friend." "Take it," the guy says, "take it and get me some more. I need a vacation." And so Vincent takes it and a week later he's back with fifty thousand. "Do it again," the guy says, "this is the easiest money I ever made in my whole life."

At this point, Jack is stirred, because Jack is still throwing his hundred in and what he picks up every week starts to seem small fry by comparison with the thickening envelopes the other guy stuffs in his pocket or folds between his newspaper. He also finds out that the other guy, the guy so cynical to begin with, has been to Vincent's apartment, has met his wife, eaten there, and taken them out on more than one occasion. He tries to tell himself he's making good money every week. He tries to convince himself it's enough. But it's not. He has a couple of bad weeks on the encyclopaedia run. The night sweats come back. There's a couple of weeks when Vincent is on vacation, when the hairy-eared smug-fuck is in there showing him a postcard of where he is, shows him the resort and tells him he's thinking of buying a place out there himself, on Vincent's recommendation. It's an investment, he says, it's for the future.

And so, when Vincent comes back and the other guy hands him the envelope back and says, "Do it again," Jack does the same. His hand shakes slightly as he hands over the envelope, his eyes avert Vincent's and his mouth tightens, because what he doesn't say and tries not to show is that the money in the envelope is pretty much all he has. It's that mixture of savings and winnings and what small pots of honey those Venezuelan bees produce.

He has another bad week. His gut aches, his head pounds most of the day and on the Thursday night he spikes a three-figure temperature that should keep him hunkered down in his bed for a few days. But no. The following night he's on the bar stool by eight. OK, his bourbon is hot and sprinkled with cloves, and whenever he moves his bones feel like lead pipes stuffed with sap, but he's there all the same. On his own. Sometimes he does get there first. Sometimes the other guy, instead of already being there with his newspaper and the wrapped cigar he rolls between his fingers, wanders in a few minutes later. It's happened. Vincent, of course, is always last.

There's a TV showing minor league baseball that Jack squints to see with his half-shut eyes that want only to close and sleep. His shirt scratches him around the neck. He breathes gruffly through his mouth and his fingers sting every time he goes to pick up the glass. When he isn't drinking his mouth shrivels into a dryness that makes him cough and blow, and when he isn't coughing and blowing, he's turning round in his seat to see if the door is opening. And when it does, leasing a near-winter chill into the place, it's a group of suited businessmen who take a table by the window.

After half an hour, the first tweaks of concern kick in. To begin with, he thinks it's just his gut roiling but then as he finishes off his drink and orders another, he realises it's not. The mouth dries even quicker, the eyes narrow, the brow draws. He loosens the collar of the shirt, shakes it. His scalp feels tender. He asks for water and gulps it when it comes and, as the four men in the window-seats laugh loudly, he gets a taste in his mouth that's more than bourbon and cloves.

After an hour, he starts to rewind the last few weeks. Then he goes back further, unfurls weeks into months and tries to get every action, every look, every conversation. He tries to get every time that Vincent took the money and every time he brought it back and handed it over, the dollar bills to Jack, right there in his hand, the visible, tangible bills, and the envelopes to the other guy, the envelopes he never once saw opened, never once saw the contents of. Take it, he said, take it and get me some more.

He doesn't know what to do. It's been over an hour and as he sits there, his stomach as tight as a drum-skin, the bourbons swilling in his head, those voices of the past start to kick in louder. Every time is the first time, he hears. There's no such thing as luck, it's a system. This is the easiest money I ever made in my whole life. Put out an extra place, honey, I'm bringing a friend. He sees the grimace again, the gesture, the way he slips the phone back neat in the holster of his pocket.

Ten minutes later, after stumbling off the stool, he's on his way to Vincent's apartment, dragging his heavy bones and his pounding head with him, the sweat streaming from his face in spite of the wind coming off the river. He gets to the building, climbs the stairs to the third floor and makes his way along the hallway. He knocks, leans up against the doorframe, out of breath, leaden, hearing nothing but those old, repeated words. With his weak, stinging fingers, he raps again, and as he does so, a neighbour steps out into the hallway in a stained vest. He looks Jack up and down. Nobody lives there, fella, he says. It's empty. Apart from a couple of days in the summer, it's been empty almost two years.

*

Jack held up his right hand in a gesture that said, for the night at least, he was done. His head lolled onto his chest, the shoulders slumped and John, standing up from the chair, went across to the bed and, holding both the back of his brittle skull and the sticky spine, slithered him a few inches further down, covering his shoulders with the quilt and the thickest of the blankets. As his father closed his eyes, he reached out and held his sallow face, the parchment skin, the cheekbone ridge, the florets of bloodshot veins, and without an ounce of pre-meditation, he leaned forward and kissed him on the forehead.

"Let's go back," his father said.

*

In the morning, he shaved him over the sink, watching the filings of his growth gather on the water. When he started to brush his hair in front of the speckled mirror, his father turned his face away, and when he went to put on his shoes, he couldn't, for the swelling, for the bloated ankles that rose up to shiny, bloated calves with streaks of indigo and lime. He packed the car alone.

Jack stayed shoeless in the diner. He'd eaten next to nothing and the coffee had gone cold and most of the time he sat and nursed himself. The medication he'd lined up carefully, like a parade, like a mix of the cylindrical and the round, the white and the yellow and the pale, eggshell blue, and then he'd swept every one of them off the table, scattering them to the floor with a growl he could hardly contain.

They headed west, back through the welter of towns and cities they'd gone through the day before, past landmarks, billboards and road-signs. The car, by this time, was showing major signs of fatigue. The pocks and crusts of the exhaust had become rust-rimmed holes that puttered and blew, the third wheel rim rolled away somewhere mid-morning and the one remaining wiper blade wore down to next to useless. Every time they stopped for longer than ten minutes, they left an oil leak. And every time they started out again the engine sputtered and strained.

Jack twitched. He was barefoot, his eyes deeper-set, his shirt unfastened, the hairs on his upper chest matted with sweat. This time it was thinner when he spoke, the pauses longer, the gathering of breath sometimes mid-sentence, mid-word even, the plosives panted and puffed.

*

He looks for Vincent and his hairy-eared accomplice for almost a year, stopping off in towns large and small in every part of the state and beyond. He goes into corner bars and non-corner bars, sits at hundreds of counters, drinks his beers and asks anyone he ever stops to talk to if they'd seen or heard of or knew of a guy who did what Vincent did. He gets nothing. And the more of that nothing he gets, the more eaten away by it he becomes, and the more eaten away he becomes so his powers of door-to-door coercion and charm start to slide, and with that his commission, and his rent and soon enough his whole ability to function on a regular week-to-week basis. It's not just the trickery that gets him, not just the itsy-bitsy mechanics of the scam, every last detail of which he goes over every night in his sleep, it's his own gullibility, it's the skewering sense of his own stupidity.

Within two years he's drunk most of what money he had left. He loses his job, his car, his place to live. He gives up on finding Vincent, on the Venezuelan bees. He sells his surplus shirts and shoes. He gets stomach cramps on a regular basis, headaches and migraines, throws up nuggets of crimson phlegm and, in a town he can't remember the name of, a doctor whose face he can't picture tells him he's had an internal collapse and he needs help.

There are months then he barely remembers; a winter in a clapboard house, sea mist every morning, the proximity of rail-tracks. There's a town bedecked in frost, drifts of feet-high snow out where the suburbs meet the open land, and, when the harshness of winter is done, there's a hospital with grounds the size of a golf course, with a network of corridors and wards with pale-green walls and radiators so hot they crack the paint.

There's medication for the stomach cramps, for the migraines, for the biliousness. There's something for the frenzy of withdrawal. And there's something, every clear, spring morning scored by birdsong, that zones him out most of the day, that makes everything in the world feel exactly the same. One day, at the pitch of that blandness when nothing moves that hasn't had its edges taken off, he's told in a white-walled office with posters of the Rockies and Christ the Redeemer that his internal collapse is permanent, that it's inoperable, and that there is a definable limit to his life.

After a few months, as the news sinks, falls into nothingness and crackles on a constant medication loop, as the azaleas bloom and the watered grounds prick with brighter colours that sometimes register and sometimes don't, there's a letter.

He doesn't remember receiving it but he remembers reading it because he remembers taking it into the glare of the bathroom and sitting in one of the cubicles. He remembers it was just before the night medications, in those moments when, sometimes, the skin and the muscles and the brain flickered enough to give him a modicum, at least, of understanding.

The gist of it is that the aunt that raised him, the stern-faced woman he's seen maybe two or three times over the last forty years, who brushed his hair with such vigour that tears would come to his eyes, has died, and that, as the sole surviving relative, he's entitled to what she left behind, namely the house she'd always lived in, the contents therein, what money there was *and* the deeds to a plot of land, owned by his grandfather, Patrick, his father's father, with a place to live on it, in a town called Mission two thousand miles to the west.

That's the gist. That's minus all the jargon and the legalese. And he understands it as he sits in the cubicle and holds the letter in his hands. The following day, after the morning medication, it starts to get faint again but over the next few weeks, after reading it over and over during that hour of slight reprieve, it gets clearer. And by the time he leaves, late in the summer, with his old hide suitcase the colour of cocoa, it's embedded.

He goes back to the house, sells it and most of the contents, some in an auction-house and most in a yard sale. He transfers the money into his own dwindled account and sits down with the deeds: The story he knows from his childhood, the panhandling grandfather, the card game and the winning of the land. What he doesn't know, what his aunt never chose to tell him, is that the land is, *specifically*, his, and that the house on it was built for him by the grandfather he never met just after his father was killed.

It's not a difficult decision to make. What is there to lose? He has an inoperable disease, nowhere to call home, no people to call family. And so, after the separation and divorce, after losing all contact with his one and only son and after Vincent, heading across the country to a place built out of love and consideration is hardly a big deal.

*

They reached the lake in the cool of early evening. Clouds had gathered in and the water shone armour-grey with the faintest patina of mist. John took the Toyota over the stones again, left it closer to the woods this time, closer to the kindling and sticks. He prepared everything, his hands always busy while his father slept in the car; the stove he assembled, the chairs he unfolded, the bowl, the pots and pans, the soft-bristled brush for his father's hair.

He knew instinctively when his father would wake. And when he did, he lifted him once more and carried him to where he'd set the chairs. He sat him down, mummified by blankets, the head protruding small and turtle-like. He made coffee, a pan of hot beans and a couple of sizzling eggs. His ear pricked to birdsong.

"Bufflehead. You hear that?"

His father shook his head, just the once.

"High metabolic rates. Monogamous. The males and females both have a large white patch behind the eye, not *behind* the eye, but…I want to fuck with his head."

The turtle head rose.

"Vincent. I want to fuck him up, badly."

A creamy half-moon sidled over the tops of the trees.

"It'll eat you alive. Find something else. Move on."

"I don't see how."

"Trust me."

John stood up. He scraped morsels of food onto the shale, gathered up the pots and pans and washed them noisily in the bowl. "You're telling me to forget?"

"Forget? No."

"What then?"

"It becomes every waking moment. That's what I'm telling you. You're either rearranging the past or organising the future. Either way, it's no good."

"But I'd find him. Make no mistake."

"And when does it stop?"

"When it's done."

"And then what? After you've fucked him up. What happens then?"

John shrugged as he swept up the kindling and sticks, the pieces of dry wood he pushed and scraped.

"It's not that simple. That's what I'm saying. There is not one thing that has not been caused by another. You can take any point in your life and figure how you got there. And then when you've figured it and traced it back, where are you but at another point? You see what I'm saying? Now, scratch my foot, would you?"

The moon sailed out into the open sea of sky. John picked up one of the sticks, bulbous at one end, sharp at the other. He held the lustrous bone at the sharp end, knelt down in front of him and rubbed at his father's soles with the other. He could hear the loose rattles, could see the sheen of his puffed feet, the face in borrowed moonlight, the faintest trail of egg-yolk on the chin. He walked back to the chair, stared out across the water, across the surface black as eels.

"You said 'lost contact'?"

"When?"

"When you were talking about going back to the Cassidy land. You said you separated and divorced and you lost contact with your son. What does that mean?"

Jack looked down into the fire.

"What does it mean?"

"It doesn't matter. Forget it. You were five years old. I understand."

"What do you understand?"

"That I was not a good father. I was unreliable. I was late all the time. I wasn't there. I drank."

"And? What is it that you understand?"

His father's face rooted down an inch or two into its scrawny neck and his spidery fingers perched onto the fringe of the blanket.

"That you didn't want to see me. That you'd had enough."

John dropped the stick onto the shale.

"What makes you say that? Why would you say that? I never said that. I was five years old. You're my father. What made you think that?"

The bufflehead sounded again from the wood's edge.

"Who told you? Who would say such a thing?"

He saw Jack swallow, the lurch of gristle in his throat. "Your mother."

"She told you I didn't want to see you? Is that what she said? That winter's day, when you came for me and drove away?"

"I tried. I tried to stay in touch. I tried every year on your birthday to speak to you."

"I would never say that. Never."

He watched his father pull at the cotton strands. He watched him pick one loose and feed it slowly between his fingers. The more he pulled, the more it came, and the longer it grew, the more separate from the rest it got. And the more he looked at it, the more he saw the twill and the weave, the more he felt it in the rub of forefinger and thumb. John saw the softening in his face as he did so, the scaffolding of the bones that held his features in place ease a single notch, the hoary skin drop a little. He saw the shoulder frame drop, the chest bone sag and not struggle to gather those pockets of breath. And he saw, on the shores of the blackening lake, with the moon no sooner set sail than swallowed up by the clouds, the look, just the once, over towards his only son, to everything he was from the day he was born, to every day that he'd ever seen him, to every time he'd held onto his hand and walked with him, to every conversation they'd ever had and every time that he'd held him, and then let him go, the look that knew, in those moments, that there never was an abandonment, there was no rejection.

John looked back at him. "She told me the same thing."

The rain began to fall as John stamped out the fire, picked up the brittle frame of his father, and lay him on the backseat with a combination of pillows for his head. He stood by the car with its mottled rust and snapped blades, and he started to imagine the version of his life with his father there, not as if airlifted into a scene, but right there, ordinarily.

He imagined him at every birthday party, watching him as he blew the candles out on his cake, breaking off a piece of the icing, raising his eyebrows at the sweetness as he ate it. He imagined him waiting outside every school that he went to, in cotton shirtsleeves and tan, polished brogues and a smile that broke open every time he came out. He imagined chess games on warm afternoons, his younger hands on a clean-shaven chin, in a calculation, just like his own, of several moves hence. He was there with him in the freight trains, there in the corners lined with straw, in the shudder of the cars, there in the barns and shacks. He was there when, for months, he stopped even trying to reattach himself to a world he could no longer connect with, there on the farmland, in the beach houses, the cheap apartments. He went to Florida with him. He could see him in the sheen of the polished cars, in the hubcaps and mirrors, always somewhere on the forecourt, the shirt verging on gaudy, the shoes canvas. He could see him in the hotels and bars, watching him cook, wait tables, rustle up a cocktail or two. He'd catch him in various places; in the surfaces of the kitchens, in the plenitude of silver, bent on the back of a serving spoon even. He'd find him in lobbies, on a sunken leather chair next to a potted palm, reading almanacs and magazines. Or, at the end of the counter, eating pretzels from a bowl, or in the corridors, the stairways or escalators, or the Zorro'd fire-escapes that zigzagged the buildings. Always there, always somewhere.

When he woke, the steam was rising off the hood of the car. Out across the lake the mist trembled like the shimmer of a thousand lockets and the hills beyond were a palette of ochres and rust, of elephant-grey, soot-black and plum. Over by the trees, he could see the collapse of last night's fire, the charred tinder, the white-rimmed remnants of bark and the bed of ash. With the window rolled down, he could sniff out the stretches of heavy sand, the plumb and gulp of deep water and faint-metal rain that hung in the trees. His cocked ear turned to get the buffleheads, teals and greygeese.

He felt warm and sticky-faced. His hair was tousled, his lips dry. There was a scarlet weal on his cheekbone where he'd leant up against the window most of the night. He opened the door, took off his boots and days-old socks, put his feet on the stone and navigated his way across the shoreline to the water's edge. He got to his haunches and splashed his face, rubbed at it, ran the water back through his hair, felt it scoot down his back. He stood up and faced out across the lake. The mist started to fritter. The low sun to the east skittered the bilberry and petrol blues of the lake, dazzled the blacks and quicksilver greys.

He headed back. And he wasn't sure why, some ten or so paces from the car, that same, sudden twist in his gut slowed him up again, or why it didn't stop right there but spread to the ends of his fingers and the back of his throat and why it dipped into his bowels or jellied his knees or made his shoulders sag like sacks of glutinous sap. He didn't know why the closer he got to the car it felt like he was wading through thigh-deep water or why his mouth dried up or what it was that tapped out those extra beats in his heart or why that frontal lobe of his felt so scrambled he could find no words to think with. Then he knew.

Part Two

The early summer dusk had melted an hour since into an evening chill. Rupture Hill to the north-west was a shadowy dung-brown, its girdle charcoal and ash-grey and the woodland at its base a soot-covered verdigris and tan. Over towards the Anderson place a bonneted Ruth checked the crucifix hung in the porch-way, blessed herself and closed the door. And one by one the lights in the house went out. Back across the uneven ground and over the path, John Cassidy stood in the doorway of the homestead, black-suited still and backlit from a tawny lamp that flickered. He looked out over the land, over *his* land. He sniffed at it, at the acuity of the berries, the damp grass and the turned, moist earth.

He'd sat with his father a long time. Sometimes he'd looked at the drain of his face, at its basted stillness and the draw of the leached-mauve lips. Sometimes he'd tidied up the blanket under his chin, the brush-mat at his feet, the kitchen bowl, the face cloth in it. The little things. Then there was the smell, the longer he sat there, of bodily moisture, of stickiness and ooze. He'd put his boots on, folded away the collapsible chairs and put them in the trunk. Then he'd driven away, over the pebbles and dirt. He'd taken a turn along a single-track road that was dusty and uneven. After a mile he came to a clearing, to a space amongst the trees where there was a general store the size of a fairy-tale shack, a low log building decorated with dinghies and surfboards and a makeshift basket of fish reels. His father in the back looked asleep. Sick and greasy, jaundice-yellow cut with lime and gruel, but asleep nonetheless.

He'd wanted to take one of the dinghies, to unhook it from the timber and pull it along the track to the slipway at the end. He'd wanted to go back to the car and lift his father off the seat and carry him like he'd carried him before, his head nuzzled in the crook of his shoulder, his nose pressed against the skin of his neck, his hair against his cheek, and put him in the dinghy, to lower him until he was almost flat, and to push him out and watch him float away.

*

The burial had taken place in the town halfway across the country where he was born, next to his father, Michael, and the mother he met for minutes only, Catherine. The chapel smelled of naphthalene and must, and the minister, in only his second ever funeral service, edged it too close to the overbearing side of solemn, his words, as well meant as they were, dissipating like the drizzle outside over the collection of motley mourners, people who Jack had either worked with or been a regular salesman to, the man in the pressed cotton shirt with the button-down collar, the one in the lustrous mulberry shoes, the men who'd bought either cars or houses or land, and the men whose lives had been blessed in one way or another by the myriad contents of his encyclopaedias.

John drifted and listened at the same time. He was both there and not there. He'd stayed that way as the casket was taken out and the rain fell harder, as the few remaining mourners stood, as gobbets of clay-coloured earth sprinkled over the mulberry shoes and his father was lowered into the ground.

For him there was no consolation. Any sense of resolution was scant. He had not been made peaceful. There was no solace that was not mauled at the moment it appeared. And, unlike his father, there was no sense of closure for him, no satisfaction in knowing the truth, that there had been no abandonment or rejection, that his father had looked for him and called him every birthday, and that the twisted lies that came out of his mother's mouth had ravaged them both and boomed them out into the world in different directions because the truth didn't and couldn't take away those twenty years of his father's absence. The knowing didn't matter. The absence was what mattered.

He made no plans. There was no grand scheme, no thought of what to do next other than go through his father's things, no thought of how long it'd take him or how long he'd be there, or what to do with the acres of Cassidy land. There was, as he stood in the honeyed glow of the lamp, no thought of the deeds, no inkling, as yet, amidst his anger and lack of appeasement, of retribution.

The town, on the other hand, or certain prominent individuals within it, specifically Ted Mallender of the Land Management Agency, were armed with more plans and contingencies than a uniformed general with a pointing stick. You see, they'd presumed, in the failure of those alleged relatives that had come and gone, that on the death of Jack Cassidy the land would be returned to its rightful owners, the town of Mission, in particular the Land Management Agency, to be built on, developed, turned to economic advantage. But what they hadn't figured on was John Cassidy, about whom they had known nothing.

*

Two weeks later Ted and the youngest, most recent member of the Land Management Agency, Doug Sketchings, from the neighbouring town of Serpentine and therefore unsteeped in the Cassidy mythology, walked the unmade track to the Cassidy homestead. A moderate breeze blew the drying Anderson bedsheets like sails and tinkled the bell-like bonnets. It was mid-morning, a clear day with puffball clouds and from the parked car at the end of the track all the way to the homestead the two men never spoke.

When they got to the veranda, Ted turned. "Stay behind me. He doesn't want to see you first. You look like a preacher."

Doug almost slipped stepping back and Ted gave him a brief glare. Bags and sacks cluttered the place still, boxes and packets, untouched. The old armchair on the veranda hadn't moved an inch.

Ted took a breath in and knocked, three short raps. They waited. The wind blew seed husks over the decking, rustled the packets and bags.

"Perhaps he's not home."

"Don't assume anything, Douglas," he said, and then whispered, "He's a Cassidy, don't forget. Now, look round the sides and the back, I'll wait here."

Doug nodded and, holding onto the rail, began to tiptoe. This was partly due to his natural diffidence and partly due to having two small children who woke at the drop of a hatpin, but mainly it was because, given Ted's snarled description of the Cassidy breed, he expected to meet something that had slithered out of a swamp.

There was no-one in the main room. All he could see through the skimpy netting was a table strewn with papers and a set of accompanying chairs. He went closer to the pane of unwashed glass, held his breath. This was not what Doug had been promised. He'd been promised charts and coloured pins and the occasional measuring of land with modern-day equipment, not what felt like a stakeout.

"Nothing here," he hissed back.

"Keep going. Round the back."

Crab-like he went, his hand staining the rail with sweat, his head looming forward at various points like a swimmer looking for air. From the back of the house, he could see the parked car and the road that skirted the Cassidy land. He could make out the rough, untended terrain beyond and the slopes of Rupture Hill. And, if he'd got as far as the other side and looked over to his right, he may even have made out the neat-trimmed edges of the Mallender estate. But he didn't.

The window opened with a swiftness and a hand grabbed his arm in a lizard's grip. "What do you want?" said the faceless voice.

Doug had nothing. In his head, beyond being a young father with a melancholic wife and twins who wouldn't rest, he had only a long-winded and officious rationale for being there, but it never happened. And the grip stayed firm.

Then Doug remembered the badge on his pocket and used his free hand to show it in the direction of the opened window. John's face appeared, pale and gaunt, half sunlit, half not. He eased the grip slightly. "Do you know who Ben Gunn is?" he said.

"Does he work for the Agency?"

"No, he does not. He's in Treasure Island."

Doug swallowed. "We'd just like to talk," he said.

"We?"

"Ted's the…"

"Where is he?"

"He's at the door."

"Shout him."

Doug cleared his throat and went for a holler that was supposed to sound clear and meaningful but came out like the bark of an old dog. Ted appeared, weighed up the situation and, speaking somewhere between John and Doug, said, "Now, what can we do here?"

"You can get off my land," John said, "You can leave me alone."

Ted had had the Cassidy legend seared into him from a very early age. But even so, though it coursed through his bloodstream, he'd never actually met a Cassidy face to face. With Jack he'd sent a couple of scouts early on but once he'd found out the man was dying, he'd decided to let fate take its course. And so John, unshaven, grimy-handed and rank-breathed, was like some sub-species of a genre yet to be classified.

"We mean no harm," he said. "This here is Doug. He's a father of twins."

Doug nodded. John glanced at the peachy skin of his face.

"We come to offer our condolences for your loss and, as members of the Land Management Agency, to ask what plans you have for the land."

"No plans…yet."

"No?"

"No."

"In that case, if you'll excuse us, we'll be making our way back to the office. And may I suggest that should you consider selling the land then the Agency might be interested. I'll leave a card."

Ted took a monogrammed card from his jacket pocket and flicked it into the murk of the room. John turned to watch it land, and let go of Doug's arm.

On the walk back along the track with the sun high overhead and the summer breeze stilled to nothing, Doug, releasing small islands of sweat onto the pale-cherry shirt he'd ironed himself, said not a word. Ted the same, all the way to the parked car, and then when the doors were closed, the air-con blasted on and the pack of cigarillos reached for, he turned to Doug and said, "You see? Animal." Then he drove away.

*

There was a hiatus then, understandably. But then that hiatus became a nothing, and the longer it stayed a nothing, the more it looked like Plan A had failed and Ted Mallender, the Land Management Agency and the townsfolk of Mission in general needed to look at the contingencies: Scouts were sent out, again. Highly innocuous and low in number, these were ordinary volunteers whose fondness for nature and exercise took them close enough to the Cassidy land for a looksee at the shovelers and teals and, hopefully, at the gruff and ruffle-breasted rarity that was John Cassidy. Then there were those edgier individuals who were willing to park their cars on the road and walk as far along the track to the homestead as possible without a genuine reason to be there. There were those who walked out of town, across the rickety bridge and out to Coronation Point and then made their way towards the homestead that way, stopping at the edge of the Anderson land as if to admire how Ruth hung out the bonnets and sheets. And there were those, fitter and braver, who risked the rough terrain and the darkness of the woods to get there from the northern side, out of regular view. Whatever, none of it worked.

Nobody saw him. Not once. Nobody even caught a glimpse of him open his door to take in the summer air, or sit in the old armchair with a cold beer, or climb into the battered Toyota and drive into town to get provisions. And, because nobody saw him, nobody knew what he was like, or what he was capable of.

With Jack it'd been easier. Jack was sick. Jack was dying. It was easier for those mild-mannered volunteers to close the door in the man's face or watch him struggle with the groceries, or, for those fitter and braver ones to slit his tyres once in a while with a pen-knife. But with John, nobody knew.

The Anderson family were visited with. They were sat down by Ted at the bountiful table and sermonised on the nature of communal duty even if that duty seemed to fly in the face of tolerance.

The following morning a starch-bonneted Ruth and her two milky ducklings crossed the path and knocked on the homestead door with a basket swollen with fruit and homemade bread. The door opened a few inches and, with an abundance of spiritual sweetness and a raising of the basket, she asked whether John would like to partake in the Good Lord's sustenance. There was a moment's pause. A bare arm appeared through the gap in the door, then a hand hovered above the greenest, shiniest apple and took it.

"Thank you," came the voice.

Ruth smiled. So too the ducklings. "And what about prayer? Would you like to join us in thanking the Lord for his gifts?"

The door opened wider, sending the rank and fusty air out onto the veranda so that Ruth's nostrils couldn't help but flicker and the ducklings couldn't help but frown and pincer those lips as if they'd tasted lime sap. The hand reappeared, returned the apple to the basket, and the door closed.

Then there was the Environment Agency, sent in by Ted and the LMA on the grounds of the risk of infestation and disease and overly high levels of Methane found in gatherings of domestic waste. The two men in hi-visibility jackets and clipboards got some way through their spiel about health issues and possible closure, but then

John, through the same chink in the doorway, said: "Chesters versus the State of Nebraska, 1956, unspecific warrant leading to the Law of Trespass and Ungainful Entry." And the chink was no more.

There were the two law enforcement officers from the town of Mission sent to investigate the Cassidy homestead while reeking provocatively of steak juice and relish who had only opened those savoury mouths before they got, "Williamson, Jeremiah, versus the Los Angeles Police Department, 1965, intimidation. Come back when you've got something."

The longer it went on, and the plans and the contingencies fell by the wayside, so the rumours around John started to spring up like bindweed: One, he was a near-savage who hunted at night in the wild terrain. Two, his antecedent, Patrick, had built subterranean tunnels, one of which came out in the cellar of the general store. Three, there were enough stockpiled tins to feed an army. And four, the body of his father was still in there, part-embalmed, hence the smell.

After two months, standing in front of the fallow ground of last resorts, they turned, reluctantly, to Jake Massey. He'd met John Cassidy after all. He'd spoken with him, and even though they neither trusted nor liked him, even though they considered him unreliable and full of bullshit, still, at that point he was their only chance to find out what was what. They talked about gentle persuasion. They talked about just getting into the house and having a regular conversation with the kind of questions you might ask over a neighbourhood fence, but Jake, with his attention span not much more than a sentence long, heard only hush-hush and camouflage.

The other candidate would've been Sophie Li. But, following Jack's death, she'd left the town. Whether it was that, apart from her neighbours in the migrant housing, the rest of the community had cut her out for her simple association with the Cassidy's, no-one knew. Whether it was lack of funds or a disagreement with John or that her sister and brother-in-law, Lee Shaw, who lived a few miles to the east of Serpentine were a better prospect, again it was hard to say. Either way, she'd gone. So Jake it was.

For John, the paradox was this; that the ungainly efforts to prise out what his plans were, actually made him give them some thought. Prior to the visits, he had nothing. OK, so his father had told him something of how he'd been maltreated by the town, mentioning the name of Ted Mallender in particular, but he was still a long way off a plan, grand or otherwise. But, with Ted and his sidekick, with the Andersons, the Environment Agency, the law enforcement men and then, on that Saturday morning of slow-rising mist, the jaunty and combat-jacketed figure of Jake Massey making his way along the path to the house, well, it made him think. For the first time, gambits started to twitch. If people wanted to come onto his land and take him on, if they wanted it so badly, then let them come and get it.

*

Jake knocked, tried, as best Jake could, to play it cool. He offered his condolences, a shake of his hand. He tried, as they sat around the kitchen table and talked about the summer heat and the dryness of the land, about the timber mill and his warnings and the new foreman, Dan Cruck, sent in to examine the efficiency of the place, to play the covert agent.

He glanced and scanned. He extended his stay as long as he could, drew out those questions up to and beyond their natural limits, so that he could skim and absorb some more. He made enquiries that may have looked like genuine interest in the house, the land and John's intentions had they not come out of Jake's mouth. They went down into the cellar to fetch up a couple of beers. They stood on the veranda. Jake used the bathroom, more than once, checked out the cabinets and shelves, the smell of the towels. John heard him, mapped him yard by yard.

"And then there's Rita and Delilah," he said, standing in the doorway. "Rita, I like, but I don't know Delilah. I don't know who she is. You know what I'm saying? She's a mystery."

John's mouth twitched.

*

The following day, Ted paid Jake a visit. He tried to be friendly. He bought beer and a pack of his favourite cigarettes. He looked at the posters on the wall: Bruce Lee, Rambo, Scarface.

"So," he said, "how was it? Did he let you in?"

"I was there an hour. You know, there must be a thousand books in there. Whole boxes of them. Everywhere. And shoe boxes and shirt boxes."

"What does he eat?"

"All kinds. He's got cans, fruit, vegetables, pulses. Meats and fish. You won't starve him out."

"And is he clean?"

"Clean enough."

"Did he talk?"

"Sometimes."

"What about?"

"The heat, the dryness of the land."

"Did he say anything specific?"

"What about?"

"About his plans?"

"He said he didn't exactly have any."

"And the land?"

"The dry land?"

"No, *his* land."

"He didn't know, but he was thinking about an offer from the Land Management Agency. Yes, he was thinking of selling the land."

"He said that?"

"He mentioned your name, said you'd given him a card," Jake said and inhaled from a cigarette at the window. "And he wanted something else," he said, "Something you could help him with."

"What?"

"He didn't say."

Ted got the smell of cinder blocks and sawdust. He walked over towards the window, gave Jake another pack of cigarettes and patted him twice on the shoulder.

"You did a good job."

"You want anything else, you just let me know."

"I will," he said, opening the apartment door, sniffing, heading for the stairway.

"Hey," Jake shouted, "do you know Delilah Morris?"

Ted drove away from the apartment building smelling of nicotine. Over to the north the ridges and crests of Rupture Hill were caught in a glare-less sunlight. Children played in the neighbourhood streets. Cars got washed, polished and waxed. Middle-aged men in pastel shirts mowed short, square lawns and the scent of grass wafted up into the birdsong of blossomed trees. And, as he skirted the town, past the railway station and on towards the burial grounds, he figured this much; that maybe, after more than a century, after the laying down of the ragged thief's threes and kings had bent every generation of Missionites out of shape, the issue of the Cassidy land may not be an issue for much longer.

*

Most mornings he had black coffee and peaches in syrup. Then he exercised, usually bare-backed so that with every sit-up both 'Restless' and 'Fearless' would ripple like indigo waves. He showered and, every third day, he shaved, using the same china-handled razor his father had. Sometimes he busied himself: He moved the single bed towards the window. He took down the netted drapes, felt them crackle in his hands. He opened all the windows to let out the fetid air, cleared all the seed packs from the veranda, and, with polish Sophie had left behind, he shined up the gargoyles.

Sometimes he did magic tricks. He wore the black suit and the white, cotton shirt, put on the gloves and, in front of the equally polished mirror of the wardrobe that remained, he remembered what Mario had done to disappear the buttons, coins and hatpins, to set free the watches and chains.

Most days, though, interrupted only by sustenance food and a bottle of his father's beer, he read: Sometimes in the armchair, sometimes leaning against the back wall overlooking the land, but more often at the kitchen table he kept clean and dry so he could lay those books down and not have them smeared in brine or prune juice or sausage meat smoked in a cannery.

It was a self-styled education, a free-form curriculum. One day he might follow a pattern or a theme. The next he might take out the blindfold and randomly choose a volume, whether it was muscles, museums or mushrooms, parliaments, parrots or particles. Or, he might move from one thing to the next, weaving those zany diametrics with the barest of threads. And, there were those things he kept going back to, over and over again; the evolution of card games, the great, unsolved disappearances, gambling scams, legal studies and precedents, poisons, examples of epistolary, of boxing, of Zen archery, of trance, of the source of the leather shoe and the cotton shirt, the myriad examples of chess sets, of opening gambits and permutations and the multitudinous ways to skin a bob-cat.

When he was done with the encyclopaedias, he put them back into the room with the single bed and turned his attention to the local histories. This was generally chronological. There was no reason why John should rope-swing from one historical event to the next in a scattergun manner. History was cause and effect. In history, one thing led to another.

The material was manifold. Some could be found in the encyclopaedias. The geographic region, for one, the Gold Rush, for another. There was information under Lewis and Clark and the aluminium industry. There were footnotes in the Modoc wars, appendices in wheat, pioneers and Godliness. Some was in smaller volumes by local writers who might attempt the historic panoply of the place but who generally focussed on more specific events; the migration west, the 'Christianising' of the native tribes, the land purchases and, of course, the gold.

They might, as they inevitably had to, mention young Nathaniel Hansetter who, in the gloaming of the nineteenth century, while contemplating a proposal of marriage to his childhood sweetheart, Rosa Carter, discovered what he thought was a sure-fire sign of his direction-to-be, a ring, embedded in the ground near Coronation Point. Except, it wasn't a ring, it was what the ring was made of.

They might tell of how, instead of heading straight for Rosa's house, knocking on her door and going down on bended knee, he got side-tracked. He had visions, golden visions of voluminous wealth that took him away from the town that very day, beyond the foothills and over the higher land to look for a buyer to make him rich. They might say that the fate of Mission was sealed then because, being a simple, dunderheaded soul who'd never left the town from the day he'd been born, he was never going to understand the guile and easy deceit that lay in spades beyond those hills. They might relate how, the day after he returned with his handful of potential 'buyers', as well as 'surveyors', 'mining engineers', weighers armed with scales and a whole posse of hardy, grim-faced prospectors disguised as trappers and traders, he was found dead in a ravine at the bottom of Rupture Hill, and the flood gates opened.

They came mainly from the south and the east. On horseback, in wagons, on foot. Some came by sea and then made that arduous journey inland, and after they'd travelled those weeks and miles, they wanted something substantial at the end of it. They were men of blunter demands who had less need for scriptural guidance and who shunned the parables and commandments for whorehouses, bars and places that sold equipment that could last the bad weather.

The look of the place changed. No longer prim and clean, it began to bear all the hallmarks of a large-sized shanty town; detritus and waste, worn thoroughfares, the sudden rise in transitory accommodation, the arrival of the railroad, the extension, much needed, of the jailhouse, the place humming to the scent of the mass unwashed. In the midst of so many changes a good proportion of the previous inhabitants left, taking their families with them across the prairie lands in wagons piled high. Some stayed. Some saw it as their duty to convert the panhandlers. And there were others who saw the whole thing not as an invasion or a collapse, but as an opportunity, to gain dividend and position. Hence, Archer's chandlery, Parker's general store, Smithson's loan company, Jess' board and lodgings.

So, they might lay the blame at the feet of young Nathaniel. They might suggest it was his stupidity that changed the town for good. They might imply that even though those treasure-hunters didn't stay for very long or even find an abundance of treasure, their legacy, apart from a few stray bastards and a greater urban sprawl, was a culture where profiteering on any scale became second nature, and goodness and kindness and looking out for others got left behind.

Other reading material came in newspaper articles, letters, a few barely decipherable maps and a small collection of black-and-white and sepia photographs, all gathered together in various conditions from pristine to ragged in a box found in the dusty belly of the wardrobe, marked 'Dinner shirts/White'.

There might be a discussion of the building of the timber mill, something about the migrant housing settlement, the refurbishment of the Station Hotel, the burial grounds. There might be a feature on the redistribution of land beyond the river, which happened to coincide with the creation and the establishment of the Land Management Agency through which every application needed to pass.

The Mallender family made several appearances, as early landowners and mayoral candidates and in various photographs of the family estate. So, too, did Patrick Cassidy. Mentioned in volumes spanning the turn of the century and once in Eke Masterson's *The People of Mission*, he also made a number of the photographs in Jack's shirt box: With John's grandfather, as a boy, on a Jeepster, the sun in his eyes. With him a few years later on the edge of a sports field and then in uniform, weeks before Utah beach.

He imagined it, the buildings and streets and landmarks of the town. He imagined its history and its geography, and he didn't need to stand on any particular vantage point to see how important the land was. Nor did he need to spend any time in the clearing of Coronation Point to figure how much of a part the gold had played. He didn't need to walk into every civic building in town to feel the hold that greed and manipulation had. No, most clear days, when he stood in that homestead doorway just as his father and his great-grandfather had before him and looked back towards the town, he could sense the righteousness skewed and bent out of shape and the godliness that was both scabbard and shield. And the gambits started to move, and make shapes.

*

Two weeks later Jake made his way across the Cassidy land again. He was there, on Ted's request, to see if there were any developments, if that something else that John wanted was imminent. He brought foodstuffs this time, perishables, dairy and fruit that had sap. He sat in the old armchair, squinting, trying his damnedest to listen, to play it hush-hush, to figure whether he was being Jake or Ted's boy out on his mission. He lit cigarettes, looked down at the shovels and saws, at the seeds in the grooves of the porch-way steps. It was difficult. It dazzled him as he sat there in the afternoon sunlight.

"I'd like you to meet Delilah," he said. "I'd like to bring her here and see what you think. We could bring Chinese. I could ask Rita."

"Maybe we could," John said.

There was a pause. Jake swilled the dregs of the coffee. "So…" he said, "was there something else you wanted?"

"I need surveys and maps," John said quickly, "All the land this side of Coronation Point, including the rough terrain, all the way over to Rupture Hill. Detailed. You think you could do that for me? You think you could get those? And then we'll think about the Chinese."

“I could try,” Jake said, and followed John back into the house. He was confused. Was he working for both sides now? Was he a double agent?

*

The Land Management Agency was situated on the third storey of a sandstone building just across from the Police department. Apart from the Italianate cornicing, the walnut angels on the staircase and the commissioned oil portrait of Edward Mallender, senior, astride a chestnut stallion, there was little fanciful about it.

A couple of middle-aged men in suits wrote in ledgers, and Doug Sketchings, father of two two-year-old insomniacs with short fuses, stared down at a chart like he was trying to hypnotise it.

Ted looked out of the window with his back to Jake.

“So, he wants surveys and maps, does he? Did he say what for?”

“Just he wanted them.”

“But not why?”

“No, sir.”

“He didn’t expand?”

“No.”

“Maybe he’s figuring how much land there is to sell. Maybe he’s working it all out.” He said and turned. “Why aren’t you at work?”

“I got suspended,” Jake said.

“What for?”

“Lateness.”

Ted popped an antacid into his mouth and piled another couple of assumptions about Jake Massey onto the spike.

“We need something,” he said. “I don’t care what it is. Something that lets us in, something that tells us what he’s up to. Does he have a weak spot?”

“Sir?”

"I want you to find me his weak spot. Sometimes it's easy to see, sometimes it's not. You see Doug over there? You know what Doug's weak spot is?"

Jake shook his head.

"Look at the eyes. Most of the time they're heavy, and when they're not heavy they're bloodshot. Look at the collar of his jacket. Look at his pants. Stand up, Doug, show the kid your pants."

Doug did so, slowly.

"You see what his weak spot is now?"

Jake was drawn to the maps on the wall and the host of coloured pins.

"It's his domestic situation. He's got two kids that won't sleep and a wife who zones out all day. He's got food stains on the collar where he holds onto the kids and his pants look like they've been ironed by a retard. You want Doug to do something, you don't ask him first thing because he's exhausted and you don't ask him last thing because he's already dreading going back to his situation. So, you give him a coffee and you ask him around midday and then he might do a half-decent job. It's called psychology, Jake."

Doug sat down again. It was three-thirty in the afternoon. Ted sat at his desk upon which stood a framed photograph of him and Lily at a property convention in Oklahoma.

"He's not here because he wants to be, is he? Neither he nor his sick father were here through choice. He wants the surveys and the maps for a reason. He's making moves, and I want you to find out what they are, Jake. Can you do that?"

"I think so, sir."

"We're smoking him out. We're getting closer."

He dusted the photograph with the sleeve of his jacket and stood.

"You see, that land out there belongs to my family," he said, "and I have a duty to get it back. I owe it to all those good people from whom it was stolen. We can do things with that land, Jake. It changes the town. It makes it a better place and what we don't need are any more of those Cassidys to sit on it for another hundred years and rub our goddamned noses in it. You see what I'm saying? If he wants the surveys, we can give him the surveys. If he wants the maps, he can have them. But we need something back, Jake. What do you say?"

Jake turned to face him, to see the flushing of his cheeks and the eyes that pierced and then settled.

"What are the red pins for?" he said, pointing.

*

And, because the surveys arrived, rolled in cardboard tubes, marked *The Property of Mission LMA* and with Ted's official seal of approval, the Chinese meal took place, in the Cassidy homestead, on 9th August, John's twenty-fifth birthday.

To begin with, it was stilted, notwithstanding Jake's fanfared entrance of waving the tubes above his head as if he'd stolen them from Fort Knox. Rita and Delilah had never met John before, even though, like everyone else in Mission, they knew the name and every connotation of depravity that came with it. What they also knew, because he'd told them so many times, was that Jake was knee-deep in a clandestine mission with more secrets than a CIA filing cabinet.

The meal itself passed off quietly. They sat at the table with the food in front of them. Delilah found a thick beeswax candle under the sink, placed it in the centre and lit it so that their faces took on fitful glows as they sat. John, for his part, was courteous. He'd sat down with Mario enough times to know how to mime the manners he needed and even though, with each course, his crooked nose burst into spasms of sniffing, it looked more like the actions of a trained chef than those of a small forest animal. He managed a couple of conversational fillers, like the abridged history of the bean sprout or why Occidentals are better at mathematics than westerners, but generally he left it to Jake and his Kung Fu films and Rita and her high-pitched enquiries as to the names of the dishes and how to pronounce them.

As the plates and containers were taken away and Jake opened up his beers and whisky, it was always likely the shackles would start to loosen. It got noisier, for one thing. Rita found some of Jack's records and put them on so that the howls of the Coyotes started to quicken and the squawks of other creatures got louder across the land, so that more than once one of the Anderson lights went on and more than once the door would open and the crucifix would swing in the slice of light.

Rita got lascivious, as she always did. She wanted to see John's books, his pictures and papers. She wanted to see the value of his land in actual figures. She wanted to, and did, rifle through the shoe and shirt boxes in his room, most of which did not contain shoes or shirts. No matter, she shuffled through them anyway, her face veiled in cigarette smoke. And, when she was done, she threw them back. Then, with insistent Jake right next to her, she wanted John to put on the black suit and the white shirt and the long ladies' gloves and do some of his tricks. John had little choice. To Rita's yelps and with hands as though in bird-flight, he made coins disappear and re-appear. He produced flowers, keys and lockets, tied hatpins in chains, all without moving a muscle on his face.

Then she wanted to, and did, put the suit on. She wanted the blindfold and the thin white gloves and to dance with John who stood white-shirted and barelegged as she moved towards him and who, with the slightest movement of the head only, refused. So, she danced with Jake instead, and when Jake let her go, she fell. She sent coins rolling from the jacket across the floor and as she slumped into the table, the candle rocked and the blindfold slipped. Within five minutes, she was asleep like a deadweight, her hand up around her face, the cherry-red nails so carefully stroked by Sylvie Buckle that very afternoon, chipped and cracked, and a snore like a flap of folded paper stuck in the spokes of a wheel.

Jake staggered out onto the veranda. He lit his cigarette and started to rant about the timber mill and how the company wanted it closed down, about Dan Cruck, the smug-fuck, and the unfairness, the harshness, the pettiness of being suspended like a school kid for lateness and for stinking of alcohol next to a whirring saw. He got raucous, and at the peak of one of his rants, he kicked out and into the gut of Jack's armchair, puncturing it with his heel. The material ripped and flapped open. Bare springs popped and stuffing the colour of earwax oozed out. He said nothing, sat on the chair, dragged on his cigarette, and closed his eyes.

John watched him from the doorway. He felt the ululations of night wind on his face, looked down at Jake slumped into the give of where his father used to sit and look out over the land, across to Coronation Point and the town beyond the wooded rises where the people despised him, getting paler with each day that passed, more wasted and wizened, the sags of skin of his upper arms dangling around the joints, the drawn cheekbones, the sallowing skull, the near-liquid breath in the bones of his chest. He walked over towards him, took off his shoes and socks and removed the lit cigarette from between his fingers. He sniffed, the ears moving indiscernibly.

He went back into the house, stepping over Rita. He heard Delilah moving around in the cellar, Delilah who'd rarely spoken, who'd finished each course of food with a dab to the corners of her mouth with a paper napkin, Delilah he'd spent only a few moments with the whole evening when, with Jake riling himself up and Rita tipping out the contents of the boxes, she'd stood on the veranda gazing out towards Rupture Hill with its hoops of thin mist in that silk turquoise dress that clung and shone in the half-moon's glow, and without turning round, had said, "My grandfather always said that most of the gold was right here, on this land."

He heard her heels on the stone floor down below. It was four in the morning. And without a single pulse of thought his hand went towards the bolt of the door and slid it across.

*

Everything happens for a reason. Everything is cause and effect. Because of one thing, so another, and so on. So, *because* the Land

Management Agency wanted the land *because* they figured it was theirs, and *because* the Law Enforcement and Environment officers and the bonneted, basket-bearing Andersons had failed, Jake Massey had been called in. And *because* Jake went to the homestead with the Chinese meal, with Delilah and, in particular, rummaging Rita, *because* the surveys came, and the surveys came *because* Jake had gone to the LMA and Ted Mallender, then John Cassidy was able to chance upon, amongst the ruin of his room the following day, amid the various boxes upturned by Rita and not put back, the one thing that would take all of his gambits and moves and put them together, that would take his grand, fermenting scheme that began only with anger and rawness, and light its fuse.

It was stuck to the bottom of one of the shoeboxes, underneath an article on the restoration of the storm-damaged Station Hotel; a page ripped out of a newspaper, mug-stained in the top right-hand corner, the stain embedded like a seal as if the article had been kept out, pinned down and looked at for a long time.

The dominant feature of the page was the story of a rescue: It was a hot, summer's day and eight-year-old Abby Weekes was walking her dog, Winnipeg, along by the river when the dog had fallen in. Abby didn't know the river. She was visiting her grandparents out east and so when the dog started to flounder, she decided to jump in and save him. What she didn't know was that the undertow was notoriously strong. There'd been accidents there before, fatalities even, and soon not only did Winnipeg go under and not come back but so, too, Abby started to feel her feet and calves as though suddenly yanked at. She was a decent swimmer, but that was it, and slowly she began to get dragged further out into the deeper water. Sometimes when the pull was heavier, she went under completely, and then she'd surface again. It was during one of those surfacing moments that she saw the man on the side and screamed as loud as she could before she went down again. It was in between the drag-downs she saw him next, *in* the river, knee-high, then waist-high, getting closer until, just as those moments when she went under got longer, she felt his hand grab hers and pull her towards him. She felt her upper arm pulled, her shoulders and rib cage, her back and her legs until she was wrapped around him, until she felt him push back to the shore.

The photograph, to the side of the text, showed the man and the girl with the river behind them. The girls' parents were next to her. They were smiling broadly, Mr. and Mrs Weekes. They were smiling, Jeff and Hannah, because their daughter had been saved, and even though poor Winnipeg had perished, their daughter was alive. Jeff had his hand down on Abby's shoulder. Hannah looked not to the camera, or to Jeff, or to Abby even, but to the man standing by the river's edge. She looked directly at his face, this stranger in town, this passer-by, this man that nobody knew.

The man of mystery was the CEO of a small company called Carpe Diem Enterprises. That was all the article said. But, to Abby Weekes and her parents, he was a saviour. To them he would never be forgotten.

His face was circled in green marker pen, more than once. An arrow came out of the circle and went to the top of the page to the left of the mug stain, just below the date. At the end of the arrow's trail was written, in the same green marker, in Jack Cassidy's shaky hand, the name: *Vincent*.

*

With the various surveys and maps spread across the kitchen table, with his peaches and black coffee done, his guests, including pale Delilah, gone and the article cut and folded and placed in his pocket, he set off for Mission. Over his shoulder was the packed bag and in the left-hand pocket of his black suit jacket that smelled vaguely of Rita's cheap perfume were the deeds to the Cassidy land.

Now, apart from a handful of people, nobody knew what he looked like and so, based on those wildfire rumours, the majority of the townsfolk expected to see some kind of deformed creature, hunchbacked, club-footed, overly large or small. They expected a slack-jawed beast, hairy-handed, heavy-browed who would rattle its way across the land on a hand-fettled cart that would be left on its side, draped in bloodied pelts and fishhooks on the rickety bridge.

When he got to the stairs of the sandstone building, he took them two at a time up to the third floor. He knocked on the glass partition and went in. And, because they'd only ever seen him unshaven and half-lit, neither Ted nor Doug recognised him, especially in the crisp, white shirt and the suit. As for the other two men in the office, they rarely raised their heads from the ledgers for anyone.

"Mr Mallender?" John said.

Ted seemed troubled. He looked up from behind the desk, away from him and Lily in Oklahoma and away from why there was a single blade of lustrous grass on the bathroom floor that morning.

"Can I help?"

"I'm John Cassidy."

The two ledger-men paused, in unison, swivelled their necks like adjustable lamps and glanced across the room. Doug went dry-lipped, felt the caffeine ignite in his system.

Ted stood. "Mr Cassidy," he said, walking toward him, "you look...different."

"I'd like to discuss the land."

"Yes. Good. Come this way."

Ted led him into a smaller, separate office, wondering why, when he'd gone for the peppermint mouth rinse in the bathroom cabinet, there was none left.

The two men sat. "What is it you'd like to discuss, exactly?"

"The selling of the land beyond the homestead. There's a stretch goes as far down as the road in one direction and hits the woods in the other."

"It's rough land, overgrown."

"It's also twenty-five acres. That's over a thousand square yards."

"And you want to sell it?"

"That's why I'm here."

Ted leant back in his chair. He looked across to the young man opposite, saw the tie-less, unfastened collar, the hair in need of a cut.

"What about the land with the homestead on?"

"Not yet."

"Yes, but..."

"My father's dead just over two months. I have things I need to do."

He looked at the crooked nose, the twitch of the ear when Doug stood up in the next room, the features of the ready, rural immigrant with his currency of soil.

"I understand that, but..."

"I can always go elsewhere."

He heard his youth, his lack of respect, his smear of the family name. "I'm sure we can find a solution."

"Let's hope so," John said, and stood. "I'll be in touch."

Ted stayed right where he was. He reached into his pocket and fished out an antacid, tasted the fizz in his mouth. He watched the Cassidy creature go, heard him clip down the stairs and tried to figure why there was a printed tread of earth on his kitchen floor.

Doug moved one of the red pins three inches to the left on the contoured map and sidled over to the window. He looked out and across, to the serrated ridges of cloud and the rooftops flat and sandstone. Then he moved closer to the pane and looked down; to John Cassidy leaving the building, to the man from Treasure Island with his packed bag slung heroically over his shoulder. He watched him cross the street, go down the hill, past the Station Hotel and further, until, almost lost amongst the Missionites, he crossed again and walked into the railway station.

*

On his way home from the office, Ted Mallender called into Harry's bar. This was unusual. This was once in a blue moon, so much so that Harry himself who'd attended every meeting of the Mission Development Committee that Ted chaired, had to look twice to see who it was. For one thing, Ted thought he might bump into Jake. For another, he was celebrating, albeit a little early, the fact that a piece of Cassidy land, no matter what it was, may be being returned to the town. And for a third, *but* for a third, he was troubled.

He knew something was awry when he watched Doug Sketchings drive away from the Agency in his small Korean car and he envied him. Despite his stained collar and his creased pants, he envied him the certainty, however dreaded it might be, of knowing, at least, that he was going home to a clinically downbeat wife and two uncontrollable boys in a place that stank of kids' sick and nail polish.

It was preferable to the uncertainty of his own home, to the instances that revolved dizzily around his younger wife, Lily, to the blade of grass, to the mouth rinse and to the footprint on the kitchen floor that had played in his head most of his working day like a tune he couldn't get rid of.

He rang her and told her he'd be late. And then he listened, to the way she responded. Normally when Ted spoke to anyone, including Lily, he was only ever interested in what they said if it was beneficial to him. But this time it was different. This time he listened for a tone. He listened to whether her voice was quicker than usual, or more delayed because she had to think or make corrections. He got nothing.

It was Jake's first day back at the mill after the suspension and he took the detour down to Harry's because he felt he deserved it. He had a couple of quick beers that sieved through the dust at the back of his throat and then, for reasons of discipline and self-control, he was about to leave when Ted motioned him from one of the booths. Jake checked back over his shoulder towards the door, towards his apartment and the threadbare grip on what was for the best.

Ted pointed to the seat opposite "I've got news, Jake," he said. "Grab yourself a beer and sit down."

The jukebox played country rock in the background. Jake sat down, his apartment sliding further away into the gloom.

"He offered us some of the land. It's the rough land behind the homestead, but it's a start. His father's dead less than three months. And he needs somewhere to live. I can understand that. I'm a patient man. There are things he needs to do. That's what he said."

Ted moved forward in his seat and drummed his fingers on his chin. "What are those things, Jake? Do you know? Has he said anything? What those things are he needs to do."

Jake took a glug from his beer and tried to feign a torch-lit delve into the nooks and crannies of the night of the Chinese meal.

"I don't remember anything."

"Think some more."

"There were books, magazines…the surveys. That kind of thing."

"But he didn't say anything? He didn't specify any particular thing that he needed to do?"

Jake shook his head and Ted sat back in the chair, folded his hands across his chest and looked around the room.

"And you didn't get his weak spot? You didn't take a good enough look."

"I tried, but…"

"You remember what we did with Doug? You remember his weak spot?"

"Yes, sir."

"What was it?"

"Food stains on his collar."

"Exactly. Shall I tell you about John Cassidy? He's a man familiar with deceit, is what he is. It's a familial trait."

"He locked Delilah in the cellar."

"That's what I'm saying."

"And he stole Rita's watch."

"I don't like him, Jake. He's disrespectful. He's a deceiver of people and he won't make me look like a fool. He won't do that. I like the truth of things. I like it all laid out where I can see it. I like it so I know what and where everything is. And I don't like it when I don't or when people keep it from me…Do you have a girl, Jake?"

"Not exactly."

"I want you to do something for me. I want you to go back to the Cassidy place and look around some more. I need to know what his moves are. He's out of town. We watched him go. Black suit and a packed bag. A few days, at least. I could drive you there right now."

Jake closed his eyes a few seconds. Dusk had descended like a veil.

"I'm not sure, Mr Mallender."

"You're not sure? What do you mean 'you're not sure'? I don't think you understand me here, Jake. I said I want you to do something for me." Ted looked round. "You see those guys over there? Those guys are wondering what you're doing sitting here. That's all they're trying to figure. What exactly Jake Massey, with his reputation, with his track record for fucking things up, is doing talking with Ted Mallender, is doing *having a beer* with Ted Mallender? You understand me? Now I can make it go two ways here, Jake. I can make it look like you're making a nuisance of yourself. I can shout. I can accuse you of all kinds. Or, I can make it look like we have a connection. I can make it look as if you're a funny guy, like you're here because I like you. Do you follow me?"

"Yes, sir."

"Are you sure?"

Jake nodded.

"Plus, there's another favour. Very hush-hush. Very clandestine."

Ted stood, mopped at his mouth with a napkin, left money on the table.

"I'll tell you in the car."

Jake waited out on the parking lot a few minutes before Ted came back out. Something to do with the grease-stains and the sawdust on the uniform and the sacking he made him sit on. Something to do with the black, toe-capped boots and the polystyrene mat he brought out for Jake to put them on.

There was a half-moon out beyond the rough terrain, angled down to the crags of Rupture Hill. Ted took the road out, past the burial grounds and on, and the closer they got to the Mallender estate, to the lawns and the colonial house, so his agitation seemed to grow. A quarter-mile short of the turning he pulled over to the side of the road with a screech and jabbed his lit cigarillo up around Jake's face.

"That greasy fucker, Jorge, has been in my house. I know he has. And if he's been doing what I think he's been doing I will have his balls on the end of a flagpole. Now I'm never there when he's there. He rolls up in his jalopy after I've gone and he's gone when I get back, so I need somebody to go on up there and see what they can see. Y'understand what I'm saying?"

"But I'm at the mill. I'm..."

"Don't let me down, Jake. I need you to help me. Now get out and don't touch the car. And get what you can on the Cassidy guy. Get his weak spot for me."

*

John got off the train at Serpentine. It was mid-afternoon. From the prairies to the south a wind that didn't carry the dust of timber on its back came low and quick across the street. He walked the short rise of the road to the town's library where, in its high-ceilinged rooms, he found surnames, addresses and contacts. He followed trails wherever they might go, any trail, any lead, any thread and a couple of hours later, with the buzz of the air-conditioning still in his ears, he came out with enough information to make his move with.

Carpe Diem Enterprises did officially exist. It was not long-established but, by the looks, had had two or three other names before. There was a motto, in Latin, and a mission statement that spoke of opportunism and risk. There was a logo, a series of testimonies that featured case studies of failing industries asset-stripped, bought at base-level and then regenerated and sold on for sizeable profits, or of tracts of wasteland purchased, salvaged and built on. There was a kite-marked guarantee. There was a telephone and fax number, P.O. Box details, but no official address, no doorway on the street of a town somewhere, no claw-shaped knocker. And Vincent Clay, for sure, was its founder and CEO.

There were two hotels in Serpentine; the imaginatively named Central and the marginally poetic Prairie View. John booked in at the Prairie View. The room was on the ground floor at the end of a dim corridor and decorated in tones of mustard and seaweed green. And it did not have a prairie view. It had a view of the Prairie View parking lot. And the bed was as springy as a trampoline.

In the early evening, he unpacked most of the bag. There were some clothes but mostly it was the surveys and maps and other materials brought from the homestead, some of which he laid out on the floor with the delicacy of spread petals, and some he stuck on the long, plain wall with strips of masking tape.

Around 7.30 he ate in the Prairie View restaurant, which did have a prairie view, and, given the stretch of virtually uninterrupted glass that covered the entire wall, wasn't afraid to flaunt it. And, apart from four men who wore competing shades of pastel sweaters ranging from peach to lavender and who bore every hallmark of being on a two-day, spouse-free golfing trip, he was alone.

He faced the road and the flat lands beyond. For a while, he imagined his father there, propped in the chair next to him, the gorges of clavicle and throat exposed. It'll eat you alive, he said. Find something else, move on. But it wasn't possible. He couldn't do it. The golfers left, their sweaters simmering like sorbets. He cut into the pinkish meat of the steak and watched the juices leak out across the plate.

When he got back to the room, he took out a bottle of his father's beer from the bag and opened it, sipped it with his eyes closed. His ear pricked to the sound of a flat-backed jalopy carrying hay bales and he sniffed at the fusty air. Before he sat down, he took the photograph of the green-circled Vincent Clay out of his pocket and set it above the surveys and maps on the long, plain wall. And then, over the next three days, interrupted only by sleep, bouts of exercise and food he had delivered to the room, he started to figure his plan.

He paced around. Sometimes he swayed and swooned. Sometimes he closed his eyes and stood in the middle of the room, flexing the muscles in his neck, feinting first one way and then another. He imagined Vincent Clay in the photograph, being looked at by Hannah Weekes. He imagined him shedding his green halo and loosening himself off, moving out of the frame. He felt the cold focus of the eyes that got animated when he wanted something. He sensed the dextrous manipulations of the hidden hands, the balance of the feet. Sometimes he heard him, tuned his ear in to the way he said things: I'm new to the neighbourhood. I can have a beer with my buddies, right? What did I tell you about the system? Carpe diem, my man. Seize the goddamned day.

It was like that for three days. Some sleep, but not much. In room nine on the ground floor of the Prairie View with the view of the lot and not the prairie or the skies above it. He tried to figure it, to gather it all in; the history, the land, the town and the gold. He gathered the greed and the resentment and what it was he needed to do. And he gathered Vincent and his hairy-eared accomplice, and how he might drag them in and snare them, like bugs in a jar.

He could've just held on to the land. He could've held onto it and made the whole thing about him and Vincent Clay alone. It would've been easier man to man, to contact Vincent and tell him straight that the vast majority of the gold deposits were buried under the Cassidy land and all he needed to do was to buy it up and dig. But that was too simple. John liked the twistier course. He liked the convolutions and complexities, the flax of the woven narratives, the risk of failure, even. He liked how all that guile and diligence, those manipulations and moves, made the suffering for the other so much greater. It was Dwayne all over again. Not the single blow, not the too brief satisfaction that offered nothing after the punch had gone.

And, as for the town, and Ted Mallender, and all the other deserving flotsam and jetsam, well, how could they be absolved.

*

The rumour of the potential sale spread quickly. For one thing, once Lily Mallender knew, once Ted had told her and looked her up and down for loosened hair and straggled clothes, then the following morning Sylvie Buckle, the beautician, knew and once Sylvie knew, it was open season. The news ran between those conical dryers like currents. Women of all ages raised thin, crescent brows and curled soon-to-be hairless lips. The conversations zip-wired around the hair-sprayed room and those women, sitting in the midst of beautification, with magazines or without, wondered again, as they always did, as they could not help but do, what the young Cassidy man might be like.

And for another, the two mousy ledger-men in the Land Management Agency had so little else to speak of in their lives that wasn't to do with columns and figures that the opportunity, for once, to be the bearers of news that, while technically confidential, would no doubt slip out anyway, was one definitely to be taken. And so speak out they did, to their wives, children and neighbours. Plus, they'd seen the Cassidy man up close. They'd been in the same room as him, breathed in the same air.

But while those nuggets were bolstering the kudos of the ledger-men, for others it was less so. Poor Doug Sketchings, for instance, told his shiny-skinned wife, Viola, with enough animation to suggest the news might affect them personally, and then watched as the words dimmed and disappeared into the deadpan of her eyes before she put on her moccasins and tucked into the tub of peppermint ice-cream she was holding.

And if Jake Massey had been around the streets and stores of Mission on that late summer morning, he'd've no doubt been doling out information like candy sticks to anyone with or without a sweet tooth. Or, if he'd been at the timber mill like he should've, he'd've been yelling it above the buzz-saws for all to hear, especially those guys from Harry's. But he wasn't. Because the morning the town was alive with the news of the sale, Jake was waking up on the floor of the Cassidy homestead surrounded by shoeboxes and a dozen empty bottles of Jack Cassidy's beer and with a headache like a fault-line, cleavered and seeped in.

He sat up. To his side the cellar door was lifted up, shirt boxes had the lids off. There was a blanket smelling vaguely of muscle-rub over his legs and feet. The window he'd prised open to get in was open still. He adjusted himself. Sunlight came in and made patterns on the kitchen floor. There was an empty pack of cigarettes by his feet, stubbed ends and ash on the linoleum tiles. He frowned at the lids of the shirt boxes, saw the skewered papers where he'd rifled and sifted. When he stood, he allowed the blanket to fall and nudged at the boxes with his feet. He got the same maps, the pages of local history both loose and bound, the hardback covers of encyclopaedias. He got newspaper articles, some of which he started to read until he ran out of patience. He got the leaflets again: a menu for Sizzlin' Steve's, the rates at the Smithson loan company, the cost of tool hire at Archer's chandlery. And he got the photographs, the monochrome and sepia prints he shifted out with the soles of his shoes, pushing them over to the sunlight and looking down at the lawns of the Mallender estate, at the facades of the Colonial house and at the bearded Cassidy man whose land it was, kneeling on the half-timbered roof of the homestead-to-be.

He imagined Delilah Morris again. He imagined her out on the veranda with John, the moonlight on the dress, the give of her stomach on the balustrade. And John looking towards her, towards the cradle at the base of her spine and the slow curve of the hips. And him then pushing the bolt of the door into the hole, keeping her breathy down in the dark.

The sound of the car broke him away. He could hear it making its way along the path towards the house. He sneaked into the bedroom and flicked the drapes to take a look, saw the two-tone Chevy stop where the path got too narrow to drive any further. Inside was a man in his thirties and a woman of similar age. They talked for a while, mostly the man, using his hands, and then he got out. Jake watched him stand, look up towards the homestead, and then start to walk. He was broad, barrel-chested, a good six feet in his work boots, and the closer he got, Jake picked out the thin, down-turned grimness of the mouth, the eyes that narrowed and the two cut-knuckled hands.

He could hear the footsteps on the rubbled earth and then on the wood of the veranda. He watched him stand in the doorway, swivel his bull neck slowly from one side to the other. He saw how the torso leant forward and the marine-cut head extended out like a hawksbill turtle and spoke with a smoker's rasp.

"Mr Cassidy? John Cassidy?"

Jake tried to stay still. But this was Jake. This was a lifetime of twitchiness and so, as he shuffled, his foot struck a tin of peaches in syrup and sent it rolling to an audible clunk against the bedroom door.

"Ok, so you don't want to come out, that's fine. I can say my piece from here."

Jake looked down at the shirt box open to watches and chains and hatpins.

"Now, I'm sorry for your loss, Mr Cassidy, and I guess you have all kinds to deal with selling up the land, but you owe my sister-in-law money. We can do this two ways. You can pay Sophie what she's owed and the whole thing is done with. Or, you can make a dispute of it. That's up to you. But ask anyone who knows Lee Shaw and they'll tell you to go for the first option."

Jake swallowed, wanted the long drag of a cigarette.

"I've got an amount written down on a piece of paper here, and I'm going to push it under the door. You got a week, Mr Cassidy. Then I'll be back. And if I were you, I'd have the money ready."

He watched the paper appear, saw the man turn and walk away. He heard him go back across the path and then he scuttled over to the drapes again to see him climb into the Chevy and drive away without once speaking to the woman beside him. He watched the car all the way back to the road, the other side of which, across immaculate, undulating lawns, along the Italianate colonnade and through the double, arched doors of eggshell blue to the elbow of the staircase, knelt Lily Mallender, with perky lashes and manicured hands spread on the wall in front of her, gulping the Venezuelan semen of Jorge, the hirsute gardener.

*

When John got back from the Serpentine hotel, he noticed nothing of the break-in. The cellar door was closed, the shoe- and shirt boxes were put back, if not in identical places then close enough, and the empty beer bottles had been bagged and disposed of, likewise the cigarette butts. The piece of paper on the linoleum floor he couldn't figure, nor the figures on it, nor the cakes of dried earth on the veranda steps, or the film of a single, oily print on the jamb of the door.

The first couple of days he spent catching up on sleep. He stayed with the black coffee and the tinned fruit, supplemented by nuts and grain, but cut out the bottle of his father's beer, which was why he didn't notice the missing ones. And he exercised. He cranked up the frequency of the sit-ups and squat-thrusts, used kilogram tins of pineapples and pickled hams as weights and, every morning, took those walks out across the rough terrain in his winter boots, the ears pricked, the snout back sniffing. And, with every stride, over ridges, hummocks and dips, past vines of sot-weed and clusters of prickly pear, he composed the letter to Vincent Clay.

On the fifth day he was back, he walked the rough terrain of the Cassidy land for the last time as its owner, and when he got back, he sat down at the kitchen table where his father had sat in his plaid shirt and wrote it.

Dear Mr. Clay, it said: *It has been brought to my attention by a reliable source that you are a man of considerable enterprise and ambition. It is with this in mind that I offer you the following proposition: To the north-west of the country, some two hundred miles inland and four hundred and fifty to the border, lies the small town of Mission. It is a remote community between the western edge of the prairie lands and the foothills of the Cascade Mountains. Given that its chief source of employment is the timber mill, which is currently suffering under the economic strain, the town is leaning towards a degree of instability, a fact that, I'm sure you'll recognise, makes it all the riper for opportunity.*

What you will also discover, should you consult your history books, is that towards the end of the penultimate century the town was the subject of intense, but largely unproductive gold-mining and was, as one local historian put it, 'chaotic with purblind greed'. More interestingly, though, that same historian also suggested in a lesser-known volume that the main reason for the lack of success was that 'the prospectors, arriving in a raggedy fashion mainly from the south and the east, had done little to no research as to the accurate location of the gold' and approached its potential discovery with 'little skill and logic and a surfeit of randomness and brawn'. The history of the town suggests that during the prospectors' stay, the very fabric of the town underwent drastic and unwelcome changes and to prevent further upheavals to the community any mention of the gold or its whereabouts was discouraged. However, according to previously unseen and unpublished documentation, it is estimated with some confidence that a sizeable amount of the material awaits excavation still. Naturally, this is by no means common knowledge and access to the areas will only be possible via private investment, but for a reasonable fee, I am offering you the opportunity for the kind of financial dividends you rarely chance upon.

For myself, a man of equal enterprise, it is sufficient to say that, sadly, I am currently not in a position to purchase the land myself but to guarantee the success of my venture I have sent this letter to a number of other companies and individuals. Each letter is the same and no-one contains any more information than the other. Personally, I have no interest in who makes the offer, so long as the offer is made.

Upon the payment of the initial fee, a detailed map will be sent indicating the lie of the enriched lands and who currently owns them. Should you not be in receipt of this map, take it that you have been either unsuccessful, too late or too provident in your decision-making. If this is the case, your cheque will be immediately returned. On this you have my word as a gentleman, albeit, of necessity, an anonymous one. If you are successful, then I wish you every prosperity and as an act of gratitude, I would consider twenty per cent of the overall profit to be sufficient reward.

Yours

Then, just over a week after he'd got back from the Prairie View, after every change had been made and the endless possibilities and permutations had been exhausted, he sent it.

*

The following day, a late August afternoon with patchy whipped clouds and a mild westerly, he went to the Land Management Agency to see Ted Mallender. Doug noticed him first, then the two ledger-men, who put their pens down simultaneously and lifted their heads to watch the subject of their confidential whisperings walk in. Ted was the last to know. Marooned in the smaller office those last few days he was curdling still in Jake's delivered bulletin that, yes, he'd seen the jalopy on the driveway, but no, when he'd peeked in through the windows, there was no sign of Jorge, and no sign either of Lily.

He broke away from his drift to stand, adjusted his tie, practised a brief, business-like smile, and unclenched his fists.

"Come in, John," he said, "take a seat."

John put the deeds down on the table, without sitting. "The land," he said.

"The rough land?"

"The thousand square yards of land. It's yours if you want it."

Ted narrowed his eyes slightly, and smiled. "OK, let's do this," he said, "let's move this thing along. I see no point in deliberation."

And, via an officious sequence of actions including the opening and closing of cabinet drawers, the flash and whirr of the photo-copying machine and a flurry of stamping, signing and sealing, that's what they did. At the end, with not a word having passed between them, there was a handshake, Ted's firm and forthright, John's intentionally limp.

The two men stood a moment. Ted saw the winter boots, the signed deeds on the table. He had some of his land.

"You don't have any debts, Mr Cassidy? I'm just asking."

John's brow twitched.

"Nothing your father owes? No payments outstanding? No four-figure sums? And is there any good reason to know how much the hire of an industrial sander is? From Archer's chandlery? Or the payback rates at Smithson's? What kind of steak man are you, Mr Cassidy?"

John looked directly at Ted for as long as it would take to skin a small rabbit, and then turned on his heels and walked away. He walked through the doorway of the Land Management Agency, down three flights of stairs with walnut angels on the rails and out into the afternoon sunlight.

"You know, I'm surprised," Doug said, "I mean, his family has that land for over a century, and he's here a few months and he's selling it." He moved over to the board and moved four red pins around the rough terrain of what once was the Cassidy land.

Ted wiped his hands on the table's sheen and stood in the doorway to the main office. "He doesn't know what the fuck he's doing, that's why. He's an amateur. He's a novice. I paid half what it's worth. He knows nothing. His ancestor stole the land. And now we're stealing it back. There are animals in the forest smarter than he is."

*

When John got back to the homestead there was a scrawled note pinned to the door, which said: *I gave you a week. You cross me at your peril*. He looked at it and tried to figure what it meant. Then he went inside and brought out the piece of paper he'd found on the linoleum floor a week earlier. It was the same handwriting, the same thick, slanted strokes from the same notebook. Plus, when he looked, there was the tack of the same oily handprint on the frame of the door.

The first thing he figured was this, that the four-digit number on the sheet corresponded to the four-digit sum suggested by Ted Mallender, and that same four-digit number corresponded to a debt allegedly owed by himself or his father. Second, that the precise nature of Ted's questions, alongside all the other shit about industrial sanders, payback rates and how he liked his steak meant only one thing, that someone had been in the homestead and gone through his stuff. And who was it knew he was away for a few days, who was it knew he was in Serpentine, and who was it wanted more information than a small-town gossip? Ted Mallender. And who would Ted Mallender ask to go and get him that information like a dopey lapdog? Jake Massey.

He checked the shoe and shirt boxes. Some of the sheets had definitely been moved and there, skewed on top of one of them were the leaflets for Archer's chandlery, for Smithson's loans, and for Sizzlin' Steve's. He went down into the cellar and noticed the missing bottles of his father's beer. Back in the kitchen, on his hands and knees he found specks of cigarette ash on the bristles of the broom and, in rummaging to the bottom of the trashcan, he came across an empty pack of Marlboros. He also figured, as he stood on the veranda and looked out over Coronation Point bathed in soft sunlight, that whoever had written the note and pushed the four-digit figure through the door had seen Jake, the dopey lapdog, and figured it was him.

It was enough for him to know that it was Jake. It was enough to know that he'd sliced open his father's armchair without a word of apology, that he'd broken into his home, stolen the beer, rifled through his possessions and fed whatever information he felt necessary back to his master. And it was enough because, standing in the late summer air with hints of fabric softener drifting over from the Anderson clothes-line, he didn't need to go and pay him a visit and hold his father's shotgun to his head. He had his own plans for Jake Massey.

*

Four days later, he got Vincent Clay's reply, to which he replied, and four days after that he watched as a two-tone Chevy turned off the main road and made its way along the path to the homestead. It was mid-afternoon, temperate, a few degrees cooler than the day before.

He saw the oil on the hands first, then the grim line of mouth. He adjusted himself by the porch-way as the man got closer, as the blades of grass flickered around his feet and the birdsong fretted. Five paces from the steps to the house he stopped. His hands went into his pockets and he spat out onto the path.

"I warned you, fella. You ignore me at your peril. You ask anyone, they'll tell you the one thing you don't do is fool around with Lee Shaw. Y'understand me?"

John stayed root-still.

"Now, I don't want to make your life any shittier than it already is, but if I have to, I will. You owe Sophie money. Either you or your father, I don't care, and if you don't pay up like a decent man, I'll hurt you. And don't for one minute think I won't."

John took a breath in. "How many weeks' work?" he said.

"The last five she was here. Plus gas. Plus wear and tear. Plus errands."

"My father wasn't around for half that."

"Not my problem. Sophie cleaned up. Sophie did her work."

"Where is she?"

"She's with us. My wife is her sister. I'm acting on her behalf."

"You got legal proof of that?"

"Don't fuck around with me, boy. Now, what's it to be?"

John stepped those two paces forward from the threshold of the door to the edge of the steps.

"This is my land, Mr Shaw, and I will not be preached at by you or by anyone else, so the way I see it is this: You've got two options. One, I'll give you the money for three weeks' work and the whole thing is done with. Or, I'll give you the five, and it's not."

"Give me the five, and I'll tell Sophie you wished her well."

John turned and walked back into the house, closing the door behind him. A minute later, he was out. In his hand was an envelope and, as the birdsong chattered and rang out, he walked down the steps, stood in front of the squinting man, and gave him the money.

"I'm a man of my word, Mr Shaw," he said.

He watched the man take the money, put it in the pocket of his jeans, and go. Over the top of Rupture Hill came a flock of whipped-white clouds in a scoot of feather and fluff, and, further east, beyond the upturned bowl of Blessings Point, many miles away, there was a single, puff-balled harbinger of rain.

*

A month later, after Vincent's reply to his second letter of understanding, he sat at the kitchen table and wrote the third.

Dear Mr Clay,

It is with great pleasure that I can inform you that your application has been successful, that the other two interested parties clearly did not share your hope and ambition, and that I am now in a position to forward you the more detailed surveys and maps, the contacts in relation to the purchases of the land, and, as promised, the further information that may guide your plan of action.

It is important here to say that the existence and whereabouts of the gold is by no means common knowledge. Indeed, you are now the sole bearer of the most valuable information and, as such, the methods of acquiring the land will need resolution, guile and discretion. Might I suggest that the reasons you give for buying the sections of land are veiled for as long as possible so as not to arouse suspicion, and might I also suggest, for similar reasons, that the sequence of buying the land be given consideration.

The purchase of the larger tract of rough terrain, formerly part of the Cassidy land but recently sold to the Land Management Agency is the most suitable starting point. The reasons are two-fold. One, it will attract little attention. And two, the head of the Agency, Ted Mallender, is the most influential man in the town but, for all his advocacy of civic pride and belonging, he hides a streak of raw enterprise. The reduced price paid by the Agency will give him the kind of leverage he relishes and he will see the opportunity either to make good money on the sale, or to take a keen interest in whatever ruse your project assumes. Either way, you will need to play him at some point. I suggest an appeal to his ego, to begin with at least.

Second, the timber mill. According to evidence, there is a rich seam underneath where the mill was built, and so it may be worth monitoring its financial decline. Potential for sale would be greatly improved should the mill fall to its knees. Or, given the time-scale of such an eventuality, not be there at all.

Third, the Cassidy land itself, supposedly the location of the larger deposits. The cheap sale of the rough terrain implies one of two things: either Mr Cassidy, an outsider who acquired the land on the death of his estranged father, knows nothing of land costs, or he is eager to sell. However, rumour has it that he is an obdurate young man and, as such, however tempting it may be to approach him first, an initial, direct contact, without the foundations of previous purchases, the potential ally of Ted Mallender and the support of the townsfolk, is likely to be both unsuccessful and damaging. In terms of the townsfolk, Mr Clay, the people of Mission are like most small-town herds, basic and gullible. They are bullish when feeling powerful, but cowardly and deferential when not. Given the right approach, you will be able to use them as you please.

Finally, it only remains for me to wish you every success, and I look forward to my own remuneration.

Yours

Four months later

The low-slung sun of a late afternoon in January. The dazzled white-lime and corn husks of the prairies and fields to the south, the land hard and rutted, ridged in places by snow.

The two men sat on the train, Vincent next to the window, watching the landscape pass and Lester Hoops, his accomplice, slavering on a health-kick plum and trying to gather the juices from his chin. Lester had hit fifty and was overweight by at least thirty pounds. His nose was bulbous and riddled with rivulets of claret and his hairy ears were as though moulded from clay by a large-thumbed boy with neither the skill nor the patience to glaze them. His hair was a thinning sawdust colour that tried to hide a hummock scalp and both the collars of his shirt and the cuffs of his jacket were on the cusp of fraying. To Vincent, though, he was the most reliable man he'd ever met.

The town became visible, slewed in the bay of the foothills whose shoulders bore the winter brunt. Closer in, as the train slowed, there was the river's bend and those southern neighbourhoods spread like old men's fingers, with their bone-coloured housing, the cuticles of owned land and that gentle rise back to the town with its two crossed streets and, across the bridge, the migrant shacks, and the stacks of the timber mill.

"Here we go, Lester, my friend," said Vincent, standing, "Are we ready?"

Lester nodded, an ungathered trickle of plum sap on the jut of his chin.

They got to the Station Hotel as the light drew in. Vincent, in his pale-grey suit and spruce-green shirt, did what he always did when he first arrived in a new place. He became porous and smart. He spoke briefly to the clerk, tipped the bellhop, commented on the chill of the day, the good size of the adjoining rooms and, while Lester flopped shoeless on the bed, he walked over to the window, opened it and looked out.

He could see the whole of the street, the long spine of the cross from the intersection at the top to the rail-tracks at its foot. He could see the sidewalks and the stores, the stretch of covered arcade and, most of all, he could see the people. He watched always for first impressions, the movement of faces, shoulders and hands tapping into him like semaphores. He watched for pace and texture. He watched for the spectrum of hot and cold, for regularities and habits. And then, while Lester slept and snored and dreamed happily of his eight-ounce steak, he unpacked his valise and propped up the photograph of his fake wife on the bedside table, just as he always did.

*

Sizzlin' Steve's was as slack as most Tuesdays in the heart of winter. The Mallenders had just left, Lily shimmering in Christmas jewellery and Ted in steak juice and suspicion. So, too, had Ned Scarratt and the two young officers who spent most of the time sneaking disbelieving glances at Rita Mahoonie and her plumped cleavage as she sat at the window table with the suited foreman of the timber mill, Dan Cruck. Neither they nor most of the adult population with half-decent eyesight could believe that Rita and Dan were an item, that they had been since early December, since John Cassidy's idle suggestion to Rita that she deserved a man with prospects. It was a win-win situation for all. Rita, even though she had to suffer Dan's pillow talk of fragile infrastructures and poor safety standards, at least got to sniff the aroma of sophistication once in a while, usually on the linen of out-of-town hotels and the tables of low-lit restaurants, while Dan got to have roller-coaster sex most nights, and, of course, John Cassidy got exactly what he wanted from Rita, whether she knew it or she didn't; regular bulletins on the state of the mill.

Vincent and Lester found a corner table out of earshot of the small coterie of bank clerks and the birthday party of three. They ordered steak and fries and a couple of beers. Vincent sat straighter. Lester hunched, his neck sticky inside the collar of his shirt. Every once in a while, Vincent reached across and picked up one of the toothpicks.

"This is the big one, Lester," he said, removing a scrap of steak, "this is the best opportunity we've had for a long time. Better than the asset stripping, the land for land's sake, the bought-up lots in the middle of nowhere. Better than all the short cons, the race-tracks, the street tricks. Better than them all."

"If it's for real?"

"If it's for real, Lester, you think my very thoughts. If it's for real. Correct."

Vincent laid the toothpick down on the table, angled the steak knife across the plate, and leant forward.

"I have only one question," he said, "everything else, the existence of the gold, the whereabouts, the volume, the ownership of the land or otherwise, is superfluous. It means nothing until that question is answered. You know what it is?"

Lester held his silence and stopped chewing.

"What does the writer of the letters gain? If it's not for real? That's what I ask myself? What the fuck is the point?" He paused, shook his head. "And I don't see it," he said, "I've looked. I've examined every suspicion I have, but I don't see it. I don't see where his gain is if it's not for real. And we take risks. This is the nature of what we do. For how long now?"

"Fifteen years."

"Fifteen years. And every time is different. And every place is different. And we play it always as it comes. You see a card, you play a card. And so on." He licked at the relish on his lips. "What was it my father used to say?"

"Yes, sir."

"What did he say?"

"Eye on the prize, boys."

"What else?"

“Eat or be eaten by.”

“And?”

“Treat failure as an impossibility.”

“And what is our motto?”

“Carpe diem.”

“Say it again.”

“Carpe diem.”

“And what does it mean?”

“Seize the day.”

“Exactly,” Vincent said, picked up the steak knife and dug it hard into the meat. “Seize the goddamned day.”

The party of three left after nine, taking half the cake with them, leaving only an out-of-town couple en route to the coast, one of the bank clerks and Vincent and Lester almost done.

“We need two things here,” Vincent said, leaning back in his seat, his spruce-green stomach rising and falling like kelp on a tidal swill, “you know what they are?”

Lester leaked out a steak-scented sigh through pursed lips. “Spades?”

“Not yet spades.”

“Diggers?”

“A plan of action is one. Something to go to the Land Agency with. Something credible. Something that makes this Mallender guy think. You know what else?”

Lester frowned, the deep-set lines as if cut into his brow.

“Hearts and minds. You know what that means? It means we don’t upset anyone, we don’t say boo, we don’t move, until we have to. We go and see the land. First thing. We go out there, out to this Cassidy land. We take a good look. We find out who and what we’re dealing with.”

*

The town, on that Wednesday morning, went about its regular business. The train from the south was due, so folks were down at the station waiting to go to Serpentine mainly, or sometimes further west and beyond. The signage was being repainted on Smithson's loan company and, in Archer's chandlery, a handful of farm labourers on their fortnightly trip to town, stood and weighed up, literally, the pros and cons of jig-cutters and buzz-saws. Further on, Mae Chattus, of Chattus' Buttons and Bows, sat on a three-legged stool and waited for any one of her dozen customers to call in for whatever yardage of material and, in Ike's barber shop, the talk, as it had been those last few weeks and months, was the perilous state of the timber mill. Old men with pale-grey hair thinner than one of Mae's cotton strands sat on those red leather chairs, some of which swivelled and some of which didn't, and allowed their husky bulletins of second-hand news to flit from one shiny surface to the next, until they fell, superseded, to the floor.

Elsewhere, the police department building was home once again to garrulous Judd and Gerty Snipe and their two teenage sons, and across the street, the older and less salacious cousin of Rita Mahoonie tried with cold fingers to use the key-cutting machine, wondering whether the widower ten years her senior she was cutting it for was trustworthy, or whether those envelopes of high-denomination cash she'd found in his apartment were signs of something different.

Parker's was busy. Over the winter months there were always a few epidemics of stock-piling, usually kick-started by old Mr Parker himself who used any hint of a quiet period to drip-feed his 'concerns'. He was shrewd. He'd stand behind the counter in his collar and tie and sprinkle those words of wisdom over his customers. Not *his* words, you understand, but words he'd heard from those sages of all things meteorological; the farmers. And those gentle, knowing aphorisms were all he needed to get people thinking, to get them feeling prepared and to get those shelves of processed foods and soups moving again, based only on the fur-change of a piebald's flanks or the drift of cattle to the lower ground.

Towards the end of the street in the new red-stone building the surgery was closing, Dr Stone having dished out his quota of diagnoses for the day. No sentence was longer than an expelled breath. There were no words of comfort, no hands across the desk. He delivered verdicts, none of which were connected to him, none of which he ever felt because, for Abraham Stone, the jury of life with its freaks and its foibles had made its decision and there was nothing he could do. So why would he weep?

He stood in the prime of his life, with the photograph of his wife and two smart sons there in front of him on the deck of the Vancouver ferryboat, and opened the drawer enough to glance down and see the five-figure cheque from an emergent east coast pharmaceutical company. Why, indeed, would he weep?

Back towards the intersection, past the LMA where, in spite of the purchase of the land for what amounted to peanuts *and* Jorge's dismissal with no more than a Christmas card, Ted still hunkered down in the smaller office, and where Doug's New Year had been bolstered by a couple of after-work beers with his new acquaintance, John Cassidy, the rumour mill that was Sylvie Buckle's beauty parlour was getting up a lacquered head of steam.

On that particular day there were any number of topics to choose from; the regimes of personal care, for one, the tips and techniques on anything from calories to cuticles. You could've gone north with the extensions and streaks. You could, thanks to Rita and her modish mid-wave, have sashayed around the lack of investment at the timber mill and how concerned Dan was with the state of the roof especially in the light of rumoured spring rains. Or, there was Jake Massey and his drinking bouts, or the sighting, more than once, of Delilah Morris out at the Cassidy homestead, the owner of which still attracted more attention than most and about whom it was said on a regular basis; he was a convert, an acolyte, a man who had 'Blessed are the meek' tattooed across his back, who had found forgiveness in his heart and would go to church every Sunday come rain or shine and stand in the shadows at the back. Or, he was a bumpkin, a simpleton, a savage. He was a trickster and a sham, a man who stole women's jewellery, who had unpaid debts, who, from his wastrel father and great-grandfather had inherited nothing but card-cheats and a crooked little finger on his left hand. He had, it was true, the black suit of a mortician and the white gloves of a strangler. And his face gave nothing away.

Or, you could've pecked and clucked at the tumbled feed of Lily Mallender's life. You could've noticed the batteries she bought from the hardware store, or how neglected her winter lawns had got, or the way, whenever she was at Sizzlin' Steve's with her gastric husband, she let the steak juice run from her mouth and never used a napkin to wipe it clear. Or, there was the commercial fact that, from the pharmacist's shelf, those bottles of peppermint mouth rinse never moved an inch.

*

Vincent Clay sat in the window seat of the coffee house at the crux of the two main streets and watched the unfolding with flat dispassion. He watched the behaviour of people, their actions and reactions as if they were marionettes pulled this way and that by the wishful and the dutiful and most things in between. He watched how they moved, how they crossed the street or walked the sidewalk, how they stopped to speak. He heard what came out of their mouths; the taste of the coffee, the strength, the sweetness, the frothiness, the rate at which it cooled. He watched how the young waitress with the pigtails deferred to the surly, older waitress who had bitterness in the tiny pull of her lips and who, in turn, deferred to the manager every time he appeared, doused in his bachelor's aftershave. He saw how Rita Mahoonie's cousin walked away from the key-cutting machine with misgivings seeping from every pore, how the stock-pilers came out of Parker's, put those goods in the trunks of waiting cars and drove away like they were better or smarter or wiser than most. He watched it all, broken down into moment by moment, one enacted thing after another.

People were pliable, he thought. They were unpolished and callow. They were credulous beasts; you could tell them anything. They were so ripe you could pick them, pluck them, and pickle them without them even knowing. You could move their arms and legs. You could lead them, pull them along, drag them this way and that and still they wouldn't know. Look at what you could get people to believe. Look at every con-trick they'd played. You couldn't do that, on that scale, for so long and so often, unless people were there for the taking. His father taught him that much. "You know what you need to succeed with people," he'd said, "to get them right where you want them, where they'll do whatever you what them to do? The right carrot, and the right stick."

*

John got him from fifty paces at least. He got the age, the bulk, the round-shouldered amble. He got his feet clomping over the hard, winter earth with the grace of a dizzy bear. He got the part-roasted face, the hair a matted tobacco across his skull and the fat-fingered hands. More than anything, though, he got the ears.

He had to calm himself, to ride that clamp that fixed across his chest and around his skull. He had to stop himself from walking over to the kitchen table and picking up the knife, to avert himself from any tin he could hold and wield in one hand, any bottle, any chair leg. He had to keep away from the rat poison down in the cellar, from the bleach and the toxic industrial cleaners. There was the spade and the rake near the porch-way, the saws and the scythes against the wall and, over in the bedroom, alongside the drawers under which the encyclopaedias piled still, there was his father's shotgun.

Lester got closer to the homestead with the slow rise of steak juice, beer and stashed tequila coming off him like steam as he went. His lungs burned, his joints pounded and, as he got up to the porch-way steps with a jerry-can as hollow as a pauper's gut, he tried, in the only way he knew how, to gather himself and play it cool; with those inward dog-like snarls to keep the fuck calm.

He sank down into the old, ripped armchair. He closed his eyes, absently rolled a wrapped cigar between fingers and thumb and slowed his breathing to a level he could speak from. A few zest-white clouds scooted over the peaks of Rupture Hill, like training poodles. He stood, knocked and waited. He heard sounds from inside, a few scratches and scrapes, the slide and fall of something heavy, then footsteps. The door opened. The two men looked at each other.

John stayed fixed on the tufts of hair in the ears of the shyster's bitch. His hands rooted down into the depths of his pockets, clenched almost to crushing point. He waited for Lester to speak, his frontal lobe twitching like a sandworm.

"Could I have some water, please?"

The voice, the same voice his father heard in the corner bar. Gruffer than he imagined.

"What's your business?"

"I'm just walking."

"You're not from these parts?"

"No, sir. I'm looking at the land. I understand it might be for sale."

John looked at the rashes of red on the man's neck, the dry, bird-meat lips, and the claret map-lines over the nose.

"Do you have a container, something?"

He watched him fish out the empty jerry-can from the rucksack, mock-shake it, and hand it over.

"Wait there."

He turned and went back into the house, ran the faucet, the pitch changing the fuller the can got.

"This is my land," he said, handing him the container and watching as Lester guzzled down a good half of the water, his eyes closed, the back of his hands as though downed in ageing fox fur.

"I appreciate that," he said, gasping.

"I'm not sure you do."

"I meant no harm. I could hardly breathe."

"Trespassing, coming to my home, uninvited."

"It was just the water, fella. I was in a bad way."

John watched him put the jerry-can back into the rucksack. Water had spilled onto his chequered shirt.

"I'm heading back into town," Lester said, "which way's best?"

John studied the grooves beneath his eyes. He took a breath in. Take it, he heard. Take it and get me some more.

"The long way is by road. That's an hour at least. Or, you can go past the Anderson place there, head up to Coronation Point, follow the track to the rickety bridge, and you're almost there."

Lester tried again to look into the house. Hearts and minds, he mumbled to himself. We don't upset anyone. We don't move until we have to. We don't say boo.

"I'll take the track," he said, "and thanks for the water. I owe you one."

He turned, and before he got to the bottom of the steps, the door was closed behind him. And before he got to the Anderson place, to the line of starched bonnets, the kitchen window of the homestead was open and the twin barrels of Jack Cassidy's shotgun were pointing at the base of his skull, at an equidistant sweet spot between his two unglazed, hairy ears.

*

"Who's this guy, again?" Ted said.

"Vincent Clay."

"That doesn't tell me a damned thing, Doug. Who is he?"

"He's a businessman, and he's interested in the Cassidy land."

"Except it's not the Cassidy land, is it? It's the land that belongs to the LMA. Are you not sleeping?"

"It's Viola, sir. She has migraines, night-sweats. We're going away for the weekend, without the boys."

Ted looked at his watch. It was 10.15. "Go get yourself a coffee, Doug, find your shape. What time's he due?"

"Eleven."

"OK, let's get ready."

The Land Management Agency, but specifically Ted as its absolute figurehead, had a reputation for not making the purchase of land as easy or as smooth as the purchasers would like it to be. Any potential buyer needed to know that it was Ted in control, and that *their* wishes, *their* clauses and sub-clauses were nothing without him as the final arbiter. And so, on that morning, he was prepared for Vincent Clay and any offers and proposals he might make.

So, imagine then, when at 10.59, Vincent breezes into the office, nods to Doug and the ledger-men, introduces himself to Ted with a beaming smile and tells him that the rough terrain, the thousand square yards of land he's interested in, is only one of a large number of potential sites for investment and that his financial backers have encouraged him to 'think expansively'.

His compliments, too, were seamless; the ergonomics of the office, the walnut angels, the Italianate cornicing and the sweep of brush-strokes that captured the majesty of Edward Mallender astride his chestnut stallion. Not to mention the effusion of civic pride he sensed everywhere he went, the generosity of spirit, the hospitality, and, of course, the quality of Sizzlin' Steve's quarter-pounders. In those moments it took for Vincent to create his impression and Ted to absorb his compliments like a sponge, the latter had gone from fierce protector of his land to a man not only willing, but eager, to sell on account of being a man of entrepreneurial spirit himself; he was keen to be a sizeable part of whatever expansive thinking Vincent and his quixotic aftershave was attached to.

Over the next hour, Ted gave him a brief history of the land. He showed him the plans, the deeds, and the Cassidy signature. He got Doug, bolstered by caffeine, to manoeuvre the pins around on the board and he mentioned a price he figured reasonable enough to work around. He told him how the town of Mission had attracted pioneers and visionaries before and it could do so again. It was a town on the rise. It was going places. He told him about the lush prairie lands and the soft, coastal wind that yearned to come this far inland. He talked about the advantages of the railroad and, when

Vincent pointed to the photographs on the desk, he told him about Lily in Oklahoma, Lily in a red organza dress, Lily in a ball gown the colour of moonlit mulberries.

He tried to tease out the more precise nature of Vincent's plans but they were skirted and sidestepped in such a way that pinched at Ted's curiosity even more and made him offer him lunch, more coffee, a beer down at Harry's, dinner at the Mallender estate sometime. He offered him one of the spare rooms in his house for as long as he liked but Vincent, politely, declined them all. There was his business partner, for one thing, his long-time, loyal associate. And there were other meetings, other discussions to be had, and other places to see.

At 12.30 Vincent looked at his watch and offered Ted his firm handshake.

"I'll be in touch," he said. And then, in the guise of an afterthought, he added, "Can I get a game of golf around here?"

"Doug here's your man," Ted said, "he plays off six. And he's a leftie, aren't you, Doug?"

Doug stood and dutifully practised a mock-swing, a mid-iron from fairway to green.

"How about tomorrow?" Ted said. "I can let Doug go for a few hours."

"Tomorrow's no good for me," said Vincent. "There's some decent land available up near the border. What about Friday afternoon? I'm seeing someone at mid-day. He's got farmland he wants to sell but I might be able to do the afternoon."

Doug paused, took a breath in, and stood there. And the reason he stood there as if spellbound, as if suddenly mesmerised, with Ted looking towards him and the two ledger-men raising up their heads, was that he had the weekend trip with Viola all planned out. Everything. Including reservations for dinner at six. He pretended to think. He picked up a diary that he opened and read like a caddie checking yardage. The diary page was a Sunday in May, as white as driven snow, and while he trailed his finger down the page and Ted's look grew expectant, he began to frown. He had visions of carnage, of surface-to-air volleys of assorted objects hurling through his domestic space.

"How about Monday?" Vincent said. "Actually, Monday's probably best."

"Monday it is then," said Ted, "and listen, the Agency's paying. Anything you need, anything you want, you send the bill to Ted Mallender."

And with that Vincent was gone, down the stairs.

For a good half-minute Ted and Doug and the two ledger-men stayed rooted, until it was clear that the potential buyer of the rough terrain, the thinker of expansive thoughts and the most kindred spirit Ted had met in a long time, had left the building.

"What the fuck was that?" Ted said, "You almost lost us the guy."

"It was just…"

"Just what, Doug?"

"Viola," he said, and looked down at the floor.

*

In that meantime, as the temperate air for early February and the extra sunlight that came with it melted some of the low-lying snow and pixels of buds and sprigs and freakish shoots popped in the woodland, the diametrics and tangents of the situation were these; that Lester told Vincent about obdurate John and Vincent told Lester about Ted. Out in the Cassidy homestead, after John had put his father's shotgun away, Delilah told him about Lily and Jorge and, later that evening, John fed that information to a tousled and distracted Doug, as ammunition, should he need it. Doug, meantime, told John about Vincent, not knowing for a moment that the out-of-town businessman with whom he was due to shoot eighteen holes of golf was in John's diabolic sights. Over at the Mallender estate, in the kitchen bereft of grass blades, gastric Ted told Lily all about Vincent, about the expansive plans and the rough terrain and how young Douglas had nearly lost him because of his indecision. And Lily, not yet coiffured and allowing the contents of a five-fruit smoothie to slide down her throat, told Ted that maybe Doug and Viola needed that time together, to touch whatever shaky base they had.

Elsewhere, the two Snipe boys were in trouble again. Old Mr Parker made a healthy and unsurprising January profit. Rita Mahoonie's less salacious cousin changed her mind about the widower and the spare key when she found a receipt from the Central hotel in his pocket.

And, one more thing, some twenty or so miles out of Mission, on the road south, the two-tone Chevy of Lee Shaw's was found nose-down in a ditch. Mr Shaw, aged thirty-four and a mechanic by trade, was taken to hospital with a dislocated shoulder and minor cuts and bruises. Upon inspection, the steering mechanism of the car was found to be seriously faulty.

*

Doug Sketchings stood on the first tee of Sermon Park on that Monday and tried, as he lined up his long-iron drive, to forget the eggshell of a weekend with Viola. Not Viola herself, but the over-bolstered bed, the under-done steak, the flecked mirror in the small bathroom, the mumbling bell-boy, the receptionist with the runny mascara, and the long-haulage trucks that boomed past and shook the bedroom window at three, four and five o'clock both nights.

It wasn't too difficult. As sleep-deprived as he was, he still loved the aesthetics of a golf course. He loved the eighteen sections of land, the subdivisions of tee, fairway and green, each with their own individual frisson of excitement. He loved the arc of the hit ball, the lushness of the grass, even the amoebic shapes of the bunkers he tried to avoid. And maybe that was why, along with being able to walk without tip-toeing and talk without every word being one of appeasement, he played better on that day than he'd ever played in his life, outscoring a more erratic and cavalier Vincent Clay by twelve clear shots.

Vincent, naturally, was never anything other than gracious as bogey piled on bogey and short putts sidled by the holes without waving. He was complementary, courteous and conversational whenever their paths chanced to cross. He mentioned the land from time to time, particularly after slicing his drive into the rough terrain of the dogleg seventh. He asked, too, about the land around the homestead, about its size, the condition it was in, what its history was and, across the tees and greens, if not the fairways of the ninth, tenth and eleventh, he got an abridged version of the Cassidy story; the great-grandfather, Patrick, the card game, the forty-year neglect, the building of the homestead, the further neglect, the sick father and that sense of genetic resentment the townsfolk seemed to have towards the Cassidy name. Vincent listened carefully. Vincent missed his three-footer on the twelfth. Resentment he could always use. Resentment was curdled fuel.

*

Doug basked in the rhythm and grace of his game. He was basking on his drive home. He was basking as he lay in bed next to a sleepless Viola, and he was still basking the next morning when Ted Mallender stood with his hands behind his back and glared across at him.

"Twelve shots? What the fuck were you thinking?"

"I played well, sir. It just happened."

"Nothing just happens. Listen, boy, when you're playing a prospective client you let them win. Golden rule. You make them feel good about themselves. How is this going to happen if you beat the guy by twelve shots? Did he mention the land?"

"Sometimes."

"Did you try to persuade him? Did you put in a good word?"

Doug lowered his head, picked up a couple of spare red pins on his desk and ran them between his fingers.

"You're a fucking miracle worker, Douglas. That's what you are."

Mid-morning Doug got a call from Viola. One of the boys was sick, she couldn't tell which. He'd hurled over himself and the kitchen floor and she couldn't deal with cleaning it up. Her head felt like it was in a vice, she said, could he come home, could he take a couple of hours out to clean everything up? He looked across the room. The ledger-men were busy and Ted was in the small office looking at the deeds of the land. He walked over, and knocked.

"Excuse me, Ted," he said, "I wondered if I could get a couple of hours out? It's Viola. It's one of the kids."

"Which one is it?"

"Both. I got a call. One of the boys, he's sick."

"How sick?"

"He's hurled over the kitchen floor. And himself."

"That's it?"

"He's three, Ted."

"And how old is Viola?"

Ted waved him away from the door. The conversation was over. Five minutes later Doug was back.

"What are you saying?"

"I'm saying after your fuck up on the golf course, you leave at your peril."

"What does that mean?"

"Figure it out."

Ted sighed loudly, stood up and put the deeds in the drawer.

"Ask me in an hour."

"An hour?"

"Yes, the time it would've taken Vincent Clay to drive from his humiliation at Sermon Park back to his hotel."

Viola called Doug again. Lloyd had hurled since, this time over his brother who, with a natural reflex, had hurled back. They were covered in the stuff, both sitting, both crying.

"I need you," she said, quietly, the TV voices louder than her own "Tell me you love me."

Doug took the call by the vending machine in the hallway. He could picture her, his prom date. He knew where she'd be sitting, what she'd be wearing; the dress with the faded roses, shoeless, no make-up, the small bottle of nail polish in her hand, the once-lustrous hair tied up, loosely. Fifty minutes had passed.

"I love you, honey," he said.

"You know it wasn't that she let the mascara run."

"Who?"

"The receptionist. It was the way she looked at me."

"I know," he said.

He went back to the office. Ted was standing as if to attention in front of a map replete with red pins.

"It's almost an hour, sir."

"Is it an hour?"

"Almost."

"Is that the same thing?"

"Not exactly."

"Then bide your time, young man. You're playing with fire."

"She needs me."

"Oh, *needs*, is it now?" he said and swivelled to face Doug, glowering in his direction with the full expectation that he would, as usual, wither like a plant. But he didn't. His face didn't tremble or rouge, and his voice showed no sign of cracking.

"Yes, it is needs."

"Then we'll decide on the hour."

In the weeks and months to come as he sat at home with Viola and the boys, he would remember how, instead of going back to his desk like a slapped dog, he moved a pace closer to Ted and fixed him straight in the eye.

"No, Ted," he said, "we'll decide now."

The two ledger-men stopped their calculating and glanced first at each other and then across to the two men.

"I told you there'd be consequences."

He would remember Ted's face turn radish-red. He would remember a siren outside in the street. And he would wonder what it was that made him stay right where he was and say the things that he said. Perhaps it was Viola. Perhaps it was the sub-scratch round of golf. Or perhaps it was John Cassidy, the novice with the crooked nose and the packed bag in whose company he felt more fearless than he'd ever felt.

"Well, you can take those consequences and stick them up your pompous ass, Mr Mallender. Because if you think anyone feels anything other than loathing for you, then you're badly mistaken. People despise you. People wince whenever your name is spoken, I've heard them. And at least I have a home to go to, at least my wife, as sick as she might be, wasn't blowing the Venezuelan gardener every Monday, Wednesday and Friday."

He would remember not hanging around. He would remember his foot slamming into the vending machine, causing a minor coffee trickle, but beyond that, nothing. Not the three flights of stairs, not the look of the receptionist as he ran through the tiled foyer, nor anyone or anything he might've seen on his way to the car and on the drive home, not the twenty miles of cornfields and prairie, nor the clouds over Blessings Point stock-piling for an hour of rain. In fact, he would remember only walking into the blast-site of the kitchen, cleaning up both boys and floor and sitting down next to Viola, squeezing her gently, and saying, "There may be fall-out, honey."

He would remember the phone-call from one of the ledger-men two days later, telling him how Vincent Clay had walked into the Agency, told Ted his backers had given him the go-ahead for the plans and how Ted, for all his business persona, all his handshakes and smiles, looked bereft while Vincent sat and signed the deeds and handed over the cheque for the land, the first of three.

*

At the corner table in Sizzlin' Steve's that same evening Vincent sat back in his seat, licked steak-juice lips and raised up his third bottle of Bud.

"To the completion of phase one," he said, "the purchase of the rough terrain. You know, by the end, Lester, he was practically giving us the land. Plus," He took another glug of the beer, "he's interested in the plans."

"What plans?"

"Exactly. The ones that don't exist. The expansive ones. Those plans."

"So, what's next?" said Lester.

Vincent paused. "What's next," he said, "is the timber mill."

"You're going to buy the timber mill?"

"That's the plan. Or at least the land around it."

"But how…?"

"Do you know what a sabot is, Lester?"

Lester frowned, shook his head.

"It's a type of shoe, a clog. It's French."

Vincent always did that to him. Made him wonder. Made him think. Made a tingle go to his balls as to what might happen next.

"Are you following me here?"

"You need a clog?"

"Yes, I do."

"You want me to find you a clog?"

Vincent leant forward. "I need the timber mill to become unsustainable," he said. "I need it to close down, to be unable to function. Now, either we can wait for the company to have an economic epiphany and recognise the place as a sinking ship, or…there's the clog. And what does the clog do? You put the clog in the machinery, and the machinery stops working, the machinery gets so fucked up it breaks. Are you there yet?"

Lester's face resembled that of a man putting something edible in his mouth, finding it didn't taste like he expected but it improved the longer it stayed there.

"So, not a real clog, you're saying?"

"Correct."

"Not a real shoe?"

"Brilliant."

"The machinery doesn't work, the mill closes down, and you buy the mill?"

"Lester, you're exceeding yourself."

"And you need a clog?"

"Yes."

"I'll find you a clog."

"I know you will. Let's drink to phase two."

Lester savoured the taste in his mouth that got sweeter and sweeter.

*

John drove away from the roadside bar where he'd picked up all the latest from Doug, including the weekend with Viola, the sale of the rough terrain and, of course, the fearless speech that'd got longer and bolder by then. But, instead of heading back to Mission, he took the road out to Serpentine and then the long loop south-west just so, on that stretch of cinder-block housing beyond the farmland, he could go by the house where Lee Shaw lived, so he could see the damage to the car; the busted headlights, the mashed fender and the hood so buckled it wouldn't close. As he slowed, he could make out the tarpaulin loose across the windshield and, over towards the house, past the foot-high wisps and stalks of grass, he could see Sophie Li in the window. He slowed enough to catch her looking out, not towards the road but down at the skewed Chevy on the track. The window was half-open. It was dusk, coal-dust and olive-green, and she was smoking, the same skinny shoulders drawn in, a ten-hour shift at the Serpentine meat factory behind her. She looked adrift, her hair loose and down.

He carried on, heading west across the flat lands with barely a border between earth and sky, picking up the road that ran north alongside the rail-tracks until it hit the Mission neighbourhoods of apartments and low-cost housing with patches of sub-standard lawn. He pulled over, squirted screen-wash over the dust of the windshield and watched as the fixed wiper swept it away. Down to the side of the car was the slow grade of the riverbank with its tubers and twines. The river ran at its narrowest there, took a course of checks and twists that straightened up and widened the closer to the town it got. He switched off the engine, and the headlights. From where he sat, slumped down in the seat, he could see the apartment block where Jake Massey leant out of his third-floor window to smoke. He called him on his phone, watched him reach into his pocket and answer. "D'you want to make some money?" he said.

Jake was having a hard time of things. He'd lost his job at the timber mill for one. He was drinking again. He'd spent a couple of nights back in the cells. He hardly saw Rita anymore, *never* saw Delilah. Plus, he'd done all that dirty work for Ted Mallender and got nothing in return. He was right where John wanted him.

"You there?"

A sigh, a smoker's rattle.

"I'm asking whether you want to make some money."

He watched him look out of the window and drag on the cigarette.

"Are you not hearing me, Jake?"

"I'm hearing you."

"So?"

"What is it?"

John could smell the blankets that'd wrapped around his father. "Get yourself down to the coffee house. Mid-morning is best. There's a guy in there looking for someone."

"To do what?"

John paused, listened out to the glottal chokes of the river. "You can't say a single thing."

"I won't. To do what?"

"Not to anyone."

"I promise."

"He's looking for someone to torch the mill," he said, in a lowered voice. "Could you do that? And make it look like an accident."

He watched him light another cigarette from the embers of the lit one.

"After the way those people treated you. After what they did. They put you in the mire, Jake, without a second thought. And the foreman guy…"

"Dan Cruck."

"Am I right he's seeing Rita?"

"I don't see her anymore."

"He comes along and he takes her away. You don't deserve it."

"I don't."

"You're a human being, Jake, you have feelings. And what do you owe them?"

"Nothing."

"What did they do to you?"

"They shut me out. They gave me nothing."

"Exactly. So, are you in?"

He saw him spit, three storeys to the ground.

"Tell me what to do, I'll do it."

John rolled the window the whole way down. He could smell the life of the river, the permanent linger of wood that came from the town. He got the sand and the silt, the metal of the rail-tracks, the gasoline spills.

He drove on, past the tracks and the prairie fields. He took the long arc of the road that swept by the burial grounds rumour said would, if the land was ever disturbed, be woken angered. He went by the Mallender estate, past winter-bitten lawns, and the house where Ted, alone since Lily had, in the wake of Doug's outburst packed up and gone before Ted had got home, laid flat, propped, laid flat again the photograph of her in Oklahoma.

As the broad base of Rupture Hill bulked in front of him, as its wooded belt only thickened in the dark and its crags stood rock-black on night-black, so the smell of his father grew, and when he sniffed up, past the chicane of the break and up to the bridge, he got not only the blankets that covered him, but the skin of his feet, the bowls of the clavicle, the fingers that scratched hair and the hair that pressed against the door when he slept. He got the woodsmoke, the half-eaten breakfasts, the myriad of linctuses, mixtures and drops. He got the flakes of his breath.

As soon as he got into the house, he put on the black suit and the white gloves and produced his hatpins, watches and coins, his face unreadable. He took out the soft black cloth and blindfolded himself and, barefoot, he got down on his hands and knees and rooted amongst the boxes, the squat shoe containers and the larger rectangular ones for the shirts. He put his head close to the floor and listened out for the thickness of the pages as he turned them and then, without once raising the blindfold, he crawled across the floor and down the cellar steps. He sat in the cool and dank, found and drank one of his father's beers and rolled tins of fruits and meats across the stone, his ear twitching the moment they hit the wall or stopped so far short he could tell to the inch.

He went into the bedroom, still blindfolded, and came across the shirt box with the photographs inside, feeling them between his fingers like the playing cards Mario would produce from who knew where; from buttoned shirt pockets, on the soles of his shoes and once, ripped and re-assembled inside of his mouth. He imagined them as he brushed them with his thumb, his ancestors, his DNA, his people. He dropped one of them to the floor and found it in his blindness with the ridge of his toes, held it there, carried it across the room to the small wardrobe, leant inside of which, next to the tallest of the boxes, was his fathers' shotgun.

He reached in and took it out, walked with it over to the table, the photograph since shaken loose with the face of Patrick Cassidy scowling out. He sat on one of the chairs, held the barrel of the gun between the white-gloved hands. He tilted it, rested it underneath the bow of his jawbone. A coyote cried out, in the dark, in the mangled, rough terrain of weed and scrub. He adjusted his finger around the curve of the trigger, tested a short, hardly detectable squeeze. He was wordless, again. He was in the various rooms he'd had as a child, with his packed bag and his winter boots. He was in the freight cars, in the beach houses on long, winter shorelines. He was behind the goofy faces of bears and ducks and mice.

*

If you looked in the box marked dinner shirts/non-white and the shoe-box black/formal there'd be some reference, particularly in Abe Masterson's *Mission: A true story*, a hybrid of hearsay and fact, to the timber mill.

The bold outline was this: The mill was established in the first years of the twentieth century by a north-western family called the Wallbecks. Because of its location, it was served not by the great log-drives of the rivers that went to the sea but by the burgeoning reaches of the railroad, meaning the work was regional rather than export-based. You might say that the Wallbecks cut their timber accordingly and, being a family-run enterprise that moved from generation to generation and looked after its workforce, it ran at a regular, if moderate, profit for almost seventy years. Ironic then, according to the historian, that it should be felled not by global conflict, market forces or the severe immigration policies of the 1950s that decimated the workforce, but by 'environmental do-gooders(sic)' in whose view the mill 'ransacked the natural resources of the earth'. Policies were revised, practices altered, regulations tightened and by the end, unable to sustain *any* profit, the mill had no choice but to close down.

But, as Abe so proudly cites in chapter 11 of his volume, Phoenix from the Ashes: *The town of Mission does not easily lie down*, and, following a few business moves and chest-beatings from a young Ted Mallender, the mill re-opened.

This time the buyer was a national company, initialled rather than named, who claimed in its literature to *understand the ways of the north-west* without once saying what those ways were or how that understanding might manifest itself. There was a fanfare. Officials from the company turned up. They ate in Sizzlin' Steve's, drank a few beers in Harry's and inhaled that smell of perpetual wood that hadn't had time to go away. But there were provisos. A down-sized workforce, for one, an obsession with waste minimisation for another, a prioritising of energy efficiency and, under contractual rules that came without a grain of consultation, most of the rights on working conditions, fought for so fiercely by the logging unions in the 1920s, were clawed back.

But ask those men that walked into and out of that mill when the siren howled what they thought of the place and they'd tell you, as they told Abe Masterson, that it was better to have it than not. Take it away, they said, and the heart and soul of the town would go with it.

The problem, though, was this; that the company had larger, more profitable concerns elsewhere and, over the years, the focus on the tiny mill in Mission diminished, as did any sign of investment so by the time they considered cutting their losses and moving out, the mill had become a burden too difficult to sell *because* of that lack of investment. Conditions worsened. Rumours of imminent closure became more or less permanent so that, every once in a while, the company sent over some lackey to ease over the cracks, to present a unified front in a company shirt and tie to a workforce who clocked in and out on what felt like borrowed time.

Dan Cruck was one of those lackeys. He was youthful enough. He looked smart. And, unfortunately for the company, he was conscientious to the point where he couldn't let go of those concerns that came out in post-coital tirades to Rita, of antiquated machinery, substandard safety measures and, of course, the perennial nightmare of dust inhalation.

So, the history books would not remember Dan for the suits he wore, or the shirts he left elliptical sweat stains on, or the ties he fastened just like his father showed him, but for his nocturnal blabbering about the mill listened to, just, by Rita, and passed on to the fine-tuned ear of John Cassidy.

*

Lester blended himself in while Vincent stayed in the shadows. That was generally the way it worked. Lester was the sponge, the ordinary Joe in the bars, coffee shops and steak houses, waiting for fate to take its course. There was an everyman look about him, the extra poundage, the gait of someone moderately burdened, and those regular actions that had become his own; the rolling of the cigar between his fingers, the way he pressed at the bridge of his nose when he got tired, or the sudden jut of the chin if someone came near him.

And, on that mid-February morning with a serrated wind blowing in from the north-east, in the window seat at the coffee house, his jawline flinched when the argument between the surly waitress and the young man in the denim jacket spilled over in his direction.

"Jake, you have to pay. Period."

"The money's at home. I'll bring it in. What's the problem?"

"You're the problem. This isn't the first time, is it? And you don't always bring it in."

"That's not true. I bring it in. How much is it?"

"Two dollars fifty."

"Exactly."

"Not the point, Jake. You pay up or you don't come in again. I mean it."

Jake looked sullen. He was no more than four feet from Lester.

"You see how they treat me?" he said.

Lester looked at the young, unshaven man.

The waitress tilted her head to one side, pursed lips, part-raised an eyebrow. "You want me to go and get the manager?"

Jake sighed, rubbed at his face. "No, I don't want you to get the manager... You know I'm not working right now."

"Not my fault, Jake. What do you want me to do?"

"Let me bring the money in. It's two dollars."

“Fifty.”

Jake sighed again, louder this time. He started to nod, to noticeably blink. The waitress stood straighter, put the tray she was holding on the table next to her and waited. One of the machines hissed out behind the counter.

“I’ll get it,” Lester said, “consider it done.”

The waitress studied Lester for as long as it would take to pour a regular coffee. She got the hairy ears first, then the veins and the folds of the neck.

“You sure?”

Lester nodded. The waitress looked across to Jake, nodded herself in affirmation, picked up the tray of empty cups and walked back to the counter. Jake stood, head slightly bowed. The nodding had stopped, so too the blinks.

“What can I say?”

Lester shook his head, waved it away.

“I’ll pay you back. Give me a couple of days. I’ll be right here. Same time. I promise,” he said, and turned to go.

He got to the door and turned up his collar against the chill. He stood a moment in the doorway, lit a cigarette in cupped hands and then stumbled forward across the street, taking the turn that led to the mill.

The coffee house fell back into its hisses and chinks. The manager appeared briefly. The surly waitress glared at the one with the ponytails for the tuft of spilled froth on the counter and the conversation found its regular volume on its regular subjects. No sooner had Jake turned the corner than Lester began to bask. He sat back and purred quietly to himself, his paws locked together under the knoll of his pendulous chin. That was the way it worked. Lester was the cat that brought his master mice.

Two days later Lester was sitting in the same seat listening to the young man seethe and snarl at the timber mill and the people in it without a single invitation to do so. There was nothing he had for that place, he said, that was not smeared in bitterness and bile. There was nothing he owed them, nothing they deserved. He blamed them, held them responsible. Anything and everything that had happened to him since the day he left was the fault of the timber mill. Plus, the foreman, the flunky, had stolen the best friend he'd ever had from under his nose because he'd got money and prospects and a suit he could wear, and now there was no-one in the town or the world that he could tell his shit to.

Lester didn't have to move. Jake did it all for him. There was the lack of funds, for one thing, there was the blame, and right there on a plate, fully cooked and piping hot, there was the resentment. With those alone, Lester was more than happy, but throw in the hubris and the bravado and the radiant inability to self-reflect and it was all he could do not to grin and stroke his whiskers. OK, there was a looseness that bordered on the chaotic, but Vincent could deal with that easy enough.

And, later that day, when he told his master he'd found him his sabot, when he licked his lips and dropped the young and frothing Jake Massey down at his feet, Vincent simply smiled.

"You know what it is about you, Lester?" he said, "You always come up with the goods. Every time. No matter what. Now, stay clear and tell me where to find him."

*

Vincent turned up at the apartment just over a week later. It was evening, a drape of rain over the prairies. He wore a twill suit the colour of charcoal, said he worked with Lester, and had a proposition that might be of interest.

The apartment was as cool as the air outside on account of Jake had left the window open to smoke. There were two empty beer cans on the table and the smell of refried beans and roll-mops seared through the nicotine fug. Vincent refused to sit, preferred to stay in the frame of the doorway with the door closed behind him. On the wall were a topless Bruce Lee and a coked-up Scarface. He flitted from one to the other as Jake reached for a cigarette.

"Don't smoke."

"Why not?"

"I don't like it."

"But it's my apartment."

"I don't give a fuck whose apartment it is. I want you to do something for me, and when I want you to do something and I'm willing to pay you good money to do it, it has to be done my way, otherwise there's no deal, and I find someone else. You understand?"

Jake's brow furrowed. "D'you want a drink?" he said.

"Look at Bruce Lee, Jake. Does he look like he drinks? Does he look like he fills his lungs with twenty Lucky Strikes a day? No, he doesn't. I don't want you to smoke or drink for three days, is that clear? Now," he said, "it's going to rain for those three days. It's going to be damp. On the fourth day temperate air will come in from the east and dry things out." He paused. "I want you to be Bruce Lee for me. Can you do that? I want you to loosen up enough to climb a log pile and get through a small window. I want you to get inside the timber mill and I want you to burn the place down. You think you can do that? You think you can do it so it looks like negligence on the company's part?"

"The place is falling apart."

"You think you can do it and not breathe a word of it to anyone on God's earth?"

"I do."

"Not even Rita?"

"How do you know Rita?"

"Good. Because if any of this gets out, or is traced back to us, there will be repercussions you don't want to think about. D'you understand?"

"Yes, sir."

"That's why we're paying you well. Some now, some in a month's time when it's all blown over."

Vincent put his hand in the right-hand pocket of the jacket and pulled out a manila envelope folded in half. He tossed it down on the worn sofa strewn with clothes and stained towels as thin as paper.

"We'll be in touch," he said. "You don't know me. You've never spoken to me. You don't know who I am or what I do. And get some sleep, you look like shit."

*

The rain came early, pelting the crags and flutes of Rupture Hill well before morning. It swept in from the north, coming over the pate of Blessings Point, down through the groins and folds of the valleys until it spattered the poorer soil of the burial grounds and headed into town where it fell on the rooftops and the covered walkway that sheltered the arcade.

It fell on the river and the slats of the bridge that led to the mill where it juiced the log pile and slapped at the tarpaulin and the sheets of the roof. It fell on the untended stretch between the mill and the migrant housing, on the neighbourhoods to the south and the land that went out to the rickety bridge, on the crown of Coronation Point and the routes that ran down to the level land and the washing wires freed of Anderson sheets and bonnets. Only the crucifix in the cover of the doorway was spared, the figure of Christ, head-angled, forlorn and dry.

It fell on the rough terrain owned by Vincent Clay and across the Mallender estate, stirring Ted from his fitful sleep to pad his way to the bathroom, to take a piss that burned and see the hang of his mouth in the mirror, to hear the patter amid the emptiness of the house in pockets of which, still, were the lingered scents of Lily's sprays.

And it fell on the Cassidy land, on the half-timbered, half-slated roof, on the porch-way and the three-sided veranda with its slats and rail. It fell on and dripped from the old, mounted gargoyles. It darkened the handles of the spade and the rake, riddled the flat side of the saw and seeped through the teeth, ran off the arc of the scythe and into the gashed armchair with its open and widening wound.

John sat at the kitchen table. He knew all about Jake, and Vincent's visit, and Lester and the coffee house and Dan Cruck's latest concerns as whispered to Rita. He knew that in four days' time, after the rain had blown over and temperate air had come in from the east to dry out the log pile and seal up the earth around it so that no prints could be made, the timber mill of Mission would be no more, that it would be history only. He knew that the livelihoods of men, women and children, all of whom directly or by association, were culpable of damage to his father, would be tightened like a noose around them. He knew that Vincent Clay would slither in with his hairy-eared sidekick and become for those people, a knight in shining armour. And he knew that Ted Mallender, Lily or no Lily, would begin to, finding it hard not to, let his own keen interest be known, and that Vincent would use him. He knew all those things as he sat there in the gloom, just as his father used to do.

*

Jake stood in the doorway of the apartment and tried to gather himself. It wasn't easy. He checked the pockets of the black hooded jacket that cowled him, felt for the lighter and the pack of cigarettes, for the silver hip-flask with the initials of whoever he'd stolen it from grooved into the side. His mouth was dry. The sweat clung to his sternum like a compress and the wiring in his head, never harmonious at the best of times, was close to sizzling out. Across his brow and cheeks he'd smeared lines of camouflage paint, mud-brown, olive and black. It was three in the morning, the first dry night in four, moonless.

He locked the door behind him and tiptoed as well as Jake could tiptoe down the stairs of the building. Outside the air was rain-free, the streets of the neighbourhood empty. He could hear the run of the river as he made his way along the trodden grass-tracks that followed it round. Seedlings stuck to him. Blades of dampened grass latched to his sneakers. Just past the railway station, the river ducked back towards the eastern edge of the town, past the migrant shacks and the unmade road. At the point where it narrowed and the track grew thin, he quickened up. Over to his right, beyond its growths and shallow bank, lay the Indian burial grounds, the hallowed land older than the town itself where no-one had dared to tread and where, so the story went, the vengeful spirits of massacred men would one day whirl up and dance.

He could see the mill, an outline of bulk against the trees behind and the sky above. He could smell the sawdust and the wood-chip, the cuts and blocks and piles. He moved towards the windowless back until he came to the log pile, pulled away the tarpaulin that covered it, showering himself as he did so with gathered rain. Then he looked up, his eyes like jellied amoebas amid the earth and oil smudges of his face. He took in the angle and the height of the wood packed and chained. It was a natural climbing frame, the kind he'd go at like a monkey as a kid, the kind he'd be at the top of in a matter of seconds. But he waited. He closed his eyes and pushed back the cowl. He felt a ride in his gut, a clench to his jaw. He set his feet right, so too his shoulders and hands. His face was shiny with paint as he looked up again to the top of the pile. His life had not panned out. The dice had not rolled his way, the cards had been stacked against him from day one. But all that was about to change.

He moved the tarpaulin over to the side and made his way steadily to the top. He balanced himself, took a vantage point scan. In front of him was the small window of the foreman's office which, like every other window and door was as old as the mill itself, so scoring the softened wood of the frames and sills and taking out the glass was no problem. And neither was laying it down, climbing inside, vaulting a low radiator and standing in the middle of Dan Smugfuck's room with a downward turn of his mouth.

The room was neat. There was a desk stacked with papers in either in- or out-trays, some stamped and signed, others waiting. Labelled and colour-coded binders and files nestled where the desk met the wall and to their right were two framed photographs, one of Dan looking pristine on his Graduation day and one of Dan and Rita outside a fancy hotel somewhere, Dan with his arm around Rita's waist, like he'd won her as a prize, a look on his face part-pleasure, part-ownership.

With a sweep of his arm, every object on the desk was sent to the floor, including, unfortunately, the unseen and sizeable paperweight, the dainty primrose ensconced sneakily into so many pounds of shot and leaden glass, which landed plumb onto the toes of his right foot. He winced, the sound of a mewling child followed by a curse through gritted teeth.

He hobbled out of the room and stood on the prow of the stairway, looking down across the insides. He made his way down, the pain shooting through his foot with every step. His eyes watered, his hands grabbed the rail and when he got to the bottom, he used every surface he could, the machines, the benches, and buzz-saws, to move across the floor. And when he found his place he sat.

He worked quickly, in spite of the dark and what felt like free-floating bones in his foot, in spite of the sweat filming his face, hands nicked by splinters, muscles cramping, in spite of the piston-like bounce between sternum and throat and the booming out of his heart through ears and chest. It was a chain. And all he had to do was to make sure the links of the chain were in the right order: Inspection box, fuses, a loosened wire, a mound of dry sawdust, a cone of pine sticks suffused with pitch and a trail of viscous oil leading, as straight as he could make it, to the almost empty can of propane, all assembled, all spaced. And then when that was done, it was the pathway out; stairway, office, open window, log pile, gone.

When it was assembled, he stood, blew the dust off his fingers and took out the pack of cigarettes. He put one in his mouth, held it there a few moments, looked round at the place of his misery, and then lit it. He smoked it most of the way down, the nicotine zinging his lungs, the taste of tobacco sweet on his lips. And then he knelt, and with its glow and its crackle, he lit the fuse.

*

People began to gather from first light; bleary, half-dressed arrivals, many in makeshift protective face-masks, in calico and hessian wraps, handkerchiefs and neckerchiefs, torn garments pocked for ventilation. They gathered once the fencing was staked out, standing at those perimeter points, staring out through the plumes and coils of smoke that towered through the breaking light, gripped by shock, across the flattened land and what was left of the mill, across the wider acreage of black, strewn with metal and glass, the blazes of oil and thick timber, the minor rages of indigo and blood-orange, and the ash that fell like snow, blessing the cindered earth, the woodlands and the burial grounds, covering the river and its banks in a patina of silver-white.

Throughout the morning, they lined the fencing on all sides, from the bridge in the town to across the river, from woodland gaps to the unmade road, watching the smoke slowly thin, the flames becalm and the metal of machinery turn to stiff and bended forms. Some went up to Coronation Point to see. Some to the arc of the road. Some went away and came back with food and drink and collapsible chairs, sitting in clusters and slowly, as the hours passed and the clasp of incredulity began slowly to unfasten itself, they lowered the masks to the choky air and began to talk. Briefly to start with, in curt sentences of disbelief, but then expanding, moving back to the history of the place, to the Wallbecks, to what the mill meant to the town, to the heart and soul, and the generations that'd walked through its doors and punched its clock day after working day.

By mid-afternoon, everything was all but extinguished. The volunteer firemen from Serpentine, called out at five in the morning with nothing left to save, had scoured and hosed and cleared, and by then the law enforcement officers, in protective suits, visors and fireproof boots had checked out the trees and land behind the mill *and* evacuated the dazed occupants of the migrant housing to a community hall, their ears and skulls still ringing from the blast. Some of the lawmen held positions around the fence. Some spent a few more hours gathering evidence. Or, more accurately, picking up a series of random objects and, with a rationale as flimsy as rice-paper, putting them in either waste sack or sachet, dependent on size. Others asked routine questions around the town, taking statements and filing them away, by Christian name.

Officials and representatives from committees and boards made token appearances, including the suited Dan Cruck, splayed still, even as he stood there amidst the pall of disbelief, between his duty to the company and to what he knew of their lapses. Plus, he was there with Rita, beautified that same morning, and herself torn on the less philosophical wrack between the good life of hotels and restaurants and the fact that if the shit hit the fan, and the talk in Sylvie's was that it would, then she'd have to drop Dan like a stone and let him sink.

Elsewhere, Sizzlin' Steve's had a lunchtime run on comfort steaks and extra-large fries. The local church had a few more visitors, as did Harry's bar, and old Mr Parker made a series of short-term killings on roofing felt, crepe bandages, ice packs, antiseptic spray, smoke, car, house and personal alarms, quantities of eggs (for the sound-proof boxes not the contents), different sizes of mesh and, with a nod in the direction of the burial grounds, a number of religious trinkets and charms he'd picked up.

The migrant workers were taken to see Dr Stone for perfunctory hearing tests and something for the persistent head-ringing. In relation to what might happen to their homes, their livelihoods and their future existences, which was essentially all that they spoke of, Dr Stone said he was a doctor not a politician. His role was medicinal not civic. The medication he handed over, the bottle of sugar-coated, snow-white cylinders was, incidentally, from the same pharmaceutical company that sent him his cheques.

By late afternoon, there was a sniff in the air that was nothing to do with the chill or the dying smoke. The majority of the townsfolk had packed away the chairs and foodstuffs and drifted home. But some stayed, predominantly the mill workers themselves, past and present, and, for them, as sentiment and nostalgia turned into tales of gashed and broken limbs, of missing digits, malfunctional hearing and lungs that rattled like wash-boards, the smell had got stronger.

Individual complaints became generic. One man's raised concern became the groups, his voice theirs until, by evening, the choral consent was that, given just how old the machinery was and how little investment there'd been, the Mission mill was an accident waiting to happen, that any blame should be laid firmly at the feet of the company and that financial compensation was definitely due.

And then, close to midnight, with only a handful of the men left, with animal clouds prowling over Rupture Hill, it shifted again. The blame became suspicion. The company had talked for years about closure, about how much of a burden the mill was, about cutting those losses and moving out, so wasn't it the case, they said, that the place was worth more to them as cinders and rubble than it was still standing and leaking profits like a perforated sump-pump?

The following day Ike's was busier than usual. And not for his notorious marine-cuts either. No, most of the day the theories buzzed louder than the razors. Talk of the insurance scam was high, talk of an unseen, unknown arsonist. There was the lone wolf, then the grievance wolf, and the unhinged wolf. There was the wolf on the inside and the wolf on the outside. There was the loose wiring, the faulty fuse-boxes, the exposed leads. There was the lack of rain and the moonless night.

And, in Ike's and Sylvie's on that day, beyond the scam, beyond the wires and the wolves and the missing rain there were those other zany curveballs that hurled out of people's mouths: What about the traumatised cattle over at Blessings Point, or the tumbled rock from Rupture Hill? What of the plague of beetles, the upturned haystacks and the curious arrangement of stones down by the rail-tracks? There was the fallen chandelier in the Prairie View hotel and the stopping, temporarily, of the station clock. And there were the corn dollies and the juju chains in Mae Chattus' store, all gone.

*

Lester, meantime, sat in his various seats; in the coffee house, in Sizzlin' Steve's, in Harry's, on steps across from the police department building and on two slats of held-together wood on the path out to the rickety bridge. He purred wherever he went. He scratched at the back of his neck, his forearms, between his legs. Sometimes he spoke, that everyman tone that went with the straggle of his look, but mostly he listened, not because he was priest-like, or because amongst his purring and scratching he was in any way empathetic, but because he was dutiful, because his master had told him not to say boo.

"They don't know what to do with themselves," he said to Vincent in the hotel room, "they're talking about formations of stones and cattle not moving."

"Good. They're almost ready to pick. How's the resentment?"

"You can see it, hear it and smell it, especially the mill workers."

Vincent nodded, looked out across the rooftops of the town, his back to the room.

"What about the company men," he said, "when are they due?"

"Tomorrow, I heard. What do we do? They'll ask questions."

"Yes, they will."

"What if they get to Jake? If they get to Jake and he spills his beans, the whole thing is done for."

"They won't. Leave them to me."

There was a coffee stain on Lester's shirt, specks of mud on his shoes.

"People don't know shit, Lester. They stumble their way through life without understanding a damned thing about it. Without people the way they are, we don't work. They wise up, we have no livelihood these last fifteen years. Now, the company men have agendas," he said, moving away from the window, "they'll look to blame, and to do that they need a good reason and a scapegoat. Do we want this to happen? No. Why? Because if the company finds a scapegoat, it doesn't need to sell the land or the price can stay high. What we want is the company on its knees, the company at the point where it's begging for a sale of any kind. That's what we want. So, neglect is what we're looking for. Neglect is what we want coming out of the loss adjuster when he gets here. Neglect on a grand and culpable scale."

*

The first thing the two company men saw, arriving in Mission in crisp suits and side-parted hair, was a collection of people standing around the formation of stones like they were watching a dog-fight. The next, as they rolled their cases up the hill to the Station Hotel, was a family, spread across the width of the sidewalk, father, mother, two teenage boys and a younger girl, all flat-footed as penguins, all wearing juju chains and the father stopping them with an outstretched arm to hawk up and spit out something the size and consistency of a small jellyfish. And, sitting on a well-upholstered leather chair in the foyer of the Station Hotel, reading a newspaper, was Vincent Clay.

The men were from the mid-east, no older than Dan Cruck, and when they'd finished up with the desk clerk and had their bags taken up to their rooms, Vincent lowered his newspaper and, in his pale-grey suit, began to speak.

He made them feel comfortable, to begin with. He put them at ease. He made it seem like that conversation in the foyer of a hotel with a complete stranger was the most regular thing to do. And, all the time, as they talked about the length and the comfort of the train journey, about where they were from and what their names were, he watched them: He saw how they checked with each other, how they looked across, made affirmations, smiled simultaneously. They were both married, just a few years, he figured, given the shine of the rings. They had new homes, young kids. One of them had a dog. They were churchgoers, non-smokers, athletic on a low-energy scale. They used moisturiser, Vitamin C products, took decaffeinated drinks and had present, dominant fathers who still tried to tell them how to manage their finances. He got the inner tension of one as around the shoulders and neck, the other as the feet, the shuffle of. And they were choosing not to say what they were there for.

"I'm a salesman, for my sins," he said. "My father was a salesman and his father before him. I guess it's part of the DNA." He lowered his voice and drawing them in to a confederate point where he could smell the sports-based aftershave and the face-cream, "but I have to say, and this is only my personal opinion, you understand, that this is not my favourite town in the world to do business in."

"It isn't?"

"No, sir, it is not."

The bellhops reappeared, handed over the room keys to the two men who, at exactly the same time, reached into their pockets and tipped them, the same amount. The company men waited, and then returned to Vincent. One of them drooped his shoulders a little, the other adjusted his feet.

"How come?"

"Well," he said, "the people are naturally suspicious, for one thing. They don't look at you straight. OK, you read the history of the place, you get that, it's fixed in, I understand. They don't trust people. They don't take to strangers too well. They think they're going to take something from them so they don't have a word for welcome. I mean, I'm a regular guy who minds his own business, but I can feel it most places I go. It's in the air. Plus, there's the whole thing with the mill."

Vincent mirrored a gesture he'd seen and done a thousand times: The tightened brow that narrowed the eyes, the pursed lips and the shake of the head. You don't want to think about it, was what it said. You don't want to go there.

"So, the mill burns down," he said. "Bad enough. It's the history of the place. It's an identity, a way of life. It's what the people know. And they're shocked. I can see that. They're overwhelmed that the place of work has gone. But then it turns. They start to blame the company. No investment, they say, no concern for safety, poor conditions, it's a blessing no-one was killed. And so on. The company this, the company that. And then they get this idea."

He enacted the quick look round, the furtive check. One of the company men tapped his toes inside his shiny, leather shoes.

"They figure the company set the whole thing up, for insurance reasons. They figure they paid some guy to come in and burn the place down."

The two men looked across at each other.

"That's what they're saying. That the mill is worth more to the company destroyed. They also say the company are sending a couple of old guys over, to seal over the cracks."

"When?"

"They don't know. But they're waiting for them. They're ready. And those cracks are not for sealing."

The one with the dog spoke, without glancing over first. He twitched his neck, flexed it. "We are those guys. The company sent us to check things out."

Vincent went slack-jawed, open-mouthed. He went quizzical. Hold on a minute. Let me get this straight here. "When you say check things out, you mean apologise, right?" he said.

"Not exactly. The company thinks the fire was started deliberately, that it was a case of arson, but by someone here in the town, someone with a gripe, maybe. And we're here to ask a few questions around the place."

"That's your opening shot? Looking for a culprit? In the town?"

The two men half-nodded, less convinced. Vincent looked around the room, at the upholstered chairs, the oil paintings of the town, the ornate clock with the roman numerals.

"Do you guys have kids?" he said, as if he was absorbing a dose of bad news, gradually.

"One each."

"What are their names?"

"Max and Dexter."

"How old are they?"

"Max is two."

"Dexter's four."

"OK, listen to me," he said, "this is from a guy who's spent time and done business here, who knows how these people think. Get the fuck out. You start asking questions, noseying around, asking about culprits, you'll get hurt, badly. Because as far as these people are concerned, the company has fucked them over. The company has abandoned them, left them to rot, with no work to go to, no livelihoods, and no futures. The company has put a nail in the coffin of the town. That's what they're saying. And you don't have to take my advice, but go home, go back to your families, to Max and Dexter."

"But the company sent us."

Vincent moved in close again. "Take a look outside," he said. "Go on. Take a look."

The two men turned slowly, tried to see through the hotel doors.

"There's a guy there already. Overweight, red-faced, keeps pacing up and down. Tell them you tried."

"But…"

"Listen, in a couple of days there'll be a loss adjuster here. Those guys are like bloodhounds. If there's anything, they'll find it. If there's a culprit, they'll track him down. Trust me."

The one without the dog shifted from foot to foot. The other checked back into the street, saw the hairy-eared man go past once more.

*

The mist sneaked in from over the hills, snaked its way through the town, suckered itself to the wind of the river. It hovered over the burial grounds, its belly like floss. It crept across the lawns of the Mallender estate and on around the waist of Rupture Hill, crawling up its bodice and crags. It wrapped like a crown around the monkish pate of Blessings Point, grovelling the valleys and groins. And it hung like dirty netting over the rough terrain, stretching its tendrils over towards the Cassidy land in the homestead of which John sat and waited, the photograph of Vincent Clay in front of him. He drank one of his father's beers, put away the watch-chains and the stones from his pocket, the containers of beetles. The lights were out, the cellar door open, the shotgun propped against the bedroom wall. He waited just like he had in the makeshift ring, like he'd waited for the amphetamine sulphate to kick in, like he did and would some more, soon, with Jake Massey, like he would with Lester, with Abraham Stone, Lee Shaw and Ted Mallender, like he would with the town itself. He balanced himself, a twitch of his snout and a turn of his ear. He waited for Vincent to succeed, to buy up the grounds of the mill and to focus his attention on the Cassidy land. And then he'd be there.

There was a knock on the door. It was Delilah Morris, in a winter coat the colour of squid ink.

*

Later that evening, under cover of the late winter mist, with most of the mill workers, including Jake Massey, gathered in Harry's bar, the two representatives of the timber mill company headed down the fire-escape of the Station Hotel to board the last east-bound train out of Mission.

They no longer wore the suits or the shiny leather shoes. Their hair was unparted, either mussed or swept-back, their cases ditched for kit-bags. The one without the dog felt the heat over his feet, and the church-going owner of the Japanese chow rolled his head from side to side to ease the grip on his neck. They'd called home, spoken to spouses and children, imagining them not as hazy and grainy from a distance but as though intensely detailed. They said nothing of heading home, nothing of the town of Mission and its mill, and nothing of their encounter with a salesman who'd saved their skin.

Down near the station a different group of people stood around the stones. The clock in the waiting room was three and a half minutes slow, and beetles scurried on the platform floor.

*

For the town, no mill meant no wages, no wages meant no spending power, and no spending power meant that every store in town took a financial hit. Harry's profits started to dry up, in spite of the few die-hards who tried to drink away their sorrows and savings. So, too, for Sizzlin' Steve and his comfort steaks. Even old Mr Parker and his ruses couldn't stem the loss. The only 'businesses' that survived, if not flourished, were Smithson's loans, whose rates were emblazoned across the store window, and Dr Abraham Stone whose short-shrift diagnoses and medications were doled out on a regular basis no matter that those symptoms and complaints never seemed to change from one time to the next. One morning alone, forty-five people, men, women and children, all experiencing a grip on their breathing apparatus and sporadic headaches, were dispensed with the same catch-all trauma medication from his company back east. Take it twice day, after meals. Next, please.

More rock tumbled from the shoulders of Rupture Hill. More haystacks were upturned. The fixed chandelier in the Prairie View, so carefully restored after its fall, shed a single, pear-shaped bulb. There were marks on the church door, indentations and cleavages, ciphered by the looks. Some of the migrant workers, usually so passive, showed signs of agitation as they watched their homes checked for asbestos levels and fissure sizes. Dan Cruck, in an act of last-ditch desperation, proposed to Rita on the crown of Coronation Point. And Jake Massey, saboteur, was quivering from the lack of attention.

He was not cut out for holding his tongue. For Jake to stand in Harry's bar, in sneakers still mud- and grass-stained, with the fading red welt of a burn on the back of his neck like a badge of honour, and listen to all those theories of how the mill had burned down and not be able to describe in glorious and meticulous detail how he'd climbed that log pile and done the deed himself, cranked him to the point where he could hardly swallow his beer for the words stuck in his gullet.

On the night the company representatives sneaked out of town and Rita said she needed more time, he heard those men talk about the loss adjuster as if he was the smartest brain in the state, as if *his* findings, *his* verdict, would offer the town the possibility of resolution, of something to move on from. He would be the one to discover the truth, they said, his would be the lizard's eye.

The rumours of his arrival spiked the town. No two were the same. So, there was the tall man with the wire-rimmed glasses and the stocky figure with perspiration issues. There was the small, chiselled man with a colourful necktie, the bearded Easterner, the straight-backed loner. There was the gaunt, pale man with a limp and a lazy eye. And, in the closest thing to a consensus, there was the detached, unmarried forty-something, the suited, pinch-mouthed city-dweller with smooth, washed hands the pink of rats' tails.

Some folks stood on the stone platform as the trains arced the prairie fields from either north or south. They watched for faces and hands and feet as they appeared in the windows and doors. Sometimes they followed likely candidates. It was not exactly scientific, and as the days went on and no obvious contender emerged, it became based on a rationale that'd slackened to anyone who looked like they could count quickly in their heads. Every trail was a cold one, including the detached, unmarried forty-something who turned out to be a surveyor with a note-taking compulsion on a two-day delineation of farmland. And the reason for every trail being a cold one, apart from detection based only on hunches and hillbilly wiles, was that the loss adjuster, whose verdict on the mill was crucial to so many, was a thirty-six-year-old, short-haired woman called Frances Harte.

Frances had walked straight past the scouts and the scurrying beetles without being given a second glance. She'd spent three days in the town without anyone knowing who she was or what she was doing there. She rented a room on the edge of town close to the rail-tracks and, for those days of anonymity, she was as diligent and devoted as always. She walked the streets of the town, the southern neighbourhoods, across the land to the rickety bridge and as far as Coronation Point and the burial grounds. She had a rib-eyed steak in Steve's and a cold beer in Harry's. She had breakfast every morning in the coffee house; three cups of hot, roasted coffee, a couple of honey pancakes and half a chocolate muffin. She bought a local newspaper, sat at the window seat and read it cover to cover, circling various items in red or black, depending.

Of course, the mill was the main event. There were photographs new and old, articles and histories but, for Frances, about whom the sleuths had been right about one thing, her unmarried-ness, it was the non-explosion stuff that caught her: The block ads, the notices, the items wanted and those for sale. It was, for a bird-like woman with a degree in microbiology, the offer of second-hand farm equipment, the corn prices, the infestation of hornets in the chandlery cellar and the sprawl, or otherwise, of the travel agents' net.

Apart from the printed page, what she got from plain observance, a good ear and an ability to absorb she was either cursed or blessed with, was that old Mr Parker was a charmer and a scoundrel both, that Lily Mallender had sent more than one scented letter of apology to her husband and that Rita Mahoonie, after some deliberation, had turned down Dan Cruck even though, so it was said, the ring glittered like a gold seam. She sensed too that, for some, the formation of stones, the beetles, the haystacks, the static cattle and the stopping of the station clock were not things of coincidence, and that, maybe, the spirits of the Indian lands were making moves.

Plus, on the day she surrendered that anonymity by walking into the police department building and asking to see the files, there was the serious house fire out on the loop road south. A thirty-four-year-old man had been taken to hospital with second-degree burns, head injuries and the effects of smoke inhalation. The two women who also lived there, allegedly sisters, were working at the Serpentine meat factory at the time.

*

The secret was out. As soon as Ned Scarratt crossed the street to Parker's store, ostensibly to buy more peppermint gum, but really to open his mouth about the skinny woman in her thirties with flecked grey hair and fingers like claws, Frances Harte ceased to exist as a nobody in the town of Mission and became very much a somebody.

It took a couple of days for the word to get around properly but by the time she made her way through the town to head for the mill site carrying more packed weight on her shoulders than a seasoned hiker, she was known. People looked in her direction. They mumbled her name after she passed them. Sometimes they pointed and, occasionally, they spoke, but never about the mill. As Abe Masterson suggested in his volumes, the default position of the vast majority of the townsfolk was deference. So, even though they had theories and accusations coming out of their ears, even the most resentful of mill workers zipped up when they saw her.

And Frances, in spite of sitting in Steve's and Harry's, in spite of the breakfasts, the root beers and steaks, was not a social animal, naturally. She lived alone. She travelled alone. She worked, whenever possible, alone. In fact, most of her six years at the large insurance company based out east had been spent in the industrial wildernesses of city-edge business parks and warehouses where her powers of detection had been trained on the world of objects found and details discovered rather than the slippery motivations of human beings. So, for her, the timber mill was different. Not only would she have to deal with people and their absurd social patterns and behaviours but also the only semblances of information she had were the files, sachets and sacks picked up from the police department, which were, at best, no more than fun-park brochures and candy-bags. Still, the company figured she could do it. And besides, no-one else wanted to travel out so far.

On that early March morning she stepped into the taped-off area as though it were a site of religious significance; on tip-toes, thin-legged, like a heron, her head extended forward slightly, the long-fingered hands plucking and picking at the equipment as she set it down, gently. She put on a hard yellow hat and a calico mask fastened at the back, changed her footwear to sturdier boots and stretched her hands and fingers into latex gloves. She took a small camera out of its case and wrapped it around her wrist, peeled the cellophane back off the new journal she bought for every investigation, wrote her name in the front and printed the word MISSION beneath it.

She was there almost five hours, this lone shape amongst the ruins, half-bird, half-scientist, and for most of that time, she stooped and pincered. She crouched and scratched among the detritus, moving larger stones with her feet, gathering up scraps with fine and broad sweeps and putting them in sealable sachets she'd later label in terms of date and time and location. She took over three hundred photographs, made two dozen pages of notes.

It was work for Frances. It was what she did and how she did it. And, in the same way that for some people a golf course was only so many acres of grass and sand but to others it was a place of aesthetic bliss so, for Frances, those areas of debris and ruin choked in dusty air were her milieu. They were her Augusta nationals.

Mid-afternoon she stilled herself, ruffled her arms and legs. The head tilted to one side, the eyes went north to listen and find light and, with the same reverence she arrived with, she made her way back to where she'd set her things down. The camera and journal were put away, the boots swapped for lighter shoes. The gloves were peeled off, turned inside out, rolled into one and dropped into a larger sachet along with the mask. And, lastly, the hat. She blinked hard, mussed her hair and stretched her arms fully upwards. Then she picked everything up she'd carried, attached them all to shoulders and arms and hands and walked, not the way she came, not under the tape like a flyweight, not across the bridge that led into the town where a small gauntlet of onlookers waited, but around the perimeter fence and out along the unmade track at the back of the mill, past where the obvious log pile was with its tarpaulin and rope, and into the woods beyond.

*

Over at the Land Management Agency Ted Mallender slumped his forehead onto the desk. "I don't know what to do," he said, "you call me up, you ask to come in and talk, and look at me, it's embarrassing."

Vincent stood in the doorway, motionless. The opened letter, one of three, mildly scented and handwritten in round, cursive script lay slack between Ted's fingers.

"It's understandable," Vincent said, "you're in a quandary."

Ted raised his head.

"But I'm not a quandary man," he said, and picked up the framed photograph of Lily in Oklahoma.

"We're all quandary men, Ted. We all have our uncertainties. Yours is whether you can trust her again, whether you can look her in the face and not feel the same hurt you felt before. Yours is whether to forgive her, to welcome her back into your life and your home and the town where you were born and raised. Those are your quandaries," Vincent said, stepping forward, "those are your uncertainties, your things to go and figure." He sighed, leant his hands on the table. "Mine is what to do with the land."

Ted let the letter fall from his grip.

"My people are pushing me, Ted. They're saying the plans we have are already there, ready to go. But without the land, there's a quandary."

Vincent sat down. The tips of his fingers touched the opened letter.

"You see, we need to buy the timber mill land cheaply. That's the whole point. That's the only way we can offer more for the third section."

“There’s a third section?” Ted said, and placed an antacid between the roof of his mouth and his tongue.

“Yes, there is, Ted. The most important section. The section we want more than anything. The Cassidy land. Where the homestead is.”

Ted sizzled, his mouth open, a pinkish spume at his lips.

“You’re going to buy the Cassidy land?” he frothed.

“We’re going to try. And then the plans can start.”

Ted pointed vaguely east. “The *Cassidy* land?”

“I can’t talk about the plans, yet. My people won’t let me. But, let me tell you this, they depend one hundred per cent on the buying of the land. And you need these plans, Ted,” he said, leaning forward again, his fingers tapping this time on the letter. “The town needs these plans. Without the mill, the town has nothing, no lifeblood, no heart, and no soul. Without *something*, it’ll fall to its knees. Look at it, already. People are wearing juju chains, Ted. They’re looking at cattle. They think stones are creating their own formations. They need something. And that’s just what the plans are. Salvation. You imagine that? You imagine rescuing the town, riding in on a white charger like a knight? You think Lily would like that? You think Lily would like to walk out with the man who dragged the town up from its knees?”

Ted picked up the photograph, looked again at the pleats and grooves of the organza dress.

“But I have another quandary, Ted. You know what that is? You know *who* that is?”

Ted shook his head.

“It’s Jake Massey. You know why? Because Jake Massey is insinuating he burned the mill down.”

“He’s a bullshitter.”

“Whether he’s a bullshitter or he isn’t is not the point here, Ted. The point is if the loss adjuster hears this, if she figures it’s Jake burned the mill down then the company gets the compensation. If the company gets the compensation, they have no reason to sell the land cheaply. If they don't sell the land, there's no plan. If there's no plan, there's no salvation. You see? Or, on the other hand, if she doesn't figure it's Jake, if Jake's not around, if you show her all the evidence of the lack of investment, the accident reports over the years, the company gets blamed for neglect. If the company gets blamed, the company loses out. If the company loses out, they sell the land cheaply. If they sell the land cheaply, the plan kicks in. If the plan kicks in, the town is salvaged from its juju chains and you come riding in on your white charger. Do you follow me, Ted?"

"What do you want me to do?"

"Be good to Frances Harte. Show her the evidence."

"There isn't any."

"Exactly."

"That's it?"

"I need Jake out of the way, Ted. At least until she's gone. Maybe he could go and look for Lily. Would you like that?"

Ted looked down at the letter again, put it to his nose and sniffed it.

"Lester can go with him. Lester likes a drive out, don't you, Lester?"

Lester glanced over at Vincent and nodded. Already he got the long roads, the backroads and the tracks off. He got the woods of spruce and pine, the snap of the undergrowth, louder the further they went. He got the covering of leaves and the darkening places where only scraps of light appeared, like tickertape, where the trees were muffle and cloak and Jake was begging for mercy.

"Can you do that?" Ted said.

"Lester can do anything, Ted. He's one of my men."

"And the Cassidy land? You think you can get it?"

"What did he say? Treat failure as an impossibility."

*

The following morning Sylvie Buckle's was awash and lathered even more than usual with rumours of all kinds. The main topic, the top of the list, was Jake Massey. And his beating outside Harry's the night before.

Apparently, so the stories went, after too many beers and whisky chasers, Jake finally snapped. Weeks, months, years even, of resentment and dislike, on both sides, popped like corks. The mill workers were cowards, he said. They were like mice, afraid of their own shadows with no balls big enough to stand up to the company themselves. They were full of bullshit. Every last one of them. They knew nothing of the truth, nothing of what really happened to the mill. And, in turn, right back at him, blow after blow, Jake was a lazy, no-good waster with shit for brains and his father was exactly the same pickled fruit before him.

It began, so they said, in the corner of the bar just before midnight, and ended outside just after with Jake unconscious on the riverbank where he was left. Rumour said he was so bloodied you couldn't recognise him. Rumour said there was a stab wound somewhere, a dragged broken bottle across his back. And rumour said that by morning light he was gone. And no-one knew where. No-one could find him.

Then, of course, there was Lily Mallender and her letters of scented repentance. You see, in Sylvie's, Lily's soap story of local girl makes good and divides opinion by flaunting it to local girl blows Venezuelan gardener and then asks for forgiveness was always a given. Most women understood Lily. Whether they were outraged by her actions or they weren't, they still recognised her as the girl from farming stock, the prom queen in pigtails who married Ted, and the middle-aged woman who took out her frustrations on a hirsute tender of lawns. For Rita, there was little choice but to understand. Wasn't she looking for the same way out? Wasn't Dan Cruck just a poor man's Ted, albeit younger, more sexually willing and less likely to visit the bathroom twice a night?

In relation to Dan, rumours were that, given the non-appearance of the company men and the kick in the balls that came with Rita's rejection, he was leaving town in the next couple of days *and* the big concern was that he might take out all his bitterness by denying every single one of his post-coital concerns to the loss adjuster, thereby leaving the fate of the town in the hands of the woman whose obvious lack of lipstick, eyeliner and anything that resembled even a half-decent hair product placed her in the camp of either spinster or lesbian. And that was without the hard hat, boots and latex gloves.

There was mention, in passing, of the Li sisters who'd visited a ninety-per-cent gauzed and bandaged Lee Shaw who, in his state of wordless shock, remembered nothing of the fire or how it started. And, even though his mystique was no longer top of the list, no blow-dried rumour session would be the same without the scattered updates on the Cassidy man. First thing was, in spite of possessing radar on a military scale, no-one in Sylvie's was any the wiser about him and Delilah. No-one knew why she was there, what she was doing, or what plans they had. Not even Rita. Next, he was a practising recluse, a hermit self-flagellating his way through winter and spring on a diet of tinned fruit. Or, he was a selective mute serving penance for past sins. And he was on medication of the tranquilising kind, collecting animal pelts in the woods.

*

Lester stood in the middle of Jake's apartment and called Vincent. "He's not here," he said, "and the bed's not slept in."

He heard his master sigh. "He got beaten up last night. Some of the mill workers got to him."

"Did he squeal, about the mill?"

"I don't know. Nobody knows where he is."

"You want me to go and look for him?"

"The most important thing now is that he doesn't get to the loss adjuster. That's it. Period. He gets to her or she gets to him, we're potentially fucked. The rest we can deal with. So, just follow her, make sure they don't meet. I'll come over to the apartment building."

"Where is she?"

"She's with Ted at the LMA. I heard she's leaving tonight. We've got so many hours, Lester, and that's it. We just don't know where Jake is."

There was a kitchen knife embedded in the sill, a strewn crepe bandage with pixels of old, dried blood. There was a photograph of Delilah and Rita taken on a stoop somewhere, and a magazine opened on Harley's and Goldwing's, one of them circled.

"What's there?" Vincent said.

"He's buying bulk, by the looks. Crates, multipacks."

"Anything else?"

"Couple of cash-rolls, loose notes. New pair of Texan boots, a map of the mid-west. He's a scrambled kid."

Lester walked over to the window, opened it. "And the place stinks."

He gulped at the air of the spring day, heard the wheeze of the southern train a mile down the tracks. The sink was an assortment of skewed dishes. There was a spread pack of cards on the table next to a half-finished bottle of beer. He was hungry, licked his lips again. He saw a stray dog slip its way down to the river's edge, and felt, as he did so, the tiny shoot of a chest pain.

*

Frances gathered the material. She folded her wings around what she'd collected. She nested, labelled her sachets and bags, dated them, took her German-made magnifier to the contents and measured them up against guidebooks and manuals she used: The journals of past cases, directories of timber and metal, lists of flammable reactions, her leather-bound bible of soil. She studied the photographs the same way, zooming in on the colours and textures of erosions and burns, looking for patterns and time-scales.

She listened back to recordings she'd made, looked through the accompanying notes and annotations. She walked around the room as she did so, her head as if pecking, making suggestions to herself, a pause, a flick of the eyes, a leg that might bend and rise a moment off the ground. She listened to Ted again, to the history of the mill, to its purchase/rescue, to his part in its resurrection, and to his first-hand observation of the gradual dearth of investment. She'd seen the photographs of the mill, one in the mid-seventies and one four months ago, the deterioration, the damaged roof slates, the rotting frames. She'd looked at the minutes and agendas of the Mission Development Committee where the concerns around the mill were raised, seen the letters sent to the company and the replies, usually months later, offering little.

She listened once more to the foreman Dan Cruck, who, with swollen corporate loyalty and no fiancée to sweeten him, suggested the investment was proportionate to the size of the mill and the company's other concerns, that any company would review its options on a regular basis and that, as far as he was concerned, it was the workforce and not the company who were slacking. It was, so he said, a case of arson, a deliberate act against the mill and the company. And he gave her a short list of ex-employees, with poor attendance records and warnings against them, who had enough of a grievance to do it. Top of the list, and underlined, was Jake Massey.

She'd seen the mill workers themselves, who'd fantailed around her in Harry's bar and, in short, barked sentences, spat out their gripes: Lack of investment, outdated machinery, poor working conditions, no consultation, the token lackeys, the days lost through injuries and illness, the missing digits, the lung issues. She'd listened with her file of notes in front of her, her head often to one side, her face giving nothing away. And she'd told them, just as she'd told Ted and Dan, that she would collate all the evidence and make her recommendations. She could offer nothing more.

As an appendix to her meeting with the mill workers, there was the following note: *Recent-bruised faces and knuckles, the odd blood stain, all upper body.*

It was late afternoon. She picked up the sachets and bags, started to put them away. She looked down at the half-packed suitcase and, on the table in front of her, at the last entry in her notes, towards the back of the journal:

There is a likelihood, somewhere between moderate and considerable, that the fire was started deliberately, and that the perpetrator was local and made his way in and out of the site via the woods behind the mill. This remains a matter of speculation. There is one more avenue of investigation still to pursue in relation to who this perpetrator might be. There is a name and an address.

*

Lester watched, mid-afternoon, as the door of the building she was in opened. He watched her pause in the doorway, check inside the folder she plucked from under her wing and draw a long, spindled finger down the page. He watched her take out a pen from her plumage and write something down, look skywards, and leave. He called Vincent.

"Looks like she's heading for the apartment," he said.

"Jake's not here," said Vincent, "there's no sign. I'll get rid of the evidence anyway."

He watched her turn into the street towards the southern neighbourhoods, the head slightly angled. He watched her take the sidewalks, go past the dog-packs and clutter. He watched her slow the closer to the apartments she got, pause again, her head down to check on the folder, look up, shake herself, and go inside. He lit the cigar, moved into the shade of the doorway, and waited. There was an ache to his bulk by then, a heat and soreness to his feet. A flat cake of sweat bristled on his chest and a beaded curve arced beneath his eyes. He blinked, hard and quick, felt the dampness on his lashes.

Two minutes later, she came out again. She'd knocked and waited, then hearing not a sneakered peep, she left Jake a note and a card she'd slipped under the door of his apartment, both of which Vincent had removed by the time she walked out of the block and into the soft, spring sunlight suffused with cigar smoke.

At just before nine the light in the rented room went out, and a minute later she was in the doorway with a suitcase she could wheel and a valise attached to her by a king-sized strap around her frail shoulders. The suitcase was lighter, holding a limited range of practical clothing. The valise, though, contained all the evidence she hadn't already sent to the laboratory, plus the camera, the rock-hammer, the magnifier, work boots, hard hat and all of the folders she kept, as well as the case journal, sectioned and colour-coded, that included the underlined name of Jake Massey, against which she'd written: *Possible suspect. No tangible evidence. Hearsay only.*

She walked past the covered arcade and the Station Hotel with a half-moon hung low over the prairies. The choke of burnt metal, of toxins and oils that'd hit her when she first came, was fading from the town, so too the ubiquitous smell of its timber, its dust less possible to sweep away with an index finger, less likely to coat windows or catch the back of the nose or throat, or, more insidiously, go down into the lungs.

When she got to the bottom of the hill, she raised her head and inhaled a last time. She picked up the river, the metal of the tracks, and the thread of that same cigar somewhere. Outside the station, the family of five, with additional juju chains, stood once more around the gathered stones. Frances walked past them and, as the coming train got louder and other passengers prepared themselves, including the single woman younger than herself, so two long, unbroken columns of beetles marched over the stone.

He watched from a cluster of trees down by the tracks. He smelled of the cooled sweat that'd strapped to his chest and imagined only one thing as he looked out; the 8oz rib-eye steak with fries and relish, the redness of the meat and the trickle of its juice. He saw Frances shiver, saw her pick up the suitcase and valise as the train shambled in and shook to a stop. He watched her climb on, lift her things onto racks and seats, sit, breathe, and settle.

She thought of the postcard she'd sent back home to herself; a rooftop view of the town, with the stacks of the mill and the loom of

Rupture Hill behind it, with Blessings Point to the north-east, with the burial grounds and the snake of the river and the bridge that went from the mill to the town. And, just before the woman younger than herself stood to make her way down the train towards her, to sit next to her, she thought of her prize possession; her bookshelf of encyclopaedias, A-Z, handed down from her father who'd bought them for her when she was six years old from a man in Cuban heels.

"I'm Delilah Morris," the woman said, "do you mind if I sit?"

*

Alabama, Alaska, Arizona, Arkansas. He could smell with one crooked sniff how the night air spiked the grass as he stood on the veranda and looked out across the land. He could pick out the berries, the ripeness of, the shoots and vines as he looked towards Coronation Point with its bare scalp, to the Mallender estate and the low hills beyond. When he turned he got the faint chance of rain, saw the gape of the armchair's wound, the tumorous stuff, the useless entrails. California, Colorado, Connecticut.

He moved towards the porch-way in the black suit full of hatpins, felt the weight of the spade and looked down at the teeth of the saw with the first hints of rust. Through the half-opened door, he could see the kitchen table and the chairs around it. He could see, even through the gloom, the photograph of Vincent Clay, as the rescuer and life-saver, face down. To one side of it was the newspaper folded to the burnt mill and to the other, signed in a gambler's flourish by his great-grandfather, were the deeds of the Cassidy land.

He walked into the house, across the linoleum floor and into the room where he slept. The mattress in the corner was the same his father had shuffled into sleep on, like a feather with bent and weakened quills. The drapes were thin and drawn, and on the bedside table was a piece of driftwood like a shinbone and a mottled stone, both from the shores of the lake. The boxes were there still, shoe and shirt, so too the volumes of history and the encyclopaedias, some of which pinned the local maps down and one of which lay open, on knots, on examples of bowline, hitch and drummer's chain.

He picked up the shotgun propped against the wardrobe and went over towards the closed cellar door. On the floor beside him was the tin of half-eaten peaches, the masking tape and the two strands of rope, one thick, one thin. He opened the door quietly, went down the stone steps with the gun held out in front of him. At the foot he stopped. Delaware, Florida, Georgia, Hawaii.

"I've been thinking," he said.

The weight in the corner shifted, the sound of a sack as if being hauled, catching grit and small stones on its way.

John sat on the bottom step, the shotgun beside him. The darkness began to drain out, revealing slowly the tins of industrial paint, the primers and undercoats, varnishes and finishes. On the far side were foodstuffs log-jammed against the wall; fruits, meats and vegetables preserved in water and brine. There were soups and fish and pulses. There was rat poison.

The weight was curled up, the wrists and ankles tied by cord and rope. There was the cloth blindfold and the strips of masking tape over the mouth. It moved again as John stood and went closer, dragging itself back into the nook of the wall, the knees up under the chin, the head down, the brow beaded with sweat.

"My problem is what to do with you, Jake," he said. "I save your skin. I wait in the dark and drag you off the riverbank where they left you for dead. I bring you here. But if I give you another chance, you'll fuck it up."

The weight shook its head.

"Yes, you will. I give you chances. I offer them up on a plate. I set you up with Lester, with Vincent. I get you money to make a new start. And what do you do?"

John laid a hand on his shoulder. "Wait here," he said.

He walked back towards the steps, and up to the kitchen, ran the water first into the sink and then with a different pitch into a bowl. There was the rip of material, the chink of small bottles and the clip of scissors. Then he went back, slower down the steps, with the lap of the water. He laid the bowl down, picked up the scissors and cut into Jake's sweatshirt neck downwards until it fell open.

"You break into my house. You rip my father's chair. You drink his beer…Let me see."

The bruising around the rib cage was all kinds of violet and crimson, burgundy and black.

"Show me your hands."

Jake lifted them like paws so John could hold them up, could rinse out and clean the cuts and grazes.

"You smoke your cigarettes, you go into my room and ransack my things, *his* things. You take information about me, you go to Ted Mallender and tell him so he can make me look foolish."

He placed a dampened cloth over his bruised and buckled ribs, a towel over his arms and back. For a moment, he pulled the tape from over his mouth and dabbed at the bulbous lips, at the maw of spittle and blood, sucked up, unspat.

"So, what do I do?"

John looked down at the row of creams, unguents and antiseptics. He picked up the masking tape, tore off a fresh strip and held it between his hands. He leant in closer.

"You said I was a human being," Jake said, almost inaudibly. "You said I deserved better."

"We all deserve better," he said, and spread the strip over the pounded, hung meat of his lips.

Idaho, Iowa, Indiana. The eyes were swollen shut and sealed, a palette of blues and deep greens, the nose almost certainly broken, hard to drag air through, the cheekbones flushed. One of his ears was puffed and torn and his forehead was riddled with bumps and rises, so too the muddied scalp. John took the ripped shirtsleeve and wet it, holding it across and around the eyes so that the wounds almost sizzled as the water ran into and over them. He dried him, patting him with the fibres of the towel. He took a dab of cream on the end of his middle finger and smeared it like a corner-man over the swell of the eyelids and brows. Then he folded out the shirtsleeve and tied it around the back of the head. He threw the sweatshirt to one side, next to the blindfold, and laid a horse blanket over him, picked up the bowl again, and stood.

"Nobody knows you're here, Jake, but if I cut that rope and loosen that cord and you manage to crawl your way out, you will either be tracked down like an animal and killed like one, or you'll squeal like a pig because you can't help it. Somebody isn't paying you enough attention. Somebody isn't listening to you. Somebody isn't giving you what you want and so you open your mouth and tell them it was you burned the mill down, it was Vincent Clay paid you to do it, and it was John Cassidy, son of Jack, great-grandson of Patrick, the gambler and stealer of land, who set the whole thing up."

He reached up and pushed the bowl onto the kitchen floor above, and picked up the shotgun.

"I can't risk that, Jake. I've come too far to let it all slip."

He watched the weight recoil under the blanket, tighten up like a drawstring beneath the makeshift mask and tape.

"So, I'm keeping you here. In the cellar. Locked up. I can't waver, not now. It's too late."

The weight slid sideways, its head up against the wall. Iowa, Kansas, Kentucky.

*

The investigation into Jake's disappearance unearthed nothing. Perhaps *investigation*, as Frances Harte had discovered in her own dealings, was something of a misnomer for what the department figured was regular police procedure; the questions around the neighbourhood block, the hours spent looking for non-specific clues and what amounted to a lifting back of the bedsheets in his apartment.

So, apart from a slovenly approach to detection, why no tracker dogs with muzzles smeared in Jake's nicotine scent? Why no sketched drawings on every available post and notice board? And, more to the point, why no interrogation of any of the mill workers who'd punched, kicked, raked bottles down or stood complicitly by, or, of Harry himself, who'd let the whole thing happen, on his land? Well, one of the reasons was that nobody liked him, that over the years those uniformed officials had witnessed first-hand what a grade-A prick he was. Plus, the more senior officials had known Harry a long time, and the rest of them had grown up side by side with the mill workers. So, they found nothing.

And the reason they found nothing in the apartment was because Vincent got there before they did and removed every item of incrimination; the bulk buying, the cartons of cigarettes, the crates of beer, the motorcycle magazine with the ringed Harley, the purchases on a grander scale than usual, the bank rolls. And the grass-stained sneakers, the Texan boots, and any creams, unguents and oils that looked like they might be used for burns.

Plus, poor beaten Jake was overshadowed by two major events: First, just after Easter, with the burgeoning of colour to the banks of Rupture Hill and the emergence of lustrous berries and buds and the return of the wintering flocks, Lily Mallender flew back in herself. She called into Sylvie's before she went anywhere else to have herself fluffed and pampered and then, with her sprays and scents, she nestled herself back in the old, colonial house with Ted. And second, in early May, the big news came through from the east, that Frances Harte's recommendation of *unconditional* negligence had been unanimously upheld. The verdict was official and the company had to pay. A week later, having little choice, the company sold the land to the Land Management Agency for peanuts, including that on which the migrant housing stood, and two days after that, Vincent Clay of Carpe Diem Enterprises walked into the Agency building and, with born-again Ted as a bona fide and contributary confederate, signed the cheque for the land and vowed, for the esprit of the town, that the plans, whose full details he could not yet divulge, would bear substantial and life-changing fruit and that he, Ted Mallender, could ready his white charger and polish his bugle.

*

"To the completion of phase two, Lester," Vincent said as they sat in the foyer of the Station Hotel that same afternoon. "To the sabot and his disappearance, and to Frances Harte and her verdict. Now for the Cassidy land."

"I had plans for Jake," Lester said and looked at the oil paintings hung on the wall. "I had the long roads and the woods. He was on his knees."

"I know you did, but the world does not run on well-oiled tracks. If the world ran on well-oiled tracks, we would be fucked. The reason we are not fucked is that it's the rank stupidity of most people that makes the world go round. It's the mistakes, the near-blindness, the inability to sniff out anything that isn't right there in front of them, the gross lack of attention. People are under-developed, Lester. They are emerging from the crawling stage, the all fours, the slack, mandible jaw. They are primitive, and any pretence to anything higher is just that, a pretence, a series of coded acts, of behaviours they've seen before, manuals they've read on how to walk and talk and piss straight and how to gather all that brittleness of being they won't even acknowledge into some semblance of solidity. And still it doesn't work."

Lester sighed and checked the time on the ornate clock, studied the numerals.

"I need these people, Lester. I need to give them faith. Without them I have an obdurate man in my way."

"So when?"

"Give me a week. Then I'll go and see John Cassidy about his land."

"And in the meantime?"

"The meantime is Madeline," he said, and sat back in the give of the upholstered chair.

*

Madeline was the woman framed in the photograph on his bedside table. She had been, over the last fifteen years, as and when necessary, his loyal wife, his errant wife, his sister, business partner, business rival, travelling companion, gambler's moll and a woman he'd met on a train. She had been Dolores, Nancy, plain Jane and, once, Conchita, had been an authority on stamps, coins, race-tracks, five-card stud, palmistry and a whole host of homespun hunches that tilted people the way she wanted. And, six years previously, she had been on the end of the phone-call that said, "Honey, put out an extra place, I'm bringing a friend." Yes, she was the cook in the gingham apron, the keeper of the warm-coloured and tasteful apartment for two days that summer. She was one half of the audience to Jack Cassidy's tales of Utah beach and the single aunt that dragged the comb across his skull, the woman with the tied-up hair who welcomed him into their home, who played and listened to music from *his* era, watched *his* feet and fingers tap along and who, over those few hours, served up a homemade stew of such persuasion that poor, trusting, lonesome Jack with his best days behind him, was hooked before the blueberry pie was served.

Madeline was context. She was usually two or three days of appearance money. In this case, she was Madeline, the devoted wife, the benefactress to worthwhile causes, the lucky charm, glamorous and homely both. She was a couple of evening gowns, some fancy jewellery, hair that looked like somebody else dealt with it and a few synchronised performances designed to do one thing; to make the people of Mission trust Vincent Clay by trusting her first.

So, as she opened the door of the Station Hotel and stood as though trapped in mid-afternoon aspic, in shoes with a moderate heel, draped in a lambswool shawl and with a clutch-bag dotted with pearls, she looked like success and money and the kind of congruence that could walk into any building in the world and induce the faith that Vincent was looking for.

And, over the next few days, that was exactly what she did. Whether it was in the leisurely parades of the town, arm in arm with her childhood sweetheart, stopping to browse and buy in stores that began to seek her custom out or in Sizzlin' Steve's smoothing over the still-wet plaster of the Mallender reunion, or down in Harry's with an increasing number of regulars swinging by on the grapevine she was there, her performances were, as always, beguiling.

It was the impact on others that mattered. It was the fact that her actions, whether small-scale, like helping the desk clerk with his puzzle, or large, like walking through the town in a mild drizzle to give a sizeable and tearful donation to the mill workers' hardship fund, offered the place and its people a possibility, somehow, of something better.

And that was how it worked. In and out. Less than a week. Any shorter, people don't notice. Any longer, the impact starts to wane. All about the timing. All about getting people at just the right time. In the days after she'd gone, people began to stop Vincent in the street. They wished him well for the first time, complimented him. They offered him thanks for the simple appearance of Madeline. And even though, as yet, there was no plan for the land, no project he could speak of in detail, still the faith in him was beginning to stir.

"They're coming with us, Lester," he said as they stood on the crown of Coronation Point and looked north-westerly over the Cassidy land, "on all fours, they're coming with us."

*

It was always Delilah that went to John. There were no arrangements or patterns. Most times she would just get in the Oldsmobile and drive out to the homestead because she felt like it, and when she was there, they'd sit at the kitchen table or stand on the veranda and feel the chill or the rain or the weak sun on their cheeks. Sometimes they'd eat together. Sometimes they'd sit and leaf through the pages of his father's encyclopaedias, or look at the maps and the old photographs. Sometimes she'd stay over, and sometimes they'd sleep in the same bed but the proximity, the warmth, the one human body against another, changed nothing.

She was an outsider, an orphan from the age of two, living first out on farmland to the north and then in one of the southern neighbourhood blocks. She had no connection with the way most people lived, neither as child or adult. She didn't see things the same way, couldn't figure, even when she wanted to, how their lives were strung together, how their days went from one to the next so simply. She switched off, removed herself. Even as a child, and as a teenager twisting inside her own skin, she had enough indifference to things to blanch them out, to drain entire situations of colour and context until they were all just mime. That was how she saw the world. And, like John, she was often wordless, like an animal.

For him she was a portal to the town and a shield from it. But of his scam, his grand construction, she knew nothing. Nothing of the letters. None of the players, none of the stars or walk-ons. She saw no strategies, no game-plans. If he asked her about the town or any of the people in it, she answered him straight, incurious as to why he might want to know. Even when he sat her down and asked her to follow Frances Harte and warn her of the town's risk of collapse if the company should win, and to modify Jake into a lost soul with a boy's breezy brain and a gift for fabrication, which was exactly what she did, still she never asked why.

Three days after Madeline left, she sat at the kitchen table.

"She wooed them. Those men, eight hours a day in the timber mill, like dough."

"What about Vincent?" he asked.

"He's here for a reason."

"You think?"

She cupped her face in her hands, her hair falling forward in tresses. "You ever gonna use that shotgun?" she said.

"It was my father's. The first time I saw him for twenty years it was pointing right at me." He turned slightly, paused. "He wants the land. That's the reason."

"Which land?"

"This land. He wants to buy up the Cassidy land, like he bought up the mill and the rough terrain. He's coming over here to talk it over."

"When?"

"This afternoon," he said, and walked to the porch-way door and opened it. He put his hand tight on the frame.

"What will you do?"

"Hide the shotgun, for one thing."

"Will you sell?"

He drummed his fingers loud on the wood, looked down at his feet, at the scuff of his winter boots. He went years back, words falling in the muffle of snow, his mother's lies, the smell of coffee, his gut turning like twisted rope. And his feet. And his hands on his knees. And the rug pulled from under him.

*

Vincent pulled slowly off the driveway of the Mallender estate, listening still to Ted tell him how easy it'd been to buy up the rough terrain, how little he'd paid for it and how John was a greenhorn dumber than a beast, with a handshake like a kitten's paw. He took the loop road west and turned onto the track to the homestead, scanning the realm in front of him with the gimlet eye of a landowner. He checked himself in the rear-view mirror, got out the car in the Texan boots, and started to walk. The sky was sunless, a thin, flat grey tufted with occasional white. He got the frame of the empty house to the side of the Anderson's, a shell of beams and patchwork brick he imagined gone. Over to his left the land rose in grades and half-trod paths up to Coronation Point and, as he got closer, as his boots crunched the grit of the path, he saw the slash of the armchair's gut and the steps to the porch-way door.

John was in a boxer's trance, hands down on the kitchen table, fingers spread, hearing only the piston boom of his heart. He'd taped and rope-tied Jake, moved the last of the encyclopaedias into the cellar and hid the shotgun, and he waited, a sudden swamp of heat to his face, a few swipes of grease under the eyes. He tilted his head to one side, cocked ear and snout, sensed him right there on the other side of the door. And then the knock. Montgomery, Juneau, Phoenix, Little Rock.

Months shrank to a few, slow moments, and he couldn't move. His sternum was gripped, his hands twitched, his head straightened. He wanted to turn and see the shotgun up against the wardrobe door. He wanted the deeds right there open on the table. He wanted to go back to the beach by the lake and hear his father tell him the story over and over again until it bled back into him. The knock came again, crisper this time, making him blink away the jabs so that he pushed back the chair and stood, in the midst of his father's kitchen, on the floor where he'd tumbled more than once, not even trying to move, even less so to shout, lying there sallow and drawn, his skin like cellophane, his bones like reeds. Sacramento, Denver, Hartford, Dover.

Vincent sat at one end of the table, leaning forward, the jut of his face ahead of his torso, John at the other, his eyes unable to meet Vincent's so that he skittered from brow to moving mouth, to greying temples, to ears close to the skull as Vincent talked, and from his introductions onwards, from the first squeeze of the clammy paw, outlined his plans. He gave no specific details, just that he and his people out east wanted the land. He wanted it for reasons of business and enterprise and for reasons that would benefit the town and resurrect it as an economic force able to sustain itself after the loss of the mill. He wanted it so that he could optimise every inch of it and for that, he was willing to pay a decent and fair price. He paused for a response, or a sign of one. Nothing. So, he took a breath and kicked in again, outlining some more, buffing the plans, explaining the benefits, glorifying the resurrection, and the longer he went on, the more he threw out those orthodox left leads, one after the other, so the stiller John sat, his guard, for all those shots, staying resolutely where it was, up.

"I have no plans," he said, "I may sell. I may not."

There were so many times as he sat there, as the light of the late afternoon began to dim and Vincent pummelled his outlines and plans into him, that he wanted to reveal everything, to stop him mid-sentence, show him the ruse, the sent letters, the maps, the selling of the rough terrain. All of it. Every last detail. He wanted him to realise who he was and he wanted it to come to him piece by incremental piece so that he could watch him sit in that chair and think back and with every recollection he had get closer to knowing. He wanted him to go back to the short cons he and Lester and Madeline played. He wanted him to go back six years and walk back into the corner bar to see Jack Cassidy sat on the stool, waiting for the money to be handed over. He wanted him to remember the moment when the salesman down on his luck gave him his life-savings with the tremble in his hands because he trusted him, because he *was* down on his luck. He wanted him to go back until it started to snag, until he looked across the table and made those connections, until the moment hit him right between the eyes. And then. And then he was a table's length away. He was a tiger's pounce from whatever violence he chose, from the spade's head to the rusty saw, from the scythe to the rake, to the one relentless blow after another of the shotgun's butt. But he didn't. Even when Vincent excused himself, nodded, and said, "I'll pay a good price. Think about it. We'll speak again," and closed the porch-way door behind him, still he never moved an inch. Tallahassee, Atlanta, Honolulu, Boise.

*

The migrant housing was to go. It was deemed to have high asbestos levels and insecure roofing and as such was categorised as unsafe. On the day of their final plea for a stay of execution, a small committee of migrants made their way from the temporary shelter of the community hall to the Land Management Agency. They nodded, in turn, to the desk clerk and the ledger-men and then stood in a neat half-circle and presented their case. They spoke about their history in the town, the number of years they and their families had been there, their work records, their economic viability and their total lack of criminal convictions. They had depositions and letters from satisfied business customers and lovers of Chinese cuisine both. They asked to be cut some slack. They asked for mercy with heads bowed and hands pressed together below their chins.

But no, it wasn't to be. Ted had made his, and thereby the Agency's, mind up already. The land was legally part of the mill site and as such it belonged to Vincent Clay, the new owner, who had a plan that involved the decimation of the paper houses, and who, as he said to Lester in a quiet corner of Sizzlin' Steve's that night, had no intention whatsoever of cutting anyone any slack and had not made a success of his life by pandering to the soft and heartfelt wishes of others.

"What do they bring to the party, really? Where has all that piety and humility got them? On a slow boat to China, that's where," he said, swallowed and pointed his steak knife east. "And it wasn't that he didn't speak, Lester. It was the way he didn't speak. I mean, who treats people like that, who is it sits and says nothing, who agrees to meet someone to *discuss*, and then lets the other man do everything and shows not a thing on his face the whole time? Who is it?"

He stopped chewing, laid the fork down on the plate.

"I've watched people all my adult life, Lester, but this kid I can't fathom." He leant forward, his elbows on the table.

"We need to know who he is before we play him again. We need to figure him, to work him out. We need a weak spot, an angle in. Find out who knows him, who speaks to him, who goes to his house. Get me a profile, get me a picture. Get me anything you can, Lester. I need to know something about him. I need you to find me something I can work with. And be cool. You're asking questions, is all. Anybody looks at you funny, tell them Madeline wants to know."

*

The actual exodus of the migrants began the day after the final plea failed. Many had seen its futility and left already. A few had managed to find apartments in the south-side neighbourhood blocks. Some ignored legal instructions not to go back to the shacks by looking for remnants and keepsakes, coming back out into the sunlight with items held aloft or stuffed into pockets and bags; a muslin drainer, a floral umbrella, a porcelain holder of buttons. Removal trucks turned up outside the hall on that bright, late spring morning and loaded up with furniture, boxes, crates, objects draped or bubble-wrapped or bound together with tape, and the smaller of the people. Others packed onto the backs of flatbeds and low-loaders or squeezed into rusted cars with their belongings crammed into every available space, like a hamster's nest they could hardly see out of. The rest, the remaining dozen or so, walked out of the hall, soon to re-open for line-dancing and cake sales, leaving with homespun rickshaws and carpet-bags and heading, like the draggled aftermath of a small circus, to catch the afternoon train east.

Mr Parker spotted an opportunity, as Mr Parker always did. You had to be ruthless, he said. That was the nature of business. You had to be timely, fearless and unimpeded by sentimentality. How it worked was this: The laundry and the migrants who worked there had suffered because much of their work involved the cleaning of the mill workers' overalls caked in the grease and oil and dust that ordinary domestic products couldn't move. So, when the mill burned down, the work dried up. But, at the apex of their suffering, Mr Parker contacted the suppliers, bought in stocks of the 'miracle' detergent that worked wonders with the overalls and sold them in his store, repackaged, rebranded, and at a mark-up price just this side of scandalous. And it worked. People bought it. Whether it was his septuagenarian schmooze or the secret ingredients or whether it was, as Vincent called it, "the abject fuck-wittedness of human beings", his profits for the month of May were his best for the whole year.

And, for a while at least, the talk in Sylvie Buckle's, the buzz between the cones, was not the mill and its destruction and sale, not Frances Harte and her judgement, nor Jake Massey and his whereabouts. It wasn't the migrant workers and the wordless way they went about their departure. It wasn't, for once, Madeline and her generosity and jewels, nor Lily and her return to the fold, nor even was it John Cassidy and his rumoured freeze-out of Madeline's sweet husband, Vincent, but Parker's bottled, blue-tinged cure-all for stains.

*

The obvious go-to for information on John was Jake Massey. Jake had spent the most time with him, after all. He'd sat in his house, had a beer with him, eaten Chinese and, separately, ripped his father's armchair, broken into that same house and rifled through his and his father's possessions. There was a connection, people said. They deserved each other. But there was a problem. Nobody knew where the fuck he was.

The next in line, according to the Mission grapevine, was Delilah Morris. But it was all speculation, rumours based on the fact that the Oldsmobile was parked on the track at all hours. That was it. And besides, Lester didn't want her suspicious. So, he *was* cool. He left her alone. He didn't say boo. Actually, the first person he went to see on that early June morning was Abraham Stone, to see what he thought about the pains in his chest and his arm and the frequency of the night-sweats.

Dr Stone ran a few perfunctory tests, took his blood pressure and pulse, asked him a series of deadpan questions about his family history, his lifestyle in relation to exercise, alcohol, nicotine and diet, charged him, passed him a prescription for antacids and insomnia and, as a general pick-me-up, a twice-daily dose of his own preferred treatment he produced from his drawer for which Lester thanked him and, in a casual aside, wondered whether he knew or had any experience of John Cassidy. Without looking up, he said, plain-faced, that as a doctor he had signed the Hippocratic Oath, which prevented him from divulging personal and confidential information. But, as Lester left, and still attending to the paperwork in front of him and checking his watch, he mumbled the word 'abrasive' loud enough for Lester to hear, and put his finger to his lips.

The town of Mission was not short of opinions on John Cassidy or the Cassidy name. Lester hardly had to poke anyone with a sharp stick to get a sizzled intake of breath. Throw a question into the pit of Ike's barbershop, anyway, and the claws are on it faster than a gunslinger's draw. On the day Lester was there, even before he got to John Cassidy, there were the corn prices and the fluctuations of, the cattle behaviour, the stone configurations, the beetles, and the meaning of the recent striated cloud formations seen in the eastern sky just before nightfall. When he did get to John though, when he dropped the name in there, as casually as he could, it was like feeding time at the fish tank. Everybody had something. Something they'd heard, something they'd seen, something they knew of, for sure, no matter not one of them had ever spoken to him. Seen him, yes, watched him walk through the streets of the town, you bet, but man to man chewed the fat, not exactly. But did that make a difference? Did it prevent them from having a conviction about who he was and what he was like? Did it matter that for most of those folks what was slung into the melting pot was third-hand at best? No sir, it didn't. Was there a reining in, a reservation of any kind? It appeared not. So, John Cassidy was, as the claws ripped; thick-skinned and bestial, stoical and sorcerous. He had, it was true, the habits and ways of a lifelong mute. He was a malcontent, a delinquent, a pococurante. He had the writing of a small child, able only to make marks. And he had a hard-backed book of exotic and everyday spells and a tattoo of a rattlesnake coiled around his spine.

From elsewhere, on that bright day, with the corn tops more swayed than blown, he got the history of the Cassidy land all the way back to Patrick, the building of the homestead, the neglect, the return, the death of his father and the scant dismissal of both Law Enforcement and Environment Agency officers using legal precedents to do so. He got the boxes and the books, the reserves of tinned fruit, his refusal of prayer and the return of the apple to the basket. "Where's there's no light," a bonneted Ruth said, quietly, as she stopped by the church doors.

Late afternoon he went to the Land Management Agency to see Ted who, for his part, re-iterated the history like a badged guide while polishing the photograph of Lily with his sleeve. He talked about the swarthy card-cheat on the rainy night, and how the land, once the Mallender land, once fertile and ripe with opportunity, had been taken and then left, twice. Until Jack arrived.

"What was he like?" Lester asked.

"I never met him. He was dying. He was the first Cassidy to live on the land. He was, for many people, no more than a reminder of a grievance long-held, so they resented him. We simply waited for nature to take its course."

"And then John came?"

"He turned up in the last few weeks. His father was there for six years, and he shows up right at the end, and gets the land. Rumour was they hadn't seen each other for twenty years. Rumour was the father didn't even recognise his own son. But you should ask Sophie Li. She worked at the place. She'll tell you more."

*

And so the following day, in his dutiful quest, he drove out to the Shaw place, going south out of Mission and then east across land as flat as a pool table. He knew the house straight off. It wasn't difficult. Part domicile, part sculpture, part ruin. Some of the basic frame, including sections of the roof, was missing, some was blackened, some boarded, some protected by tarpaulin and rope. The use of the tarpaulin, though, meant the windshield of the old Chevy lay exposed to the fates of the weather like a maw of jagged teeth, and so was either rusted, crusted or wet. There was still the buckled, un-closable hood, the axle unfixed, the nose nuzzled into foot-high grass. There was the box-garden hooked onto the grille, a few vines held by planted canes and, as he passed, with the fist of his arm clenched, there was a moment's rise of sweet pea and clematis amid the resident choke of the burnt and charred.

He stood in front of the door, its hinges loosened, its paint more or less gone, and knocked. The pain in his arm came after breakfast, after his supersized eggs, grits, and coffee, sweet and strong.

"Hi, Ma'am," he said as Sophie opened the door as wide as the smallest garden cane was long, "my name is Lester Hoops and I am the legal representative of Carpe Diem Enterprises." And with jellied eyes, with the tributaries of blood vessels over his cheeks and nose, he explained that it was his role to investigate any possible mitigation in relation to and in advance of the undertaking of whatever project the company was involved with, namely, in this case, the acreage to the west of the town known as the Cassidy land. And would she mind if he asked her some questions?

Sophie looked him up and down. She hardly spoke anymore. She hardly did anything anymore, and she was afraid, of becoming tongue-tied for good, of becoming thoughtless. She was afraid of living out the rest of her days in that godforsaken place. So, she would've let him in even if he'd been selling car insurance, garden furniture or solar panels for the bare-boned roof. He was company for a while. He was a chance to speak and be heard. Plus, he reminded her of Jack, a man beyond fifty seen his best days gone.

The inside of the house was like the inner malfunctions of a sick man; the wheezes, the slack pumps, the air trapped in swarms. The furniture was old and damaged, the kitchen no-go, a suction pad only for grease and grime. Upstairs was sealed off by cycle chains and thick wool and, in the corner of a downstairs room, to the right of a hallway towered with boxes, was a makeshift smaller room sectioned off by drapes, behind which was the bandaged figure of Lee Shaw.

On the two right-angled walls were pictures of car parts and the various paraphernalia of white supremacy, hung there to prod and provoke him, to remind him who he was, to help him back to the land of the fully conscious. Because, in the grip of trauma, riddled with burns like atolls and reefs and lungs full of smoke, Lee couldn't speak of or remember a damned thing.

Lester sat down at a table full of vinyl records and posters of freak-shows.

"Did you know who he was, when you applied?" he said.

"There was no name."

"And when you got there?"

"I guessed."

"And people ignored you because you worked there?" he said.

"Yes, they did."

"Because you were helping a Cassidy?"

"Yes."

To Sophie the questions were like rainfall after a drought, the inflections nudging her skin, the word "you" more than once.

"I needed the money, Mr Hoops. They want to shut me out, they shut me out. What can I do?"

She lit a cigarette. Lester glanced over towards the drapes, then back.

"What about Jack?"

"I felt sorry for him. What else was there to feel? He was a dying man."

"You didn't know his story?"

"I needed the money. What concern did I have for the history?"

There was a murmur from behind the drapes, the hum of a song.

"He was divorced, I think. He had books. He was a salesman once upon a time. The land was family land. He never said too much."

Lester laid his paws down flat on the table. "And what about John?"

Sophie paused. She squashed the butt in the ashtray, and whispered, "He put his step-father in hospital. Poisoned him until he snapped. His mother's a drunk. He stole money from her. And Jack wouldn't see him at first. He didn't believe him. Hadn't seen him for twenty years, didn't recognise him. Plus, there were others. Another son, nephews, nieces, all came to the house, all claiming to be connected to Jack."

He digested, licked his lips with his crusty tongue.

"So, twenty years," he said, "then he turns up. There's a man about to die, a sick man, a man with money and land and no-one to leave them to, and this long-lost drifter he doesn't even believe to begin with comes along?"

"That's about right."

The humming stopped. Lester noticed, Sophie didn't. She tied her hair up, shifted the vinyl sleeves like giant playing cards.

"And then he took him away," she said, and leant back in the wooden chair. "He got him up one morning and then they were gone. No word, no nothing."

"You didn't know where?"

"He never said a thing."

"And Jack never came back?"

"No, sir, he didn't. I never saw him again."

"And the burial?"

"No. Don't even know where it took place."

"Can I ask you something?" Lester said, clenching one of his paws, "Did he leave you anything?"

She shook her head.

"Nothing? No keepsakes, no mementos?"

"Not that I know of."

"So, you look after the old man. You clean him up. You wash his clothes. You cook for him. You are, until this stray dog comes along and takes him away, his *only* carer. And there's nothing?"

She shook her head again. He moved his paw closer to her tiny pink pads, looked at the bare skin at the back of her neck.

"Did he owe you anything?"

"Lee sorted it. He went to the house."

"And?"

"John paid him what was owed. He gives some to me and keeps the rest. Then his car goes off the road."

The eyebrows arch. "Continue, please."

"He loses control, in broad daylight, on an open road. Ends up in a ditch. He's a car mechanic, Mr Hoops. The steering was never faulty. *Then* there's the fire."

"He remembers nothing of?"

"Not a thing. Look at him."

Lester turned, saw the body-shape against the drapes hung from a homemade rail. The hum started up again, got louder, hit a chorus. He saw her flinch when it stopped.

He stood, felt the tack of his soles on the floor. He got to the door, looked over at the grease of the cycle chains, at the boxes piled high. He walked out and got level with the angled nose and the box-garden, the sound of Sophie's dainty boots behind him. "We never leave," she said, "Between us we're here twenty-four-seven. We do alternative shifts. Meat factory and here. We don't have health care, or insurance. We can't take him anywhere, or do anything with him. We're stuck, Mr Hoops."

Lester saw her look down.

"We could help you out," he said and took a good handful of notes from his billfold and held them in his hairy paw. He reached out, took her pink pad in his, opened out the fingers, put the money in, and closed them again.

"Here, take it. You've helped us."

Sophie looked up at the frisky clouds, then over towards the flatlands. She made a single glance towards him, and took it, with a nod.

"Anything you can think of," he said, "anything we can use. People'd speak to you again, if they knew. They'd help you, fix the roof, do something with the car. Anything that gets the stray dog off the land. Anything that puts a nail in his coffin. That's what we're looking at."

*

The sound of a medium-sized dinner plate hitting a kitchen floor from approximately two and a half feet. Then another, and another, and a fourth. And, at the very point of each smash, the squeals of little-boy laughter, doubled. Doug was on the phone to John.

"Vincent wants me to play golf with him again. There's a proposition," he said, and walked the length of the hallway to see hands skittering over the marbleised kitchen surface like crabs, feeling for anything else that might break extravagantly. He saw them by-pass boxes and cartons, crawl quickly by anything wood or plastic and close in, even at that young age, unable to make a mark for their name or dress themselves, on the sugar bowl and cookie jar and the ceramic coffee pot laden with dregs.

"Something to do with new land. Viola! Help me out, here."

He watched her appear in the doorway, looking, even though dusk had gathered, as if she had only just got out of bed, untouched by the healing powers of daylight. Her hair needed a wash. A horse blanket was draped around her shoulders. She had so little left, so little gas in the tank.

The carnage paused. Doug gestured towards the telephone in his hand as she shuffled into the room.

"He mentioned your name. He said he'd like me on board. Something about the pins."

He saw the two boys watching her, dawdling by the bowl, tapping fingers like cartoon cats. The bowl started to move, as if nudged by a colony of ants, towards the edge. Viola dropped like a sack to her haunches.

"I'm not a deserter, John."

"Doug, listen."

"I'm not a mercenary. I need you to know this."

"Do you need the money?"

"We're way into the savings."

"And Viola? And the boys?"

"They start kindergarten in three months."

"Then go and play the golf. Talk to him at least. See what he wants."

Doug pointed with a wince towards the bowl. Too late. As if in slow-motion, granules jumping ship on the way down, and a mouse-like squeak into the folds of her skirt from Viola. Doug put the phone down on a brutalised kitchen table, picked up the two boys in both arms, their legs kicking against him, and set them down outside without saying a word. He walked to a cupboard, scored by crayons, took out a brush and pan, and handed them to Viola.

"Honey, let's go," he said, "one thing at a time. The door's locked."

Viola looked up at him and across at the shards and splinters, at the scattered sugar over the floor. He smiled as best he could, picked up the phone again.

"Are you selling the land? Is that what it is?"

"Who knows? Now, go and do yourself a favour. You need the money. And let me know, I'll be in touch."

John put the phone down. Outside across the Cassidy land, across the rough terrain and beyond to Rupture Hill and its lattice of crags, a sky of chain-mail grey and lobster shell, of streaked vermilion and bruise-blue. He walked over to the table, to the peach segments and spoon, to the rope and tape and thinner cord.

He could feel them getting closer, moving in towards him with every day that passed. He could sense them making those preparations. Vincent, practising his moves for the second meeting in the roadside bar, Lester, his sparring partner. Ted Mallender in his office. The town's recruits and volunteers, on whom he could sniff out the righteousness a mile away.

He jockeyed the bowl of water down the cellar steps, lay it down on the floor and peeled away the old tape and bandages from Jake's listless body. The eyes that looked back at him were fearful no more. The appearance of the shotgun never flinched him, nor the scissors and rope. There was no longer the anticipation of pain from the cuts and bruises being dealt with, with his body being shifted and untwisted. There was no fear of the dark, of wounds not healing, of gangrene, of rats and rat poison, of malnourishment or dehydration, of not enough protein, too much sickly brine, toothache, retinal damage, paralysis. No, for Jake, what was worse than any of those was the relentless biding of time. He was not cut out for incarceration, or confinement of any kind. He was not a survivor. He was not a man of mental or physical resources. If he had little to no concentration *before* John Cassidy picked him up and carried him back from the riverbank, then he had none after. Whenever John came in to pull back the tape from his mouth he had less and less to say. There was no pleading, no presentation of his case. There was no will to understand anymore. He was a shell, a casing only of bones slow to heal, of pastel bruising and scores that left pale, fossil-like marks. He stared out at some mid-distant point on the far wall, above the tins of food and paint, above the opened tin of rat poison. He gulped at the water John gave him, swilled it around the tenderness of his mouth and spat it down, some on the floor, some into the bowl, and some over John who took the tape from his hands, picked up the dampened cloth and mopped at the cheeks and brow, who wiped at the nape of the neck and round under the jawbone and throat. Sometimes he pulled out the sweatshirt and squeezed the cloth so that the water ran down over his chest and belly, so that whatever bruising was soothed and whatever openings rinsed. The body stayed slack and disinterested, the sinews and muscles unmoved.

"I don't know what choice you think I have, Jake. You forget how easy you come into my house," he said, untying the ligatures around his feet, "you forget how quick you were to rip open the chair my father sat in, to get your hands over things not yours to touch. You forget you stole from me. You forget you had no thought or respect for who I was because you don't know or care who I am. I mean nothing to you. I *am* nothing to you," he said, snipping the cord, fraying the thicker pieces with a knife. "To you I am only a name and a history. To you I am only cruel. I am reacting badly."

He sponged the still-swollen feet, ran water over and in between the toes, the crusted soles and heels, the indigo slopes. He took a dry towel and ran it over grooved ankles and shins and calves weakened from lack of walking.

"But you forget, just like the others forget. You forget this simple thing; that if you don't fuck up in the first place, if you don't presume you can do things to people and not get something back in return, then we're not where we are and I have no need to keep you here. It's not difficult," he said, wrapping clean tape back around his ankles and wrists and mouth, "it's cause and effect. Oldest equation in the book."

*

Vincent was the first to arrive. He sat in a window seat and waited in his pale-grey suit for John to step through the ropes. It was a temperate day, the dome of Blessings Point clear to the north and, as he waited, with a wheat beer in front of him, he began to align his body and the features of his face, to hide the disdain, the dislike, the dismissal he felt. He'd played people so many times in so many ways over the years. He'd told them what they wanted to hear, showed them what they wanted to see, but this time it was different, and when John walked in forty-five minutes late, in T-shirt, ripped jeans and sneakers, with no word of apology or explanation, sat down, picked out a point on the far side of the road close to the ditch's edge and fixed it, he had to clench his jaw and look down at his beer before he smiled and spoke.

"If this is about family, I understand," he said. "If it's about you father, your flesh and blood, the attachment to, history of, I get it, you have my empathy. But listen," he said, sat back, sipped at the beer, "these are different times, John. You would not be letting down the family name, you would be selling a piece of land. That's it. Your father's not here anymore. It's about you. These are your choices. Do you know what carpe diem means?"

John nodded, once, still looking out.

"My father seized the day. In fact, he seized the day every day. And for that this company owes him a debt, for that he is still its beating heart. He is my attachment, my bloodline. My work is his work," he said, looking towards the half-profile, the marine-cut temple, the bent snout, "but if he was here now, he'd tell me one thing. He'd say, 'Vincent, it's your life, do what's best for you. The past is the past. It's done with.' And, if it's about the money, I understand that, too, believe me. But if you want a good price, I'll give you a good price. If you want a deal you can walk away from and not feel you should've got more, come to me. You need any contacts out east, let me know. You need a connection somewhere, tell me, I know people, I have favours to call in. Somewhere to stay, somewhere to work, tell them I sent you. You need to look after yourself, John. Make whatever peace you need to make and move on, make a fresh start. You've got your whole life ahead of you. Think of it as an opportunity."

There was a moment's pause while a Cadillac passed, sending up whorls of dust and dirt. A moment to look up and see the young man not even looking, not listening. A moment to feel the acid rise up in his throat.

"I don't know what more to say to you. I have nothing else," he said. "But I wonder why you care so little for what people think of you. Where you find the insouciance, the presumption, the arrogance. I wonder why people think of you as having no light."

John looked at him for the first time. Not for long, and not studied, but enough to catch the shift. He watched the hay-stalks scoot across the road, the sidling by of a flatbed truck half-full of sliding boxes. His breathing was good, the forearms strong.

"Why you are no more than a gypster to people, why you are only speculation and rumour. You know it beats me why you stay," he said. "You live out there in your grief-shack on the land your family stole, with your tinned food and your father's beers, unspoken to, resented, despised. You don't understand the force of your presence, Mr Cassidy. These are not rational people. They're twistable, open to manipulation. Wind them up and point them in the right direction, boy, they'll go. And I wonder why you would set fire to Lee Shaw's house," he said, leaning forward, a relish to his tone, "why you might poison your step-father, why your mother is no more than a drunk who never wanted you in the first place and from whom you stole money. And why your father wouldn't let you in, didn't recognise you, didn't believe you were who you said you were. He thought you were an imposter, didn't he, a charlatan after his land and his money, a trickster, a mountebank, an ass in a lion's skin? Why did you take him away, John? Where did he die? Where did you bury him?"

John closed his eyes a few moments, took the combinations, felt a shudder in his facial bones. Vincent was a reach away then, an arm's length only from the throat he could sense the gristle of, from the empty glass he could pick up and push into his face, feeling it break so that he could grind and twist the edges hard and deep into his skin and bone. And the more he'd try to wrestle himself loose, the more he would get torn at, ripped open and pulled until he was nothing but cut fruit, all sap and flesh and pulp.

He stood, an old jalopy about to pass, and looked at him. And then he leant in, hands arched on the table, his head moving to within inches of Vincent's pinned face.

"Do you want the land or not?"

Vincent nodded.

"Say it."

"I want the land."

"Louder."

"I want the land."

"Say I am the fucker that wants the land."

Vincent swallowed. John moved a notch closer. "Say it."

"I am the fucker that wants the land."

"I am the bastard that wants the land."

"I am the bastard that wants the land."

"Say I am the cunt that wants the land."

The crooked snout pushed into Vincent's cheek.

"Say it."

"I am the cunt that wants the land."

John pulled away. From the other side of the room the jukebox kicked in. The jalopy passed, sending straw out across the land.

*

It was only natural in a place like Mission, with its *demeanour of moral rectitude*, as Abe Masterson called it, that the news on the unpardonable word would spread faster than a bush-fire in a heatwave. The context was meaningless. The use of the word enough to make people feel violated. The womenfolk, especially, even those who knew what their husbands had done to Jake Massey, felt defiled, and Sylvie Buckle's, in the days after its utterance, was not a place to casually blow-dry around the latest gossip but instead was one of whispers and asides. No-one could mention the word. No single, coned woman, pretending to leaf through a magazine for fashion tips or otherwise, could possibly repeat what the diabolic Cassidy beast had said to poor Vincent.

It was similar in Ike's, but less whispered. Amongst the younger men who went in there once a month there were equal measures of disgust, disbelief and a seething desire to get out there and do something. The older ones remembered. They went back, shackled themselves like captives to the decency of the place, to its history, to its land and to the wistful contents of Abe Masterson volumes. They went back to its upright nature, to those values and ways that existed *before* a stranger could walk into town and use such a word.

Ruth Anderson fainted. She was in Parker's buying starch for the sheets and literally collapsed in a heap of billows and tufts when she heard it. Old Mr Parker did what he could. He put her in the recovery position, cleared the airwaves, delicately parting her stiff collar. He called for medical help and, as a sure sign of that decency, he sold her the starch half-price when she left, still shaken. Later that day there was a sharp rise in the sale of earphones, comfort blankets and bubble-wrap. And for the younger men, the new, hastily improvised foam sacks to let those frustrations out on.

Sizzlin' Steve's had a couple of good nights, too. People eating to feel better. People consoling themselves with large steaks and fries and extra-hot, flagellating relish. Church attendance upped. Dr Stone drew a few more folks in to seek pharmaceutical relief for their shock. And somebody, just like Lester Hoops said they would, did indeed, in an act of community, drive all the way out to the Shaw place and offer to fix up the roof. Someone did invite Sophie and her sister to go and eat with their family, and someone, an ex-mill worker with impaired hearing, volunteered to sit with Lee once a week, as respite for the sisters, and read aloud from the white supremacist literature he had around, in the hope that he might find his mojo again.

For Vincent it was too good a chance to miss. It was the essence of seizing the day. So, contrived and promoted by a day-only, crowd-pulling appearance by his loving and supportive wife, Madeline, he generated a sense of unification in the town. Any petty disputes that people might've had over money owed or grazing rights or farm equipment borrowed and not given back were all forgotten in the face of that growing communal resolve. Men and women, young and old. Ignoring what had happened was not a moral possibility. You let such things pass at your peril, he said. There was a duty to act, for the sake of the town, for its past and, as he reminded them, its future.

*

The first posse was made up of a dozen men, ex-mill workers and men from the southern neighbourhoods, all masked and hooded, who came through the woods on that early evening in mid-June. They'd been fed by Steve and watered by Harry and they walked over Coronation Point, down onto the level land and past the Anderson sheets and bonnets until they got to within twenty feet of the house. It was windless, in the low 70s still. The striated cloud formations stretched behind the turrets of Rupture Hill.

They lined up like a drilled unit and, from sacks made up in homes, tied in Harry's and Steve's and carried in turns along the way, they took out the manifold rocks and stones and, on a given and silent gesture, either by hand or from makeshift slingshots, they released them towards the longer side of the house, shattering every pane of glass in a ten-second burst.

Two days later, an ex-mill worker involved in the beating of Jake Massey, so incensed that his wife and children had heard the word, picked up his shotgun and from a vantage point on the southern edge of the Cassidy land fired a single bullet into the frame of the porch-way door.

They drove, most days in convoys of four or five cars, along the unmade track that led from the road to the house. It was a show of strength and unity, of preening gestures that hid the fester and churn they felt inside. And they needed a result. Without the outcome of John Cassidy packing up, leaving and selling the land so that the grand-scale plan could start, it was just moral fury and retaliation. So, imagine the frustrations of those righteous men when instead of being gripped by a fear of escalation, of sensing that none of it would stop until he was gone for good, the young Cassidy bastard simply boarded up the broken windows with plywood, nails and planks, sealed over the bullet hole and for most of every day thereafter sat on his veranda and looked out. Sometimes he took his black coffee and tinned fruit, sometimes a volume of something to read, and always, right there next to him like a trusty, owl-eyed spaniel, his father's shotgun he picked up and turned in their direction every time they got out of the cars.

He was taunting them. That's what he was doing. He was inviting them to get closer. It was his own form of provocation. And the longer he stayed there on his veranda so the townsfolk and the posse and the man who'd fired the bullet, instead of feeling like they'd done their duty by the town, felt only the further twists of impotence.

For a while, the stakes shifted. Given the failure of intimidation they moved, without any consultation, sideward. A painted black X appeared overnight on Delilah's apartment door. Her best friend, from kindergarten onwards, Rita Mahoonie, stopped answering her calls and wouldn't go to the door when she came. People crossed the street to avoid her. They looked the other way. For some of them the shunning was enough. It was enough for those who'd walked to the edge of the Cassidy land as part of a larger group or those who'd let close a door in Jack Cassidy's face or stood by and watched as he struggled with groceries. It was enough for all those whose contributions to the cause was to fry the steaks, pour the beers, help tie the sacks, fill up the cars with gasoline, wash hair, paint nails, pluck brows and listen to every word of hearsay and rumour, and to lay out the hymn books on the old wooden pews so that forgiveness, asked for or not, was only a short prayer away. For others, it wasn't.

Two weeks after the slingshot attack and a week after the painted X, simmering with the kind of inadequacy that no church service, no late night in Harry's or comfort steak with fries could ease, the posses and convoys and neighbourhood men got their chance and, with no talk of how or when or where to draw the line, they took it.

*

After a morning spent on the veranda with his hardbacks and coffee, John had gone back into the house around mid-day and come out half an hour later with a medium-sized valise the colour of cocoa that he carried over to the Toyota, opening up the trunk and laying it down flat. Then he brought out a number of shoe boxes and a couple of shirt boxes he put either next to the valise or on the back seat, depending. Over the next few hours, on an afternoon of clear, blue skies, with every crease and line of Rupture Hill plain to see, he took items that belonged outside, the spade, the saws, the shotgun and the ruined armchair with its belly full of stones and carried them back into the house. Around three he came out with a second, smaller valise that he propped on the front seat, went back to the house to check each and every board and panel, locked the porch-way door, climbed into the Toyota and drove away down the unmade road, the dust rising up behind him.

That night, with the Toyota not back, a second posse of six selected men, the one who'd fired the shot, three of the slingshot posse and the two teenage Snipe boys, drove out from Harry's bar in two trucks. They parked at the end of the track, close to the road, and walked towards the house, the bottles strapped and stoppered around their waists, the mix of motor oil and gasoline thickened with dish soap and tar, the wicks soaked in kerosene. None of them spoke. The veranda smelled of syrup and varnished wood.

The slingshot three walked round to the back of the house. There were two unbroken windows, one that looked into an unused bedroom tiled with papers and books, the other into a room criss-crossed with tools, with spades and saws and cutters splayed in a zany stockpile. The Snipe brothers hammered on the porch-way door, and the gunshot man, with the material of a ripped shirt pulled up over his mouth and nose, stood stock-still on the veranda. Just once he looked round, to see a light go on in the Anderson house, and then go off again in seconds.

Five minutes later, with clouds passed and gone over the Mallender estate, with Lily applying strokes of night-cream and Ted dreaming of white chargers, over the prairies and the farmlands, with Doug in TV light while Viola slept, and Sophie pulling back the cycle chains to sleep in an upstairs room for the first time in months, the six chosen men lined up on the dark side of the house, lit, on the gruff count of three, the modified wicks of bandages, cloths and rags, and let those bottles loose.

Part Three

John drove south and then east. The land was open and flat, plains patched with corn and rapeseed, hills low and rolling, bearded with occasional woodland. If he stopped, he did so for provisions and gasoline and to check on the Toyota pieced together with tape and grease, on the rusted sills, the slow leakage of oil, the wiper fixed but shorter. Whenever he needed to rest, he pulled over to the side of the road, just like he had done before.

He sat with the car door wide, opening up his tins of peaches or apricots and pulling out the contents like fish. Sometimes he listened to the radio. Sometimes he read, one of the handful of volumes he'd brought in the shoe-box, one his father had made a mark in. The nights were warm and clear and he settled himself either sunk down in the seat or curled in the back, one of the blankets loose over him, another folded or rolled as a pillow. He tried to find sleep, an hour here or there, but it didn't come easily. He named constellations, knew their places in the summer sky, could figure directions by them. He placed the late birdsong, the animal sounds, checked his pockets of pins.

He knew how close he was. He knew from when he got to within an inch of Vincent Clay and made him admit to who he was. He knew he was a phone-call to the LMA and a matter of signed deeds away.

*

He got to the lake in the early evening of the next day, left the car on the same pebbled shore and walked over the stones and the shale, looking towards the line of trees and the westerly shoreline sketched with driftwood and scree. The sky was soft-blue, stroked by midsummer pink, and as he walked, with the same buffleheads, shovelers and teals, he went back to the ferrying of the kitchen bowl, full, empty, full again, to the unbuttoning of the plaid shirt, the pallid and paper-thin grooves, the visible bones, to the filing of the skin on his feet, the feeling of his scalp through the brush handle, the chin through the razor, the piano-key ribs and spine through the fabric of the towel.

He walked further along the shoreline, closer to the narrow spit of land. He stopped at the cuticle whiskered by seed-grass and listened out to the water as it lapped at the shale. There was the way his father sat, the reeds of his voice when he spoke. There were his parchment hands that rested like a bound collection of sticks on the driftwood of his legs. There were eyes all but lost in the folds of his skin, in the scribbled rivulets of blood. "It'll eat you alive," he said. "Find something else. Move on."

First light pricked around four, along with the birdsong he picked with a tilt of his head. He knelt and splashed his face with water, swept it back through his hair and allowed it to run down his back and his chest. He looked across the silvery-black surface of the lake to the dun and palest-blue of the hills on the far side. Then he stood and headed over towards the line of trees, following the narrow track cut through.

He walked for almost an hour until he came to the small general store with its hung dinghies and surfboards and, beyond its baskets of fish reels, snorkels and masks, a call-box. He waited at the tracks' edge. Sunlight spliced through the trees, and to his right the track widened and led down to a slipway to the lake. A car pulled up outside of the store and a middle-aged woman in a gingham dress got out and went inside. The man sat at the wheel and leant forward. Then he rolled down the window and lit a cigarette.

His crooked snout twitched. The woman came out of the store with provisions. She put some in the well of her seat and some on the blankets and duvets and boxes in the back. The man watched her, without speaking. He watched her get into the car and close the door behind her, glancing back as she did. He pulled one last time on his cigarette and threw it to the ground.

He got to the call-box, heard a bufflehead sing out. One of the dinghies twisted in the riddle of wind that came off the lake. When it was over, when he no longer felt the heaviness in his limbs and the acid in his gut, when the need for closure was done with, when he'd played everything out, made the call, said the word, posted the signed deeds and made it all happen, he would walk away and leave it all behind, just like his father said. And when Vincent had bought up the land and begun that ruination of self and town and every one of the deserving people in it, he would let them all swing. He would let them tear at each other, let them ransack themselves, with no reprieve, no quarter or mercy shown, and Vincent Clay would sink to his knees as a beaten, fooled man.

*

Ted Mallender wasn't there. He wasn't there to run to Vincent Clay with the news. He wasn't in the Agency building to imagine himself mounting the white charger and grabbing his bugle. And he couldn't call Lily, his flower of atonement, and tell her the Cassidy name and the Cassidy land and the Cassidy beast with his Cassidy word would all be gone, and how the lawns would get tidied up, soon. No, it was the least-mousey ledger-man who took the call, who listened as the young man told him that he was selling up the land, that he would haunt the town of Mission no more, that he would no longer be an affliction, a bugbear or blight. He had lived on his land long enough and it was time to move on.

There was a pause when he stopped. The lake shimmered, a thousand bracelets and lockets dancing over the water.

"Don't you know?" the ledger-man said. "Your place is burned to the ground."

He stood, looked back towards the clearing, his gut twisted, his joints jellied and loose. He saw the woman change her mind. He saw her get out of the car and begin to re-arrange some of the things in the trunk, to take one of the duvets from the back seat and lay it out, to take out the bags of provisions and put them on the ground by her feet and start to swap items from one bag to another, making a heavier bag, and a lighter one, to pick up the lighter one and put it in one of the boxes on the seat, where once the duvet had been, and take the heavier one over to the trunk, pushing it in against the side.

He got the faint music coming from the general store, the smell of pine-treatment and sawdust, the sniff from the slipway of kerosene and oil. He got the lit-olive and the pale, but lustrous mulatto of the tree trunks.

"Was there anything left?"

"Nothing," the ledger-man said.

"Anything saved?"

"No."

"Anything…found?"

"No, sir."

He watched her look at the trunk, top to bottom, side to side. The duvet she picked up by its two lower corners and arranged over the top of the things, including the pushed, heavier bag. He watched her reach up and close the trunk, check the lighter bag of provisions in the box on the back seat and close the door. He saw the man look towards her. He saw him speak, not for very long, roll up the window until it was almost shut, and then start up the engine. The woman fidgeted in the dress and looked behind at the box with the provisions in it. The car moved forward. The man paused a moment, turned the car full circle in the dust and drove away.

"Mr Cassidy? Do you need anything?"

"No," he said, and put the receiver down.

He imagined his great-grandfather on the land, a young and bearded player of cards, oblivious to risk or threat. He imagined the land left, bunch berried, strewn with sot-weed and liverwort. He imagined it returned to, the near-septuagenarian Patrick, still immune to the townsfolk's wrath, building the place for his grandson Jack to live in, not knowing that the single aunt would keep it from the boy, through spite or protection, who knew, not knowing that the boy would never in his adult life go back to her to be told and would not discover the existence of the land until he was sixty years old and had nowhere else to go.

And now it was razed, nothing but rubble and wreckage. Scorched, cindered, mounds of embers and ash only. There were no memories left to look at or touch. Nothing to distinguish. Mentioned in Masterson's volumes only, the history and geography of the Cassidy land, how it became what it became, what grew on it, walked on it, ate and left fur on it. And now, underneath that ragged pile, those mounds of ash, the tumbled, crumbled roofs and walls, underneath what once was slept in and lived in, under the smells of his father's dying days, of Sophie Li's detergents and sprays, under the faint traces of Delilah's perfume, of unguents and creams, of a once-eaten Chinese meal with spilt whisky and cigarettes and an armchair ripped and ruined, were the left bones and teeth of Jake Massey.

A week later the deeds were on Ted Mallender's desk in the Land Management Agency, the third cheque was signed, and the land was Vincent Clay's.

*

Of the fire itself there was little to no information. No-one had seen or heard anything. For their part, the Serpentine volunteers, as with the mill, given the distance and the delay, got there way too late to salvage anything worthwhile, and the Mission police department, busy celebrating Ned Scarratt's birthday at the time, set up only a token investigation the day after, which, unsurprisingly, bore no fruit whatsoever. They figured this much: if it was arson, they were looking at a few hundred suspects at least, six months' worth of paperwork and the nuzzling into people's lives that would get them no thanks. An accident, on the other hand, or something of a self-inflicted nature, was a single sheet and a signature. End of. Plus, the disappearance of the Cassidy stain and the selling of the land was proof that he himself had no stomach to contest it as a criminal act. As for the six men, they were neither named nor named themselves.

If people knew or suspected them then they never said, and it was never spoken of.

Once the sale was announced, though, the town ditched its zippered mouth and was uplifted. To the townsfolk, regardless of age or gender, whether they'd been involved in the Cassidy war or they hadn't, the destruction of the house and the sale of the land felt like a victory. It felt like a century-long, multi-generational dispute finally resolved and laid to rest, and a triumph of the Good Lord over spirits blacker than pitch. Business was good again, so too church attendance. People gathered in Harry's and raised glasses to righteousness and hope and to the riddance of the young Cassidy brute who made their lips curl. They had larger steaks and extra fries. Old Mr Parker, never one to miss an opportunity, had a bonanza day. Special offers and reductions and a run on objects of a vaguely commemorative nature; mapped tea-towels, candles by the bulk load, playing cards and a fire sale of tinned peach and apricot segments, amongst others. People flocked, people bought, people loaded up their trunks and drove away.

The talk in Sylvie Buckle's was like the short twists of the curling tongues, full of sizzle and hiss. John had gone. John had finally packed up and left because Goodness had knocked on his door and he was not able to look it straight in the eye. He'd flinched. He'd averted his eyes. They heard that before he left for good, he seared the earth around the house, scorching the soil with signs. They heard he skinned and sawed animals he kept in the cellar, that he roasted them on a makeshift spit and with some he didn't even wait for them to cook so you could smell the burning flesh for miles. It was true they found satanic items, that the walls were black before they were blackened and were strung by catgut with all things craven and deprived, with pelts and skins and juju dolls. And it was true, too, that if you followed the signs on the walls and joined them up it was like tracing a road map to the devil himself.

If there were any doubters, anyone less uplifted than the rest, they were Dr Abraham Stone, for one, for whom happiness of any kind was a financial kick in the balls because there was less of a need for his coated pills, and, surprisingly, for another, Ruth Anderson. You see, even though she considered John Cassidy to be without light and beyond salvation, and as a Christian woman she recognised the sizeable role that fire and destruction played in the scriptures, she was less convinced of the Lord's contribution to this particular case. She understood why He might get involved but questioned, kneeling at her bedside, His specifics. She asked for guidance.

And it was different for Delilah Morris on that morning in late July as she sat in her apartment with the painted-on door. Not only because, as she dressed and listened to another half-baked apology from Rita on the answerphone, she'd been vandalised, abused and rejected, but because she had a connection with John through the aches and pangs she felt since he'd gone. She missed him, was the truth. She missed driving out to the homestead, being with him, having him there in her life. She missed the encyclopaedias, the tinned peaches, Jack's beers. She missed the seed packs on the veranda, the kitchen table, and the shoe- and shirt boxes. And she was thinking of him on that morning when she walked out of the apartment, stood in the quiet and shade of the hallway and opened up the mailbox with a key. There was an envelope. Inside it was a piece of paper with two words written on in John's child-like scrawl: *Follow Madeline*, and two thousand dollars in bills. That was the connection. That whenever she thought about him, he would somehow be there.

It was different, too, for Doug Sketchings, sitting at the battleground of the kitchen table, with Viola asleep and Lloyd and Floyd shackled to their high-chairs like baby escapologists because, for one thing, he was not a born and bred Missionite and so the whole Cassidy rancour had not invaded his bloodstream, and for another, just like Delilah, he had allegiance. And it was that allegiance to John that he considered on that bright morning as he sat and thought about the phone-call he'd had from Vincent the day before, telling him the unveiling of the plans was a week away and there was work if he wanted it, measuring out the land.

He sighed, as the toaster pinged and Lloyd poised with a spoonful of wetted oats. You see, Doug had found something through that allegiance. In the midst of all the bedlam around him, he'd found his importance and worth. The problem was, or were, as he opened the letters from the mailbox that morning, amongst others, Dr Stone's medical bills, the utilities, the dwindling savings, the upkeep of the Korean car, the cable package, ants, in-laws, numerous breakages, the boys' rampages and Viola's continual slide, none of which lessened his worth, but all of which added to his headaches and to the sense of his tether being stretched to snapping point.

But on that day, rising up to the late 70s already, with the sound of Viola up and stirring, the shower on, so too the TV, he opened the last envelope on the pile that lay on the kitchen table, splashed with milk. The oats got flung in slo-mo, hitting Floyd flush on the forehead. Inside was a cheque for five thousand dollars.

And for Sophie Li it was different, both because of her sympathy for Jack *and* because she had been made to feel like a migrant. Different, despite the part-fixed roof, the cooked dinner and the offer of respite, despite Lester's handouts and a room to sleep in that wasn't full of junk. Different, even though she'd dished the dirt on John and left him to the lions' claws. Different, as she left the house that same morning and lit a cigarette, as she walked past the nose-down Chevy and stopped at the mailbox. Inside the mailbox was a cheque for three thousand dollars.

And for Margaret Sweeting, formerly Cassidy, formerly DeMille, who lay in the bath of the apartment out east she could only just pay the rent of and frazzled over what drink was in the place, and where. She was not familiar with the north-west of the country, nor the Cascade Mountains. She was not familiar with the town of Mission nestled in the crook at the edge of the prairie fields, nor with its brief but turbulent gold-mining history, nor, of course, with the plan of her only son to sell the Cassidy land and entrap Vincent Clay until he was a ruined and fractured man.

She got out of the lukewarm water, dried herself with a threadbare towel and walked around the apartment naked. She was forty-six years old and the last ten had not been kind. She looked in cupboards and drawers, in every compartment, blocked or otherwise, of the refrigerator, in and on top of the single wardrobe with the broken door. She got down on all fours to see if anything had rolled under the old sofa and stuck, and it was in that position, her ear on ground level, her hair matted by bathwater and sweat, her face blotched claret, with the sag of thin-dough skin and the vine of pubic hair, that she saw the letter by the apartment door.

Her first thought was of eviction, of a landlord's notice, a writ for late payment. Or it was a janitor's bill, a neighbour's gripe. It was a prosecution, a demand for money she didn't have. It was the sheet of test results, the grim news on bloods and liver functions, on scans of heart and lungs and brain. It was Dwayne up there in the hospital she visited twice a year when he barely recognised her and she barely recognised him. Or, as she crawled across the creaking boards, it was written confirmation of what she feared most; a dry day.

She picked it up, didn't recognise the scrawl on the envelope she ripped at with cracked nails. She held the letter up in the shake of her hands and twisted herself so she could sit with her back against the door, her knees and feet tucked in. TV noise came from the neighbouring apartment, a siren wailed in the street outside. Her lips were salty and dry, and moved along to the words she read:

You lied to me and you lied to him, it said. *You told me something that wasn't true and from that moment on I am the way that I am and all that time is lost. You fucked me up and you deserve nothing. If you'd raised me like you should've, if you'd given me a chance, given me anything, things might be different. But you didn't. So, I have no sense of mercy. I owe you nothing. You told me where he was because you wouldn't raise a finger to help me when I needed it. You told me not out of kindness but spite. And I had him for six weeks when he was skin and bone, when he had a rattle for breath. I had him to shave and to wash his feet, to see him scooped out to nothing. I had him to bury. I had him to mourn over. So, this is not forgiveness*, it said. *This is not a change of heart. I will be gone from your life and you will be gone from mine. This is a choice you never gave me. Do with it what you will.* And, folded next to the letter, was a cheque for five hundred dollars.

*

The people of Mission knew the revelation was coming. They knew Vincent Clay had bought up the land for something, but what that something was and when it would be unfurled, they had nothing. Rumours were rare, any guesswork based on estimations of Vincent's stock, on Madeline, and the fact that he'd told them it was a grand-scale thing of hope and opportunity.

Vincent had opened up the land. He'd invited anyone from the town to go and walk on the earth that no-one, apart from the posse of six, had ever walked on. He invited them to go up close, to stand on that cracked, black stone where the homestead had been, to take a look over to Coronation Point and to Rupture Hill and to try and sense the dark and dreadful presence of the Cassidys. When they'd gone, when the last of them had headed back down the track to the road or trailed across the land to the base of Coronation Point and up in small, none-the-wiser clusters, Vincent and Lester stood on a rise in the late afternoon light. Without the building, the veranda, and the steps that led to the porch-way with its armchair and its seed packs, the land looked different, like a rotten molar pulled out and left.

Vincent watched the last car drive away. He listened to the engine shake and the exhaust rattle, looked down at his hands. "This is the moment when, Lester," he said.

Lester's neck was itchy. He was hungry and dry-lipped.

"It works like this. We get the people into the hall. We set up a table on a raised platform and put four chairs behind it. And we explain. With Ted, with Lily, with Madeline. We tell them all about the financial backers, about our wise men in the east with their power and their vision and the money they want to invest, about how they see in the Mission venture only the floodgates of possibility about to open. And then we tell them about the gold."

Lester looked over towards Rupture Hill, across the rough terrain. His feet were sore and he wore an Oilers' cap to keep the sun off his threadbare scalp. He had three days' worth of stubble scratching at his chin.

"Where am I?" he said.

"What?"

"In the hall. You have chairs for the others. What about me?"

Vincent paused and turned towards him. "Lester, you are where you belong. You are where you are best. Amongst the people." He clasped a hand onto Lester's shoulder, onto the faded, chequered shirt with the collar starting to fray. "These folk are readable," he said. "Look at the faces, look at the way their bodies move and twitch. They know reactions, and that's it. Look at the anger they have, look at the resentment. They don't possess refinement of thought, Lester. They don't know nuance and guile and the playing of one thing against another. They have limitations, and one of them is the mental equivalent of not being able to turn around physically."

Lester squinted out. His lids and lashes were sore and a line of sweat ran from each temple. On those days when the temperature nestled snug up in the 80s and stayed there, when he was outside and bearing the full brunt of the heat, then Vincent's puzzles and abstractions made the bones of his head ache.

"How long are we here now?" Vincent said, looking back over his shoulder towards Coronation Point.

"Months."

"This is the eighth month, Lester. Winter, spring and summer. We live here. We work here. And now we wait only for the people to sit and listen. You know why they will? Because they're expecting something, they're in a state of anticipation. It's like Christmas Eve out there. They want something to happen. Trust me, Lester," he said, holding out the palm of his hand, "I have them right here."

They drank lukewarm water from a canteen and walked down the rise and on past the house that was shell and neglect only. They took the path that led them close up to the Anderson place, to the breaths of the white sails and the porch-way in shade. And then the slopes and the jags up to the pate of Coronation Point, where they stood, Lester bent and billowing, his face plum-skin, a monkish bowl of sweat where he'd taken his cap off, Vincent still, taking a breath in and looking out, over his dominion.

"What did he say? We are animals with brains. We are urges and drives and if we see something we want, we go out and get it. What did he say? The world is up for grabs. If you don't take it, you don't deserve it."

A hundred yards ahead and to the left, the figure of Ruth Anderson, minus bonnet, hung out the laundry on the line. She worked quicker than usual and when she was done, she took her empty basket, lodged it against her hip, and walked back towards the house. When she got to the porch-way she stopped, her hair loose and over her shoulder, with a noticeable lack of ribbon. Something else was different that day as the sheets and the aprons began to sway. Despite her husband's pious protestations, the crucifix had gone.

*

Two days later, after he'd gone to the Mallender house and told Ted to prepare his charger, after he'd made his confederate asides to Harry and Steve and old Mr Parker, and made his call to Madeline, Vincent was ready. And, in the community hall that had its residual haunt of rice-steam and blankets, of starch, lemon-grass and ginger, with the majority of the town either gathered or represented, flanked by Ted and Madeline, with Lily to the side in a sea-blue dress and a new diamante brooch, he stood and unveiled the plan.

He told them life was about more than just survival, more than living day to day, week to week, hand to mouth, not knowing from one month to the next whether it would get any better or not. For him, that was not enough. There had to be more. He told them the plan he was about to present to them was a long-term plan, not just a like-for-like replacement for the mill. It was about expansion and enterprise and the chance of prosperity. It would provide work and financial stability. It would, by necessity, require that sense of civic responsibility that every citizen would be able to wear like a badge of honour. And then he paused. He waited for Madeline to lean forward and place her hand on his, for Ted to straighten up his back and put the bugle to his lips, and with the steeliest look in his eye, his jawbone set, and the firmest tone in his voice, he said, "We're digging for gold."

And, with barely a pause for breath, as Lester looked out for those twitches and signs of unease, he told them that the location, the rough terrain, the mill, and the Cassidy land, and the estimated volume, which was substantial, had come from reliable sources, that he'd seen the maps and the written evidence himself and of its existence he was one hundred per cent convinced. He told them that what had happened before, the ruination, the tearing apart and the filth, had done so because of the naivety and the short-sightedness of a single young man; Nathaniel Hansetter. The town had not been prepared. It had no time to prepare. It didn't know *how* to prepare. This is not the same thing, he told them. This is nowhere near the same thing. The excavation, the digging up of land, as surveyed as it is, as measured out as it will be, is not an act of pillage or piracy. There will be no invasion. There will be no hordes. You will not be at the mercy of cutthroats and heathens. You will not be swamped by the unwashed and the uncouth. You will not hear blasphemy and profanity or be preyed upon by the darker sides of man. This time, he said, there will be no strangers.

He talked about stages and time-scales, about what would happen when and where and how, about those solid and guaranteeable things that made people feel more secure. He talked about planning. He talked about structure. And, with his shoulders set back, he talked about hope and ambition and risk. His voice soared out over the hall, over the heads of the gathered and represented. He became evangelical, a believer who made others believe, who carried them with him and took them, with their years of only the tack and the sniff and the rattle of things, and he gave them a sense of the beyond, of the possible.

He asked for commitment and trust. He asked for optimism and faith. He talked about a good and fair wage for anyone wanting to work, a bonus scheme, an incentive. And he asked those who doubted, those who feared the upheaval and the change, who had concerns for his conviction, to ask themselves these simple questions: Why would we buy up the land? Why would the backers do the backing? Why would we dig up the land if there was no gold? Why would we come all the way out here on the strength of nothing? And then, as Ted stood and moved alongside him, so too Madeline, and as Lily sneezed and dabbed at herself with a silk kerchief, he nodded, once. That, ladies and gentlemen, is the plan. Have faith, he said. Trust me.

*

Over the next few weeks, as late summer moved into early fall, the sense of belief and assurance began to take hold. Optimism was greater, faith stronger, and if there were any creaks in trust, they were smoothed over by Vincent's confederates. So, Harry convinced his drinking clientele, Steve his steak-eaters and Ted, basking in his associative glow, spoke at every opportunity of the man's credibility and vision and his ability to make the town prosper again. He was backing him, he said, and there was a sizeable cheque to prove it.

All this was helped, of course, by the presence of Madeline. For the people of Mission, Madeline was balm wherever she went. She was pacific and good and able to eliminate all traces of doubt simply by standing next to Vincent and breathing. And if Vincent was next to Ted and Lily, or if the four of them were seated like royalty at a corner table in Steve's, then everything had to be hunky dory.

People did react, just as Vincent said they would. In the first few days alone the majority of the ex-mill workers, including most of the first posse and half of the second, along with some of the neighbourhood men, responded to those advertisements for work, as drivers of rock trucks and bulldozers, as operators of sluice boxes and water-pumps, or as labourers paid to maul and dig and pan as soon as the machinery arrived. They came into the community hall, one after the other, and Vincent, sometimes with Lester, sometimes not, with every contract signed and every shake of the hand, made them feel responsible again. He made them get their importance back. He made them think they were of value and impact and not the inevitable by-products of a backwater town with grievances and gripes, nor made out of clay, or dough, nor credulous beasts, nor fruit ripe for picking or plucking. No, they would turn up on time and give him no grief, and he would pay them to find him the fortune he'd make.

They reacted to the promise of work and a steady wage by buying boldly on the strength of it; farm equipment they'd wanted, truck parts, cattle and cattle feed in bulk, barn doors, fences and posts, the industrial sander on the list a long time. There were conceptions, proposals, and renewals of vows. Plans were made, futures decided, whole lives shifted. The man, so enraged he'd fired the shot into the doorframe of the Cassidy home, donated his shotgun to his one and only son, and bought himself a new one.

The Mallenders had their house decorated. They had the woodwork varnished, the floor tiles cleaned and polished. They had the lawns cut and tidied by a man from Serpentine older than Ted himself. Lily, for her part, back in the fold, and forgiven, had more jewellery, more dresses, and more shoes. She went into Sylvie's and had colour added to her hair. Not just a lightening, or a darkening, not something on the same spectrum, but streaked, in Lily's case, and in numerous cases to follow, a lustrous pink, the same shade as her venturesome nails.

And they started to dream, those people. Even though they were only workforce, paid to begin with for panning and digging and mauling, though they were not those grizzled and hardy men who'd carried their lives on their backs all those years ago, still they dreamed of being the one who was one minute burrowing and sifting through soil and silt and the next seeing it right there in front of them. They dreamed of it under their nails, in their hair and on their scalp, inside their shoes and shirts. They dreamed of washing themselves at night and watching it drift off their skin like glitter.

*

"We've come a long way, Lester," he said and held the steak on the end of his knife. "We've worked it until it's wrung out. And tomorrow it starts."

He bit the steak, chewed and swallowed it and sat back in the chair. He put the knife down, drummed his fingers on the table.

"What is it?" Lester said.

He paused, looked around the place. It was nine-thirty. Most of the people in Steve's had gone.

"This is almost all we have here. *We* are the financial backers. We are the men from the east. Carpe Diem Enterprises. We are the ones buying up the sections of land, paying for the machinery, the equipment, the surveyors, the wages of the men, et cetera. We are the takers of the risks, Lester. What did he say? Life is nothing without risk. You learn nothing. You gain nothing." He took a breath in. "And if the maps and the locations are right, if the documents are real and the volume is what the volume says, if it's the same northwesterly pattern, if there's the carbon and the quartz in all the right places and it's been right there on the Cassidy land all those years and just not reachable, then men from the east or no men from the east, Lester, we're in the fucking money."

He closed his eyes, pushed at the handle of the knife. "But I've asked myself the same question over and over again. You asked it when we first got here and I've asked it most days since. You said 'if it's for real'. And my question has always been this: if it's *not* for real, if it's a trick or a ruse of some kind, then what does he gain, this mystery man? I still have the land. I leave town. I move on. So, where does he gain?"

He picked up the knife again and dug it into the meat, watched the sap run out. "And I have no answer. I don't see it. I've looked at it from all sides and I still don't see anything. What did he say? You play what you see."

He bit into the flesh, licked the juices from his lips. "What did he say? I dare any man on earth to cross me."

*

And, on that historic day, when mid-scale, independent gold-prospecting came back to the town of Mission for the first time since the dregs of the nineteenth century, as the convoy of multi-purpose trucks made its way west from beyond the prairies to become components in a series of camps, as town-based caterers set up to keep those camps fed and watered and the workforce themselves, the diggers, the panners and the drivers, walked across the rickety bridge or over Coronation Point or on the long road round to the rough terrain, so Madeline Clay packed her bags and prepared to leave.

Having tipped the bell-boy handsomely, there was only the walk from the hotel to the station left, one last couple of hundred yards of pretence; the measured gait, the relaxed mouth, the eyes alert and the head aloft at the precise angle that suggested self-assurance but fell short of hauteur. It was a role she'd gotten used to, the loyal wife with a healthy independence, the good cause lady, the honorary Missionite who spoke kindly to passers-by as she walked, who smiled, and said, yes, she did have to leave, for a while at least. She had things to do, places to go, those people to see back east. But, she said, and waved over her shoulder, she'd be back.

It was late September, a skittish breeze that ruffled her hair or brushed at the hand that held the packed bag. The clouds were high and puff-balled. She had ten minutes to wait. She checked her clutch-bag, blinked at the blown dust and grit and adjusted the lambswool shawl around her shoulders. She held her peace, stepped onto the train when it came, lifting the bag behind her. She found a seat, settled herself, the twitch around the mouth kicking in, the muttered curse as a nail chipped, the first signs the pretence was beginning to slip.

And she would not be back. This was, and would be, the last time that Madeline Clay, previously Dolores, Nancy and plain Jane, the authority on race-tracks, five-card stud and palmistry, and once the provider of a home-cooked stew for Jack Cassidy, would see the town of Mission where she was, and had been, close to regal.

And one of the reasons was that the woman who moved quickly from the waiting room, across the platform and onto the train just as Madeline was chipping her nail on the clasp of the clutch-bag, was Delilah Morris.

*

The whole thing was just as Vincent had planned it; a mid-sized operation somewhere between a draggle of lone prospectors heading out with hand-drawn maps and the fully-equipped efficiency of a registered mining company with its own logo. He'd accounted for it. And, with enough research and advice, he'd graded it so that the first findings, along with Ted's investment and the 'money from the east', would bankroll any later investment in more heavy and intensive machinery.

He'd done the same with the layout of the land, marking it out in sections, paying Doug Sketchings good money to draw its lines and limits. Vincent was always thorough. He was not prone to acts of randomness or impetuosity. Every risk he made was a calculated one, and once those calculations were done, he was, just like his father before him, meticulous in their execution.

So, the camps were separated, according to function and need. The one that governed the panning and dealt with all things wash-planted and cradled was on a flat, shingly stretch close to where the river forked north-west. The basic diggers were set up near the bluffs and outcrops of the rough terrain, next to land quartered by Doug's ranks and divisions, and the flatbed trucks and the transport used primarily to move the freight that couldn't be carried or lifted by hand lay somewhere in between. The caterers made choices on the hoof. The larger numbers of men were panning along the river's edge, but the more physical and exhausting work was done by the fewer in amongst the rocks and bluffs. The first group could work for longer but when they stopped, they stopped in bulk. The second needed more breaks. They needed drinks bedded in ice, and by mid-afternoon, they needed the ice itself, scooped and sold in see-through bags.

If the panners were the pioneers and scouts, the diggers, made up mostly of ex-mill workers, were the bedrock. The work was harder, no doubt. It was the non-stop ridding of debris and rock, the pummelling and battering, hour after hour, of granite shelves, of chalk and mudstone and shale. Hands and feet would blister, repeatedly. Lungs would strain to gather in breath and sweat would sting the eyes. Lips would dry and crack open and every break, whether they ate or drank or sizzled ice onto some part of their bodies, they took it in turns to kneel on each other's backs and knead out, with elbows, knuckles and thumbs, the knotted wires of muscles and flesh.

For the panners, mostly men from the neighbourhood blocks, men whose lives until then had been largely without zeal or shine, the days from the onset were long. They set out at first light and didn't get back until dusk at least. They spent every waking moment swinging a pan or rocking a cradle from side to side or sifting through the gravel on the riverbed like pearl-fishers. They watched for nothing else. Their heads and their eyes trained to no other thing, their lives, even in sleep, even in the wrap of home-life, saturated.

But none of that mattered, not the hardship or the length of days or their inability to function at home when, in the late afternoon at the end of the first week, one of the panners, an unemployed, single man in his late twenties working the shallow gulley at the river's curve, looked down at his tray of black sand and there, in its midst, were those solid pieces of shimmer and glint.

News got round quickly. The men gathered in from the rough terrain. The caterers came. Everything changed from that moment on. Every single one of those men paid to look for the gold in one way or another felt different. The panners, the diggers, the drivers. All of them. They felt like the men they'd dreamt of being, felt it in the rise and fall of their chests and the firmer jawlines. They felt like men who counted for something.

*

The following week there was more. Every day, something. Every day a whoop and a yelp from somewhere along the river, and every time the same sense of success, the swell of pride, of optimism and hope. The men, whether they were panners or diggers or drivers, went from homespun hunches and guesswork to experts overnight, to aficionados on methods and techniques, on how best to hold the rocker-box, how to work the jig-plant and gin-wheel, on the lie and the run of the river, the qualities of silt, the proximity and likelihood of other sign-posting elements, on the silver, quartz and calcite from which the routes of those placer deposits might be traced. They sat in Harry's bar and discussed such things at length, and then they left, to get some sustenance and rest, because, almost overnight, there was purpose and reason in abundance to head out when it was still dark and stand knee-deep in river-flow for twelve hours to root down some more.

Vincent was at the helm, well and truly. Whenever and wherever news of the findings came in, he was there. His was the first handshake, the nodding of the head, keen for every detail of where and how much. His was the smile and the slap on the back. His were the figures kept, the notes made, and the directions drawn. People stopped him on the sidewalks. The women thanked him for giving their men their lives back. They thanked him for what he'd done, for dragging the town off its knees and making it boom time again. The panners thanked him, the diggers thanked him, the drivers and the caterers thanked him. The store-holders and store-workers thanked him. Harry and Steve and old Mr Parker thanked him, and, in those first few weeks, he became so synonymous with success and good fortune that he hardly had to pay for anything anymore. Not a beer in Harry's, nor a steak in Steve's. He bought no coffee or pastries. His flat tyre got fixed. He could park anywhere he liked. Even the Station Hotel reduced its rates for him and his adjoining rooms. If he wanted a haircut or a cut-throat shave, Ike would do it for nothing, and for nothing he'd tell him about the history and the people and the what was what, there and then. Two of the conceptions wanted Vincent for a boy and Madeline for a girl. The pumpkins were larger this year, the cattle were breeding, and the wedding plans were nascent but bold.

And if he'd had the need for a manicure, a pedicure, a facial or a wax, then he'd've heard in Sylvie's fresh-painted, flesh-flowered parlour with its gold bunting and its glittered mirrors all about Sophie Li's disappearance, about her resignation from the meat factory one day and her departure the next. He'd've kept up to date with Lily's latest fashion extravagancies, with the modes inspired, it was true, by the early fall collection of Madeline, his queen. He'd've heard of Rita's various beaux, of Ruth Anderson missing from church, and of Delilah Morris not seen for the last couple of weeks, gone looking, so they said, for he who made them shuffle and squirm still in ways they would not care to explain, who was, if you believed it, deported, destitute, or drowned, who was wanted state to state for felonies too many to mention, who was speaking voodoo of some kind, who was cultish up in the mountains somewhere, mumbling nonsensical and repetitive prayers to a bug-eyed guru five times a day until he was raptured.

He could've heard all the other talk in there, the same talk as on every street and sidewalk and in every store; the gold, the gold, and the gold. What it looked like, no, what it *actually* looked like, this close. What the panning men said it was like to see it for the first time in amongst the gravel and the silt. Like a vision, they said, like something they were in the presence of and not something they mastered. They spoke of moments when God had moved into their lives, whether He'd stayed or not, when their lives had felt something *other*, something beyond who they were and what they did.

*

Vincent and Lester drove past where the homestead turn used to be, and on, up to the edge of the rough terrain. It was the first Sunday in November, mid-morning. Vincent got out first and walked over to the fence-posts that held the southern belly of his land. He looked up ahead, saw how the path had been worn into by the panners' use, how its route cut across to get to the river, and further on, the thinner, less-worn track, used by the diggers on their way up to the ravines and bluffs.

Lester stayed in the car. He leant forward, let the fleshy back of his hands take the weight and the tack of his forehead. He breathed heavily, moved only when Vincent summoned him, and then eased himself, a good twenty pounds heavier than when he first came, out onto the gravelled road. He shambled over, his shoulders slumped, as Vincent turned once again to face the land.

"Our mystery man is not letting us down, Lester," he said. "The locations are right. The patterns are right. The volume is what the volume says and what he gains is his twenty per cent. We doubted him wrongly. He's a man of his word."

Lester blinked out, took a half-finished cigar from his pocket, and lit it.

"There's an estimation of at least four or five seams that lead out from the river. We trace them, Lester. We follow them across to the Cassidy land. We match them up with those from the rough land and the rocks and any there might be coming down from Coronation Point, and we dig. And if we can't dig, we drill. And if we can't drill, we blast. Now, Doug figures the land is shallow land, mostly vegetation and dirt. He figures we don't have to go down more than fifty feet to get to the hard rock. We have enough made already to rent the dozers and trucks, but it's how many. So, I need you to go and ask Ted for measurements, and pass them on to Doug. Then we can figure how many and what size."

Lester tried to lick the dryness from his lips. "I've done some digging myself," he said.

"And get me a duration if you can."

"There are three possibilities." Lester felt a tingle in his hand, enough of a sudden numbness to make him drop the cigar to the ground. He could only watch it, didn't bend to pick it up nor move his foot to tread it out. He saw the soft breathing of its burn, the ululations of orange and ash.

"And the panners split, some further north as far as they can get along the river, the rest back towards the town, up to the mill and the woods behind it. And keep an eye on them, Lester. I know the scales are here, the checkpoint's here, the trucks are here, but some of those fuckers I don't trust. This is more than just gold here, more than the nuggets and the flakes and the shine of the stuff. This is where people lose their heads. This is where they step off the treadmill and don't come back. What were you saying?"

Lester moved his mouth to speak, but nothing came out.

"What possibilities?"

The light of the cigar began to dwindle.

*

A pale Lester Hoops walked into the basking glow of Ted Mallender's office two days later and picked up the measurements. He drove out and took them to Doug who, after Lester had gone, unrolled them and splayed them out over the clean surface of the kitchen table. The boys were at kindergarten, Viola at the shopping mall. They had money for the first time since he'd left the LMA. The bills were paid up, the savings healthier. The car was fixed, the ants gone, the breakages repaired, and Viola, free since the delivery of her children of Dr Stone's prescriptive medication, put a brush through her hair once in a while and bought shoes she didn't shuffle like a drunkard in. Everything in Doug's life was going swimmingly. Except for two things; those allegiances of his. On the one hand, Vincent had given him the kind of opportunity it looked like he might never see again. He paid him well. He trusted him. They played golf together. But then there was John. And when he sat with those measurements in front of him, he felt like every line he drew, every route he geometrically traced over the contours of the land, was cutting into him, A to crooked Z.

*

Once the measurements were done, Lester could figure the number and the size of the dozers and trucks. He could go along and order their arrival five weeks down the line while they waited for the diggers to finish up with the mauling of the boulders and stones and to take those few days extra to prepare for the Cassidy land. And while they soaked those bones and sealed those gashes, the panners, on Vincent's instruction, split. Most followed the river back towards the town, building pontoon bridges so they could work either side, but a smaller, single-figured group, hand-picked and bonussed by Vincent, including the Snipe brothers, carried on up-river to the northwest, edging into the wilder foothills where even to get to the river was perilous, and when they did there was little shale or silt to work with, only ice-cold water that hurtled and boomed its way past on the way down.

They set up makeshift camps, skinny tents exposed to animals and wind, and slept there instead of going home, their cradles and pans and boots at their heads. They took what whisky they could and drank what survived the clashes and falls of the trek. They took cartons of cigarettes and smoked them grim-faced in the dark, talking of silver they'd seen, of calcite under the water and quartz in the veins beneath their feet, of places they figured might be better, easier to drag their pans through. They listened out for carrion, and the shuffle of hooved feet.

Each day they emerged from the tents more raggedy. They ate and drank from dwindling supplies and they carried on, because Vincent was right. Their heads, if not lost, were turned at least. They had become insatiable and slavering, unable to go back, unable to think of, speak of, or look for anything but the promise of gold. It had bitten into them, whether they were paid their weekly wage or incentivised to find more, it didn't matter. It had burrowed its way under the skin and into the bloodstream of every last one of them, so that all they could do was work those inside bends where the river might slow enough, or score the fissures of obstacle rocks, their eyes searing the water's surface and every flicker of light underneath, as hopeful and as desperate as ever.

*

Now, if the selling of the Cassidy land and the burning down of the homestead were historic moments for the townsfolk, if they were victories overseen by the Good Lord in the guise of righteousness, then the plundering of its topsoil and the peeling back of its earth was just the same, and so most of them turned out on that second Monday of December to watch the dozers and trucks arrive. They drove out first thing. They brought food and blankets, some fold-up chairs, binoculars and cameras. They found places to watch; between the fence-posts, on vantage points of risen land, on Coronation Point, or on the arc of the road itself as the convoys shimmered across the eastern lands, looming and rattling until they shuddered past on a cold, metallic wind.

Old Mr Parker had sold five hundred improvised flags and they were raised as the vehicles were positioned and waved as the first ripping and plunging began. People cheered the grind and the churn, the mounding up of soil. They tried to get closer, to watch and listen to the savagery of the machines, to the butchering of the land by loaders and skidders with back-fill blades and boom-swings. To them, it was the brutal removal of cankerous skin. It was the exodus of black, unwelcome spirits in twists of smoke that seared of whatever it was that evil smelled like.

Vincent stood on the homestead site with Doug's estimations in his hand, Lester on one side, and Ted on the other. Lester, cold and unshaven, Ted, straight-backed, minus only his charger and his shiny bugle.

Apart from where they were, the best view across the Cassidy land was had, not by any of those gathered townsfolk with hampers and flasks, but by Ruth Anderson at her bedroom window. Ruth was aware of the dozers before most. She knew of the skid-steer and the knuckle boom because Vincent had told her they were coming when he sat, in the mild disarray of the kitchen the previous week, and tried to break bread with her.

The two milky ducklings were at school, the husband working farmland to the north of the town as he had done for the last quarter of a century. She was lost to him those last few weeks. He'd tried all kinds to get her back; homilies, parables, sermons. He'd tried putting the crucifix back in the porch-way but she'd taken it down within the hour. He couldn't speak to her. He dared not touch her anymore. She was as though suddenly and overwhelmingly complex, given to thoughts and ways that no longer moved in simple and unambiguous lines. Food was not always on the old oak table. Beds were often unmade, the sheets unpressed. The name of Dr Stone and his medication had been mentioned by him more than once.

"I cannot say with any accuracy, Mrs Anderson," Vincent had said, "how far the seams may go. Such a thing is not yet knowable. But what I do know is that if they come this far, this is not your land and I'll take it if I have to. I can speak to the letting agency. I can put them in the picture. I can listen to what you have to say but ultimately your choice in the matter may be dissolved because the Cassidy land is now my land. I am not haranguing you, Mrs Anderson. This is an offer, not a threat. If it comes to it, you can take whatever price I pay and buy elsewhere. I am not a callous man. I will pay for your removal and make compensation. And I know that you would put the future of the town before your own."

Ruth sat at the table and watched him get up to leave. She saw him stop in the doorway, turn and say, "I know that you are a woman of faith, and that there are times when the voice and the reassurance of that faith is not so clearly heard, but it is there nonetheless."

"This is not the Lord I know," she said.

She watched most of the people drift away as the dozers and trucks started to wind up for the day. She saw them climb into cars or walk in clusters past the house, go up the paths to Coronation Point or on through the woods. She could see them slow down to look over for the missing cross and the gentle blow of the white sheets, for her husband kicking off his boots in the porch-way and for the dainty, pale hands of the ducklings holding baskets of apple-sheen, palms and sprigs.

She looked out again at the tossed sea of riven earth. And then she went to the bedside, and knelt, next to the wooden cabinet with its napkin of lace, her elbows on the spring of the bed, her eyes closed, her hands clasped together. And she waited for that voice of reassurance, that guidance she'd known all her life and needed then more than ever. She listened out for its mumble of kindness, for the words that would take her by the hand. But she heard nothing.

And, in the days that followed, when she could barely go to the side of the house that faced the ravaged land, she listened for the voice in all the ordinary things, in the washing of clothes, in the simple preparation and offering up of food. She looked for it in those first flurries of snow that fell on the uprooted soil, that covered the crags of Rupture Hill like a crown of thorns and that lined the ridges towards the monks' head of Blessings Point. But it wasn't there either.

*

In spite of the relish he felt to see the dozers and trucks tearing at the land like beasts, Vincent's plans stayed resolutely time-lined. So long for the preparation, so long for the excavation, and so long for the tracks to be marked out and the routes to be transcribed from pencilled line to scored earth. And even when the land got flatter, when the sections were cut and took shape, when the diggers themselves had rested and prepared and were keening like hounds on a leash to be let loose, still Vincent was composed. He was holding his course, he told them. His was the hand on the tiller, cool and unshaking. Have faith, he said. And they did.

*

The days moved into weeks. Christmas and New Year came and went in a fizz of celebration. The mood was upbeat. Everyone felt good about themselves. Not just the panners and the diggers or straight-backed Ted and his primped and prodigal Lily, or Harry in his bar or Steve in his steak-house. Not just Doug Sketchings and the most wrapped gifts his house had ever seen, or the two ledger-men who treated their squeaky wives to an hour of unpronounceable cocktails. No, this was the town at its peak where everyone felt like they belonged, as if they were part of something bigger, something hopeful and grand, and if you asked them, they'd tell you, they were ready to go.

Everywhere was busy; the feed-store with its farmhands ticking off those long winter lists, stocking up and piling high their flatbeds. The hardware store full of panners and diggers buying up equipment and discounted tools they'd need for the days to come, buying belts and pouches to hold them all, buying ribbed-sole boots, knee-pads and thick, bolstered gloves. Old Mr Parker went more leftfield than ever. Instead of the obvious woollen hats, the thermal undergear, the wraparound scarves he could shift with ease, he went with something of his own devising; the small, plastic container he called the termite tub.

He'd heard, from reliable sources, that termites carried gold, that they burrowed so far down they absorbed it until it came out naturally. So, his two-fold idea was that if you followed the termites, you'd find the gold, and then, if you filled the tub, you'd have enough termite shit, eventually, to make a healthy dollar or two. Whatever, people believed him, and bought his containers just as they'd bought all his other homespun inventions over the years, and off they went looking for bugs.

Everyone, that was, apart from Ruth Anderson and her missing faith, Dr Abraham Stone, with one drawer full of redundant pills and the other empty of cheques, and, of course, Delilah Morris, who'd made her way quietly back into the town and kept herself to herself, who didn't feel like she belonged because she'd been away or because of Rita's snubs, or because of the painted X she'd scrubbed off with turpentine, but because, in the midst of all that colour and noise and the fizz of celebration, she knew things about Madeline that others didn't.

*

The day the diggers were set free to go with their tools and their termite tubs, climb onto the backs of trucks to head out, and tear at the Cassidy land was a cool, January one with a chance of light snowfall. The panners had gone already, an hour after sunrise, crunching their way through the frost in those ribbed-sole boots still smelling of leather, the first group over to the river-stretch close to the town, the second on with their tents past the rough terrain and up into the foothills where, in that very first week, they would split again.

That same morning Vincent and Lester had a cooked breakfast together at the hotel during which Lester tried, and failed, with one eye on his fatty intake, to tell Vincent of his three possibilities; all short cons, the ex-marine at the rail station, the art dealer, or any of the victims of the gambling scam that he and Vincent and Madeline had trailed across the north of the country some five or six years ago. They were all possible.

After Vincent had finished up, picked up the surveys and maps and driven out with Ted to check on the unleashed men, Lester went to his room, lay on the bed and, with the thrum of his lower arm, tried to go back to those towns and street-corner bars and remember the people; the ex-marine with the prosthetic arm and the scar, the loud-shirted lover of European art and, vaguely, somewhere, sitting in a corner bar, a middle-aged seller of encyclopaedias.

Most were easily fooled, he remembered. Many took only weeks or days. There was always a flaw in them, a weak spot somewhere. Often, they couldn't stomach being a nobody who mattered to no-one. Life had cut them adrift, and they knew it. It had not panned out, and they were stuck with themselves and whatever failings that beat into them like blows to the gut. They were often inadequate men, resentful men, shrouded in loneliness or despair, and yet, in spite of being bedevilled by those inadequacies and resentments, they all had this thing in common without which Vincent and Lester had nothing. They all believed, even with the shit that lay around them, with the proof of alimony payments and empty pockets and the reflection in every mirror they looked into that told them time was not looking after them, that they had one last shot left inside them. And who better to give it to them than Vincent Clay and his foolproof system.

He felt no mercy for those people. You have a choice of your own volition and what you do with it is your own call. If you fuck it up, you fuck it up. Period. Life is one good aim and shot. You deal with it or you don't and if you don't, you deserve whatever you get. There was no such thing as fairness, no place for bellyaches and gripes or wishing it had gone otherwise because there was only what was, what is and what will be. The rest was powder and smoke.

Dr Abraham Stone wasn't like that. He didn't fit the profile. He was neither resentful nor inadequate, nor was there a sorry tale to tell. Dr Stone's flaw was simple. He was arrogant. He believed himself to be better than most, which was why he sat at his walnut desk on that morning with a semi-incredulous frown on his face. In front of him were three letters. The first, arrived in the last hour, was a termination of the agreement between himself and the pharmaceutical company in the east. He had failed them, was what they said. He had not delivered. The numbers were not sustainable. The second was the anonymous invitation, sent two months ago, to invest in a number of medical research projects, the long-term efficacy of which he saw not in terms of their ethical value or their pioneering spirit but in the purely financial returns he was guaranteed. He had measured out his drawers. He had looked at the growing imbalance between cheques and pills and, with the only element of that profile that he did fit, the desperate last shot, he'd sent his money. His wife didn't know. He hadn't sat her down and told her just how legitimate and bona fide the projects were. He hadn't explained how much of an opportunity they represented. There was no mention of their philanthropic nature or that they'd be headed up by eminent, if unnamed, physicians. And there was no discussion about the money sent, about the loans he'd taken out from Smithson's or the life-savings he'd gone deeply into.

He'd heard nothing. There was no acknowledgement of any of the investments, no confirmation of receipt of the cheques or when or where or by whom they'd been cashed, and no reply to any of his enquiries. The third letter was a bank statement and an accompanying letter.

And, as he sat there, with the family photograph still propped on the desk, he started to feel like those other men felt, that acid riddle of foolishness somewhere in the gut, the sense, as a brief flurry of snow gusted past, of the kind of stupidity that leaked into the system and couldn't get out. He opened the drawer below the empty one and looked down at the snub-nosed pistol.

*

Lester tried to sit up, a sudden pain to his chest, a pincered grip that got his breath and rolled him onto his side, pushing his face into the pillow. His hands made fists, his knees shot up, the sweat gathered quickly on his sternum and brow. It ran in rivulets down his cheeks so that he tasted it on his lips. It matted in his chest hair in a mix of cigar smoke, whisky and bacon salt.

And the irony was this; that, in those moments when he felt like he was dissolving, like he was noiselessly falling apart from the inside out, he wished that it had gone otherwise, that he could just get to the door and shout something, that if he could've gathered himself and made his way through the soft-falling snow to get to his appointment with Dr Stone and explain the scale of his pain, things might've been different.

At some point, too, the callous doctor may've leant forward and offered up a reason for his surliness and furrows, for the discarding of every one of those sugar-coated cylinders into a dumpster and for why there was a snub-nosed pistol, barrel-down, on the desk. He may've shown Lester the bank statement, may've index-fingered the termination, the failure, the lack of delivery. He may've even pushed that anonymous letter across the desk for Lester to look at and make slow, incremental connections to the other anonymous and persuasive letters he and Vincent had read that would make him stand and walk like the reliable and devoted Lazarus he was, out to his master who, right then, was walking over the land, high with anticipation, with Ted and his silver, monogrammed hip-flask. But he didn't.

*

The two men walked and drove most of the day, going from one site to the next, from the diggers to the panners and back. Vincent monitored. He followed the routes across the upheaved land and stood on as many vantage points as he could to oversee and check. He carried binoculars, duplicated maps, zoomed, and zoomed again sections of land marked like meat. And when he wasn't being hawk-eyed and fastidious, when Ted, a panting mix of crimson and bronze, either held that silver teat to his lips or talked of Lily and his lawns and the age of his balustrades, he figured his plans.

He was not a paterfamilias. He was not a philanthropist, a benefactor or Samaritan. He was not an altruist or a substitute giver of balm. He had no concern for the well-being of the town or any of the people in it beyond that glorious moment when he would pick up his treasure and leave. He would have no fondness or nostalgia, would sell up the land as soon as he could. Ted would buy it back, either for himself or for the Agency. He would build stables and paddocks and parlours for Lily. He would have his portrait commissioned, done in oils, framed and hung in the hallway. He would be the king of Mission, wearing a golden crown.

*

The snowfall came in the early afternoon and stayed an hour. Some of the diggers used it to rest, to watch it slip out of the slit pillows of cloud from the backs of covered trucks or under the caterer's awnings, their faces keen still, pinched with cold. Some held up the termite tubs they'd later spill out and sift through on paper-lined tables. Some sent back for more. Some used the time to put ice-bags on swollen hands and feet, to mend cracked skin, and some stayed on the land, not stopping to eat or drink or repair, but using the give of the snow-padded crust to heel the shovel and break into the hardness of the earth.

By the end of the first day, though, those diggers, the panners who'd worked from first light both sides of the river, and those up-river men who'd gone into the perils of the foothills, had found only occasional and moderate amounts. They expected more, was the truth. They expected every day to be a Eureka day. They expected every trawled strip and stretch, every dragged and surfaced pan, to hold something at least.

By the second, third and fourth some of the panners had crossed the river, trying the bends on the northern sides and then ditching their superstitions at the pontoon bridges to go where the burial grounds banked down into the water. The Snipe boys pushed on and found gulleys and crooks a mile or so on where silt and black sand had gathered. Each morning they rose and packed and headed out, but every time when they twisted down to look at the swaying bowl of the pan, they saw only stone and shale. On the fourth day they gathered up their tents and moved higher still, picking their way along tracks of dead-ends and drops, setting up in the near-dark behind a ridge of cannonball boulders where every crack was one the wind could howl through like a banshee. The diggers, as each day passed, simply stared down at the bedrock, at the mean and riddled grains.

By the last day of the week, the panners had hacked at and loosened the riverbank into a mulch of rock and mud-slides, and the muddied diggers, the men of missing fingers, the men of dough and clay and expedient prayer went back into town beaten and confused. They had next to nothing.

For the Snipe boys, the words between them lessened with every hour that blew by. Thoughts gusted away. Any talk of going back, of taking what morsels and dust they had and giving up was snapped shut before it started. They were no longer turned, but lost. They were not neighbourhood men any more. They were not sons or brothers. They were but bags of flesh and bones with pans for hands.

Dr Stone, meantime, was pulled back from blasting himself into a debt-free netherworld by the visits of the mothers-to-be, and Lester Hoops lay saved, but seized and speechless in a Serpentine hospital while his master looked out from Coronation Point in that chilled Friday dusk with his biggest flaw of all right there in front of him; the belief that he was beyond flaws.

*

The cold hit him like a combination of slaps. Snow fallen overnight had drifted on the sidewalks and he stood on the steps of the stone building in the town he didn't know with the packed bag at his feet. He looked different. He was bearded, for one. His hair had grown to shoulder-length and, on that chill-bitten morning, he wore the white shirt and black suit of the magician's apprentice, with the old winter boots.

He closed his eyes and took a long breath in. When he looked up his nose twitched at the small bakery and the deli next to it across the street. He fastened the buttons of the jacket across his chest and, from the inside of the bag that he bent like a pelican to reach, he pulled out the pair of washed, white gloves and put them on. He scratched at the thicker growth of his chin, licked at bagel crumbs and coffee stains, and drew the collar of his shirt tighter around his neck.

He'd spent his winter months in a string of beach houses on the eastern coast, moving from one to the next every time the nets closed in around him, or whenever people he got to recognise got to recognise him. He cooked, ate his tinned fruit, walked over the sand, mostly at night in his peacoat, watching the skies for constellations he could chart. He read his father's encyclopaedias again, cover to cover, from the aardvark to the zebra, the atom to the zygote. And he tried, on a daily basis, to drain out the dyes of his past, to forget the Cassidy land, to do as his father had said and leave Vincent Clay and the townsfolk of Mission behind before it ate him alive. But he couldn't.

With every grain of information he got from either Doug or Delilah he wanted tenfold and more. He didn't want notification of the failures, didn't want them in bulletins or second-hand or rumoured out of shape. It wasn't enough for him to know. He wanted to be there. He wanted to watch it. He wanted to see the suffering and the unravelling for himself.

He picked up the valise and began to walk down the steps, his boots printing the snow. Behind him, through the thick, wooden doors of the building, along a corridor that'd echoed, in a room a storey down of near-brutal quiet and glare, was a small box of personal belongings that he sifted through, but didn't take. And next to that, in a larger box, with a pickled liver and cancerous lungs, was the body of his mother.

*

"Draw me some fucking lines here, Doug," Vincent said and slammed his fist down hard on the kitchen table. He loosened the collar of his shirt. "You are my leftie, my fairway to green man. You are my reader of the lies. And this is not happening."

He started to pace, sidestepping the loose toys and picture books as he did so. He stopped at the end of the table and leant against its edge.

"I'm telling you straight," he said, "I am not coming all the way out to this godforsaken place for this. Lester is not lying in his hospital bed for nothing. You understand me?"

Doug nodded and glanced over at the washing machine with its guarantee still plastered to its side and its protective cardboard corners next to it on the floor. He moved to the window, looked across the hoar-frosted land, at the new trampoline and the shiny model race-cars, feeling Vincent's stare aimed somewhere round and small between his shoulder blades.

"Most of the gold is under the Cassidy land. That's what the letter says. And I won't leave until every inch of it is covered. I will not be beaten by this. I have not cajoled and coerced those fuckwitted lumps of clay for nothing, not dragged them off their knuckles to give them purpose for the first time since they chopped their own fingers off for peanuts down at the mill. I have not purchased land, not spent all that time chewing the fat with Ted and his walking, talking clotheshorse to walk away with nothing. With what to my name? Sections of useless, dug-up land, a lifetime of free steaks, free beers and a free haircut whenever I like? I don't think so. So, take another look at the maps. Be imaginative. Go wider. Go random. Go anywhere."

He kicked out at a ball that squeaked, that bounced against the ultra-white door of the refrigerator.

"Get your boys to do it. Grab their hands and let them scrawl, I don't care. But draw me the lines, and make sure they go under the Anderson place. I will not be left wanting by a woman choosing to question her faith on my land. And we'll drill by the river no matter what. We'll drill its bends and its curves all the way back into town, both sides. And if we rile up the Indian spirits, then so be it. Let them fucking wail."

Doug half-turned towards the room. Everything was going so well. Viola was getting better, if not tidying up better. She was spending more time in daylight, more at the mall. She was driving again. The TV was on less, the shower more. The boys actually liked kindergarten and, with a few provisos around violence, kindergarten liked the boys. There was more money around, in bulk from John and in wages from Vincent, hence the washing machine, the refrigerator, trampoline and race-cars, and there was relative balance and calm of the kind they'd once known and since almost forgotten. And really, all he had to do was fabricate something, to close his eyes and slide his hand across the page and make whatever lines he made. But it wasn't as easy as that. Lester had asked him to measure up land already sold, and over which he had no say. But Vincent wanted him to put his name, his authorship, not only to the wholesale sunder of land but to the destruction of a family's house and home.

"I can't," he said, his throat catching.

"I'm sorry?"

"I can't."

"You can't or you won't?"

"I won't."

Vincent stood by the table, tilted his head to one side, half-smiled. "Is there a reason for this, Doug?" he said. "Something I need to know of?"

"It doesn't feel right."

"Did you say 'right'?" he said, and gripped the table's edge. "Is that what you said? It doesn't feel *right*? Let me tell you something about right, shall I? There is no such thing. Period. Right is somebody's hillbilly version of the world. It fits when it suits. That's it. It doesn't exist. There is only what needs to be done, and that's it. There are words and deeds and the rest is powder and smoke. We are animals with brains. We do what's best for ourselves."

He let go of the table and moved a couple of paces across the kitchen floor. "Are you telling me this is what's best for you, for

Viola, and the boys? Are you telling me what's best is to cut off the hand that feeds you? Is that what you're saying?"

He looked hard at Doug's profiled face, which peached and reddened. "You play a foolish game, Douglas. And you play it like a novice, because I'm going to drill anyway, whether you draw the lines or you don't."

Doug looked down to the cardboard corners.

"You know, you disappoint me. You really do. I offer you the possibility of paid work. I give you money to breathe, to gather yourselves with. I give you something to go on vacation with and something for the boys at Christmas. And all you have to do is to use your charts and pins, to make your calculations and to pass on any crumbs of dirt on the Cassidy man, the pariah. I thought we understood each other. I thought, once upon a time, there was trust between us. I thought you were stronger than this."

He turned and walked towards the door. "And let me tell you one more thing," he said, "if there is any duplicitous reason for this, if you oppose me in any way or prevent me from getting what I need, if I find out you're taking the side of the devilish man with the crooked snout who *violated* me, I will fuck you over and no mistake."

*

Vincent was true to his word. With or without the lines, he drilled anyway, turning the land into something unrecognisable in a matter of days, a vast spread of soil tossed or mounded or flattened by rollers and tracks. He was true to his word because on the morning of the third day's drilling the Anderson family left their home of fifteen years behind. They packed away their plain belongings onto trucks that bumped over the shapeless ground, the ducklings haloed in pale, winter sunlight, carrying objects like offertories, their father beside them stoic to the last, loading up the crucifix first, then the carpetbags and crates, accepting, in that bow of his head, the fate of events as if already carved in stone. And Ruth, in her final minutes, going over to kneel by the bedside, next to the cabinet, her eyes closed, her hands clasped together once more. To wait. To wait again for that voice. But she heard nothing. And by the afternoon the house was gone.

He drilled by the river, bore into its bends and curves until even its mulch was mulched, until there was no visible bank or shore and its downstream flow was so slowed and checked it splayed out into gulleys and troughs where land became thick, viscous river with nowhere to go. And still he found nothing.

*

John crouched in the woods near Coronation Point. It was late evening, the end of the first week with the Anderson house gone and only the spread of soil to see. He'd made his thousand miles west, from town to town, over flatlands and prairies and wheat-fields, and it was time to bear witness.

Why would he not? Why would he not want to be there when Vincent Clay was reduced to nothing, when he was only flesh and bone and rank humiliation? Why would he not want to get close to the unravelling and the falling apart, to watch those people who'd burned his homestead down, who'd slashed his father's tyres and spat at the sick man's feet, to watch those who felt gleeful and victorious and righteous to see his land so exorcised, those men and women who cheered, who waved old Mr Parker's flags and smeared themselves in justification and pride because they were part of that riddance? Why would he not want to see them, with each day of empty returns, start to sink, their hope of something better fading, that wish for something more starting to wither and die?

Why would he not, in the hours of night, go out and arrange the stones again, let loose the beetles and bugs. And why would he not walk across the fields in the black magician's suit, stand in front of those cattle and, with a few swings of the watches' chain, make them unable to move?

He watched the diggers and the panners first, men he recognised, men he'd pointed his shotgun at more than once. He watched from outcrops, from places he knew could conceal him, beyond the burial grounds, down by the river on the neighbourhood side. He saw the diggers follow the drilled earth day after day, mapless and lineless, with no more precision than a blind man's swing. He saw the panners cross the pontoon bridges back and forth, wading through the sluice and the mud, trailing those tributaries nuzzle-down, and their pans aloft.

He climbed into the foothills to watch the up-river men, to see them slither out of blustered tents like pupae in their gloop and slime, hardly able to get upright anymore, hardly able to speak but in grunts, their purpose all but gone, narrowed to a near-invisible pucker somewhere in the back of their gusted, blowsy heads.

He went further up, towards the ridges and the sheer falls, to find only one of the Snipe boys, to see him bent into the gush and boom of the water, shirtless, crusted with dirt, his pan washed away. The other he looked for higher up, scouring for signs of him on the tightrope tracks and along the wind of colder creeks, his wet snout twitching. He found him barely conscious as dusk fell, at the bottom of a ravine cut like crooked teeth into the rock. Both legs were shattered, the cheekbone collapsed, the jawline gone. Most of him was caked in blood two days old.

By the time John got down to him dusk had crumbled into dark. He wrapped him in his peacoat, picked him up like porcelain, lifted him across his shoulders and carried him out like a bloodied deer for two hours over land not possible to see by until he came to the up-river camp. He hid and waited, cradled the boy in his arms until the slingshot posse and the shotgun man puttered out their broken talk and crawled back into the sag of the tents. And then he laid him out, on tarpaulin and horse-blankets, covering him with any material he could find and setting his head down on the give of a saddle-bag.

He took his coat and left him there. The others could decide his fate.

*

“My father never spoke of failure,” Vincent said, as he stood in the community hall, in front of at least a hundred townsfolk, many of them diggers and panners, “in even the most difficult of times.”

It was an early evening in February, cold and blustery, and he was trying, minus his devoted Lester, without the balm of Madeline, and with only Ted and his antacids beside him, to persuade those people that more needed to be done, that, yes, the returns had been disappointing, and yes, it smacked of last-ditch desperation, but that blasting the bedrock with explosives and using cyanide to get to the hidden gold beneath were not only options, but necessities. Have faith, he said. Have belief. Most of the gold is there.

It was not as thankless a task as he might’ve imagined. For one, even without Madeline by his side, he was still the man who’d dragged the town off its knees and given it hope. He was the man who, only a few weeks ago, was being slapped on the back as a hero. There was even talk of a statue. And for another, a good proportion of those people were as far down the line as he was and so were just as driven to not calling it quits because a few obstacles had got in the way.

That didn’t mean it was easy. For some of the townsfolk, diggers and panners included, the root forms of logic and reason were screaming at them to stop, or to hold fire and reassess at least. For all kinds of reasons; the unlikelihood of success, for one, the potential destruction of the town, for another, but also because that fear of looking gullible, like the malleable hicks some of their forefathers were, had started to rise. And the other thing was this, that even in the hall, let alone the town, the naysayers and the doubters were starting to match the yea-sayers, and for the first time they were starting to ask their questions aloud: Where were the assurances? Who were those reliable sources? What about the wise men in the east? What was the chance of leakage and pollution? What about the cattle and the stones, what about the juju? Who was it, they said, had been so far up into the foothills to save the Snipe boy if it wasn't any of the panners? And where was Madeline these days?

The toughest question, and the simplest, came last. It came from Ruth Anderson, who stood, without raising her hand to ask to speak and, in the midst of one of Vincent's rallying sentences, said, "What if there's nothing there?"

The hall fell silent. Ted swallowed. The townsfolk shuffled on their wooden seats. Vincent stopped speaking, and wiped a line of perspiration away. He was not in the mood for holding fire. He was not feeling a reassessment.

"Whose money is this?" he said. "Whose risk are we talking about, here? Whose head is on the line? Who is it that, if it fails, has nothing but land he could now only give away? So, why am I doing this? What is it that brings me all this way?" He looked out over the room. "I am a man of business, that's why," he said. "I take chances. That's who I am, and it's what my father was before me. 'Life is nothing without risk,' he used to say. 'You learn nothing, you gain nothing, you go on with nothing.' Now, I have compensated you fairly, Mrs Anderson. I have treated you and your family well enough, but if you want to come here and talk to me about failure, I won't do it."

Ruth remained standing. One of the diggers next to her tried to pull at her sleeve to sit down, but she resisted.

"This is not the Lord I know," she said, "You have buried him from me, Mr Clay. You have lost me his voice."

"I have bought up some land, and I am digging for gold on it, Mrs Anderson. That's all. If you no longer look upon the world in the same way, then that is for you to question, not me. I have buried the Lord from no-one."

He walked out from behind the table and stood on the platform's edge, holding his arms out wide, to the panners and the diggers, to the yea-sayers and the naysayers who sat, apart from Ruth, and watched him.

"I'm asking you to be there. Because I still have faith and hope, and I still believe there'll be something there. If I didn't, why would I carry on? I'd be foolish," he said. "And the truth is, I imagine the chance of leakage is, like most things, down to human error. And I don't know about the cattle, or the stones, or the juju stuff, or who it was brought the Snipe boy down. I am a man of business, like I said. And Madeline is back east."

John watched them leave the hall, saw them hitch up collars or blow into conch-like hands and walk away in clusters, either over the bridge to Harry's, or to Steve's, or down towards the rail-tracks and the neighbourhood blocks. He saw the yea-sayers and the naysayers both, walking side by side, not yet torn apart, not yet snarling at each other's throats like dog-packs.

He watched Vincent and Ted linger on the steps, Vincent in jerky remonstrations, Ted listening, but holding his gut. For a while, as they stood there in the cold, in the mist that started to form, he watched Vincent alone, paring him down, cutting through the pale suit to get him right down to flesh and bone, to reduce him only to that heartless streak as plain as a shark bite the length of his flesh.

He saw Ruth Anderson, the last to leave, her hands deep in the pockets of a modest black coat, her hair looser and longer. The servility was gone, the humbleness leached to the point where people hardly recognised who she was anymore, hardly knew what to say to her, as if she bore that crisis of faith through the streets of the town like a cross on her back.

Ted drove away, almost hitting a stray dumpster as he did so. He headed towards the rail-tracks to take the road out, past land impossible to delineate anymore, past borderless earth that piled and skewed and leaked across to where the burial grounds used to be. He was edgy. He'd been there the whole way with Vincent. He'd made his sizeable contributions. He'd stood right next to him when the digging and the panning started, when the drilling had begun, when Lester was taken away to hospital. He'd sat beside him in the hall, nodded and applauded and made stiff, sure faces in all the right places. He'd shaken hands on the way out; with the meat-like diggers' mitts, the long-boned panners, with hands used to slingshots and shotguns and those a digit or two down. He was edgy not only because of the lack of returns or the fact that the outskirts of the town, the very land of which he was supposed to manage, looked more like a battlefield, but because his whole life was built on sinking sand, on the kind of conviction that gave him enough bluster to get by but beneath which there was nothing.

And when he was under threat, the Mission Mallender with a wife young enough to be his daughter was not a man of substance, and if you looked beyond that bluster there was only flatulence and creaks and pill-regimes. There was a weak and shrunken bladder and fingers bloodied on the flailing strips of Vincent's coat-tails.

Lily herself was no better. At best, a poor chooser, at worst, mercenary and unscrupulous, she was beginning to see the true wizened nature of her plucked fruit. She was no longer envied by those who wished to be in her place so she padded her way through the gastric and colic spaces of the house, with its views over the battered ranges of soil, with her ball-gowns gathering dust, and her oils, unguents and fillers lined up, ready for the fall she sensed was imminent.

He moved from one shadow to the next in his peacoat and boots, watching Vincent walk pestered through the mist. He watched him take the turn down to the hotel, pause a moment outside and take a long and lofted sniff at the air, at the pungency of the earth and the metal of the rail-tracks. And then he waited, twitching his own crooked snout until the light in the first-storey room went on and the light in Lester's empty, adjoining room did the same. He waited until Vincent Clay went to the window and put his puzzled face to the pane, as he knew he would. He watched him open it, stick his head out into the grizzled mist and peer, first one way, then the other, with that look of a man whose room, in his hour-long absence only, had been entered into with stealth and a hatpin, whose items, clothes and furnishings had been touched by white-gloved fingers, whose pillow had been pressed into, whose mirror had been gently printed on, and whose loved one, or photograph of, was no longer propped on the bedside table, but moved and flattened, face down on the bed.

*

The blasts, when they came, were like nothing seen, heard, or felt in the town of Mission before. There was nothing in any of the Masterson volumes. There were no log-falls louder, no canon-fire, gunfire or musket-fire more voluble. There were no landslides or rock falls, no quakes or fault-line shudders that went anywhere near them. The land was ruptured beyond rupture. Great schisms and rifts appeared like open, brutal wounds. Fissures and abysmal chasms cut into its paste. The coyotes ran, the birdlife scattered.

People went out there nevertheless. They drove to some point on the arc of the road, under the loom of Rupture Hill, and made their way as best they could to the rough terrain and the river alongside it. Most of the diggers and the panners were there, most of the yea-sayers, the more hopeful, those who still believed in Vincent Clay and his conviction, his reliable sources, his men from the east.

They watched still in anticipation, predicting nuggets like hailstones, expecting showers of swirling flakes, termite-storms and a whole rain down of shimmering dust that would light up the winter skies. They watched for those first few days, some bringing fishermen's waders to get through the mud, some earplugs from old Mr Parker, and some with pans to catch the fall-out in. Even the up-river panners, halved by then by those who'd carried the Snipe boy back into town, and stayed, stopped to listen to the booms.

With each day, though, things began to change. With each blast that shuddered the land beneath them at regular intervals, whether they were standing in the calf-deep squelch or sitting amongst the detritus of the camp, they understood less and less of what was happening. Even the diggers who'd hacked remorselessly into the rock and stone for weeks on end, even the ex-mill workers who'd dealt in the din of whirring machinery for most of their adult lives, couldn't quite fathom the magnitude or the scale.

For others, it was more: For some of those who went only for the first couple of days and then stopped, those who went with pans and left them there empty, those who walked back into town along what was left of the river and saw the last throes of the trout in the toxic waters, and for some of those hardened men, those with shotguns and slingshots who'd torched the homestead, slashed the tyres, left the doors to slam into the old man's face, what started to happen was doubt. Not only in the whereabouts of the gold or in the existence of its volume or the methods used to find it, not only in Vincent Clay, the out-of-town man of business and his grand-scale thing of opportunity and hope, but in themselves. It wasn't sudden, and it wasn't seismic. It wasn't a moment of epiphany for any single one of them. It was when they looked in the mirror first thing. It was when they stayed those few extra seconds longer than they would've, when they caught the eyes, the flesh, the turns of skin, they began to see something about themselves that was different.

By the time the blasting season was over and Vincent Clay had driven his frantic routes from site to site, it wasn't just the yea-sayers, diggers, and panners who noticed the difference. It wasn't even confined to those who'd played some part or another, somewhere down the line, in the destruction of the Cassidy land. It was most of the townsfolk. It was people waking in the middle of the night, men and women, not sure what it was that riddled them. It was people hesitant for no reason, losing concentration and purpose, feeling like they were suddenly sinking. For the men, it wasn't spoken of, or shared. But for the women, for those it began to affect the most, it was.

You see, the womenfolk of Mission had, for the most part, simply bore witness. They'd waved flags. They'd fed and watered and cheered the men on in ways more dutiful than belligerent and yet they felt the doubt just as much. They were culpable. And they were culpable because they'd allowed it to happen and not one of them had raised a word of protest to stop it.

They spoke and shared in small numbers, in groups and loose meetings. For most of them, it was less to do with whether the gold was there or not, less about looking gullible or foolish, but something more internal. They spoke about that scurry across the top of the abdomen or the weight that plumbed and sat further down. They talked about those mists and squalls that befell them out of nowhere even on the brightest of winter days. They talked of moments in the food aisles, moments in the kitchens, moments when who they were and what they were supposed to be doing seemed to vanish.

Some of them edged towards Ruth Anderson. They wanted to understand her, to know whether her crisis was as internal as their own. They wanted to know how and why her Godliness had gone. And if it had gone from Ruth, the woman with the heavenward face, the carrier of fruit and bread, with the ducklings always behind her and the crucifix in the porch, then what might become of them.

*

The news, on that first, crisp day of spring, with the bite of an easterly coming over the prairies, that there *was* nothing there, no seams, no nuggets, no flakes and no dust, was more resonant than any blast.

Vincent got the call first. Scattered and imploding and barely able to keep himself sane, he drove out to the Mallender estate to tell Ted. Ted, incapable of reconfiguring the lines on his face to anything other than shaken, told Lily. Lily sank. She looked across at the two men for as long as it might take Ted to put on one of his socks, and then she moved. She drove into town to tell Dr Stone who, missing his contracts out east and his savings gone west, could not even reach into his drawer and offer his patients those mounds of sugar-coated cylinders whether they worked or they didn't. And so he just told them the news as they came in, one after the other, with their ailments and their babes-to-be, with their doubts and mists and squalls he never listened to a word of, so that within the first few hours every tendril of the news had spread and the town was covered in vines.

Most were struck dumb. Households as if slapped into silence, not knowing what to do or how to reel back to figure how it'd all got started and what had led to what, how it'd come along out of nowhere and picked them all up like scraps and tossed them from side to side in its slavering jaw.

For the yea-sayers it was worse. For all those diggers and panners who'd gone out there for months, it was a collapse like no other. It was every flame of hope snuffed out, every plan, every investment, every dream, gone.

In Sylvie Buckle's the bunting had drooped anyway, the glitter fallen from the mirrors and the fresh flowers fresh no more. The lustrous pinks were the colour of pig-snouts at best and Sylvie's buzz had lost its sizzle. The talk was muted. Internal problems were more those of a darkening soul than anything ovarian or womb-based. There were no calories or cuticles any more, no streaks or extensions. Gone were the people. Gone were Frances Harte, Jake Massey and Dan Cruck. Gone were Rita's beaux and the migrants. And gone, even, was John Cassidy, the enigma, the boogerboo, no matter he was there all along.

Just after mid-day, some of Sylvie's sullen few under their driers and cones watched as Ruth walked up to stand outside and study the price-list in the window. They watched the way she checked her nails, her reflection in the mirror, and the small leather purse she took from her bag. They watched, as behind her, Delilah Morris, the woman they'd never understood or tried to, the woman they'd left behind or crossed the street to avoid, was crossing the very same street to get to Sylvie's. They watched as she smiled, briefly, towards Ruth, and walked in, not waiting to sit or go to the counter, or to make any acknowledgement of any of the people she knew in there, including Lily and her kindergarten friend, beaux-less Rita.

She stood instead in the middle of the floor with its thin carpet of curls, and said, "Madeline is not for real. She works for him. She's not his wife. And there are no men from the east."

*

John watched the unravelling from any shadow he could find. He hid himself in the porch-ways and stairwells of neighbourhood blocks, stood under the cloak of trees down by the rail-tracks. He broke into empty apartments with his hatpins, into the Station Hotel, the back room of Ike's, the storeroom at old Mr Parker's. He looked down from rooftops and second-storey windows at the town twisting out of shape beneath him. He saw the wracked faces and bodies bent double as if something was eating at them from the inside, sinking its teeth into abdomen and gut and not letting go. He saw and heard the mewl of bewilderment, the snap of men getting worse by the hour. He saw more than one smashed mirror, more than one rock-hammer get pounded into table-tops and surfaces where indigestible food shook on rattled plates. He saw pans and cradles and rock-boxes get walked out or carried, then ditched into the sludge of the river, and left.

The yea-sayers started to blame the doubters, the doubters the yea-sayers. The diggers flipped at the panners, and the panners bit back. There was a brawl in Harry's bar that spilled out like an unfurling spool that John watched from a cyst of trodden soil, his head tilted to one side, the shuffle of the hands in his pockets of pins.

With Madeline, it was worse. Because for Madeline they'd changed. When they'd gone out there to dig and to pan, when they dreamed of what they'd do with their brighter and better lives, they were still attached to who they were. But with Madeline it was different. She made them become different people, made them say and think and feel things that they would not have ordinarily done. And that was worse. That was cruel, to have been played in such a way, to have been stripped and hung out to dry like dumb, bewildered beasts.

For the women who left Sylvie's after Delilah had said her piece, it was the same and more. They'd been pulled inside out. They'd tried to get her look for themselves, to put on that same style and grace, and by late afternoon on that spring day those shallow pretensions had started to leak into them like poison. Some of them, half-powdered, half-painted and unable to go home, gathered in the community hall as pallid husks whose pain rose up with every heave and sob. And, with every guttural noise they made, came the realisation, as the town tore at itself around them, that they were not only culpable, but weak and lacking, that they'd fallen badly short, day after day, week after week, month after month.

John heard them. He was there. He watched the pain and confusion and suffering. The pins dotted his fingers with pricks that drew blood.

By dusk, with the brawling done but the blaming as raw as an open wound, the men began to turn their growling attention to one figure, Vincent Clay. And within the hour, against a violet and bruise-black sky and a wind that gusted over the foothills, three trucks of men drove out to the Mallender estate to find him; the slingshot men, some of the diggers and panners, the shotgun man and his boy, both armed, and Mr Snipe, with one son gone and the other broken, who sat with his ten-inch scar and his cut-throat razor and said not a word.

*

Lily didn't want to be a nursemaid. She could tolerate the lifestyle, the jewellery, the ball-gowns and shoes. She could manage the hotels and the fancy restaurants with Ted, just. But ask her to administer his foot-cream or deal with his nightly flatulence, ask her to tiptoe through his senescence with a smile and a lit candle, she couldn't do it. And so, when she got back from Sylvie's late that afternoon, she knew what lay ahead. Ignominy and shame, for one thing, the burden of association, the fact of being seen so often in the company of Vincent and Madeline that they would become equal pariahs in the eyes of the town. It was too much. Put together that level of blame and hostility with nursing Ted in his twilight years and her life was done with.

She packed her belongings quickly and without fuss. Ted didn't know. And Ted didn't know because he was retching in the bathroom. He was trying, with every spat-out noose of bile, to undo all the moves he'd made since Vincent first walked into the LMA to see if any of them were salvageable. By the time he was done, and the trucks choked up the driveway, Lily was gone.

*

The men faced Ted in their muddied boots. Some were cut from the brawls, some limped, and some smoked and drank from bottles and hip-flasks. The portrait of his great-grandfather looked down on them from the wall behind him. Even with the flattering strokes of the oils and the light that fell upon it, the slit-eyed meanness, the ungenerous mouth, the weak chin and arrogant whiskers couldn't be glossed over. Judd Snipe played with the pearl handle of the razor.

"Where is he?" he asked.

"Gone."

"Where?"

"I'm as duped as you are. One minute he was here, the next he wasn't. He left only the letters."

Eyebrows raised. Heads tilted to one side. The looks, to a man, said, go and get them.

Ted coughed. He walked over to a set of walnut drawers. The men watched him, not so the boy. The letters were folded, loosely.

"Read them out," Judd barked from across the room, the mauve scar from temple to scapula, twitching.

Ted held the letters with trembling hands. Night was falling over the quiet of the house, over where Lily used to sit, over the lawns and the ruined land beyond. The crown of Rupture Hill was grey on slate-black as he read, his voice quaking and stumbling.

The men leant forward to listen, their faces, in the glow of the lamp, like the worn leather of saddle-bags, beaten by wind and dust. As they did so, the words started to prick the skin, to catch them with combinations and jabs.

"Again," they'd say, at certain points. And Ted would read it back.

"The town is leaning towards a degree of instability," he read, "a fact that, I'm sure you'll recognise, makes it all the riper for opportunity."

Their heads buzzed with the punches.

"The methods for acquiring the land will require both resolution and guile."

"Again."

Harder, more insistent blows that sent them reeling.

"Potential for sale would, I needn't tell you, be greatly improved should the mill fall to its knees. Or not be there at all."

"And again."

He swallowed and paused. "The people of Mission are like most small-town herds," he read, "basic and gullible. They are bullish when feeling powerful, cowardly and deferential when not."

Cigarettes were lit and re-lit, bottles finished and dropped to the floor. Faces went tight and bloodshot.

"Given the right approach you will be able to use them as you please."

They flopped, slack and useless onto the ropes.

"You fucked it up," the boy said, his hands around the shotgun's throat.

"Vincent acted on the letters. He played us all, and he used Madeline to do so."

"What about his money?"

"Spent. He got played himself."

"So, he lost? He invested it all for nothing?"

"Yes, he did. He bought the land. He dug it and drilled it and blasted it. And there was nothing there."

The boy dug his heels into the leather of the sofa. "So who wrote the letters?"

"No-one knows," he mumbled, a gastric knot curling in his gut. "Whoever wrote the letters played every last one of us. From the start."

"My boy is lost," said Mr Snipe, the razor out of his pocket, at right-angles on his open palm, "I have to find someone to blame for that. What was your part, Mr Mallender? What were you to blame for?"

"I went along with Vincent Clay. I believed him. Just like you did."

"Did you invest anything?"

"Yes, I did."

The boy sat and watched, looking at the shiny world around him, at the furnishings and ornaments.

"Were you a stupid man?" the boy said. "Were you a dumb fuck?"

Ted swallowed.

"You let it happen. You fucked it up?"

He frowned at the boy.

"Didn't you?"

"Yes."

"Say it again."

"Yes, I did."

"What did you do?"

"I fucked it up."

Ted looked down at the floor, his rheumy eyes imagining Lily in the red organza dress, in Wyoming. The boy tilted the barrel of the gun upwards in his direction. And the men blinked out. They wanted, dimly, to call it a day. They wanted the save of the bell.

*

The town was quiet. The townsfolk, Vincent figured, had wrung out those last drops of woefulness and self-pity and hunkered down in their nests for the night. He left the rented car in a side-street by the neighbourhood blocks. Outside the hotel was too dangerous. He sat a few moments, took in the dumpsters, the trash and the few stray dogs, and then went, scuttling his way street to street, crab-like, until he got to the covered arcade across from the hotel. He waited, gathered himself. A car passed by, heading slowly down to the rail-tracks. Inside were four men.

When it was still again, he scurried over and stood in the doorway. He watched the night-clerk with the deadpan look, waited for him to get wrapped up in his puzzle again, and then crossed the pale-honey glow of the foyer to get to the stairs. He listened out, pausing at every turn, taking the corridors soft and shoeless. He stopped outside the room, took the handle in the slithery grip of his palm and opened it in notches. There was a faint smell of soil and night air coming from somewhere. The drapes were open, the windows shut. He checked around him; surfaces, wardrobes, drawers, bathroom shelves and cabinets, the same in Lester's room.

He moved quickly. He pulled to the drapes, picked up the empty valise and placed it open on the bed and with scant concern for the forethought that had run his life, he packed away his belongings and anything left behind in the adjoining room. He took what was left in the mini-bar, the toiletries, the photograph of Madeline, and within five minutes, he was ready. What he didn't notice in his haste to get out was this; that the valise had been moved away from the wardrobe and closer to the bed and that the lining of his pale-grey suit had been slit like a scar the length of a mannequin's hand.

He stood a moment in the middle of the room, his mouth dry, his feet still shoeless. And then he went, tip-toeing the corridors. If he heard anything, he darted back, held himself taut and still, his eyes invariably closed. Somehow, back and forth, he got to the last turn of the stair next to the foyer. He looked over towards the desk clerk, who glanced up and laid his puzzle to one side as the lights of the same passing car slowed up again and stopped by the doorway. Two of its doors opened, and then slammed shut.

He turned and ran back up the stairs, up and up, second, third and fourth storeys until he came to the fire-escape door. He pushed it open, looked down at the rusty zigzag of the metal. Below him were the line of dumpsters and the half-lit windows of the kitchens. He'd had little to eat or drink all day. He felt dizzied, like a spun top on its last reels. He could see over the prairies, over the felt of the charcoaled land where the rail-tracks bent east. He closed the door behind him, stood on the metal prow. A few sudden claps of wind rattled the frames and sent up the trash-scents from below; the thrown, spiky foods, the rancid dregs and spillages. He imagined he could hear the squeal of sizeable rats somewhere, the scratching and scraping of dogs. He went down slowly, the tan leather shoes in one hand, the valise aloft in the other.

When he got halfway, something moved in one of the dumpsters and, in spite of being a leanish man with a teenage past on the sports field, he started to lose his balance. The shoes went first, spinning out of his grip, over the rail and into the mulch of the neighbouring dumpster. The valise was not far behind and, by the time that something moved again, and louder, and quicker, he was bouncing like a pinball rail to rail until he landed at the foot of the steps, crawled between the dumpsters and scrunched to a near-ball, head down and every spike drawn in.

The valise, meantime, was upright. It had proved its considerable expense by being solid on landing. The downside, though, was that two four-legged animals, not quite close enough to dogs to be a hundred per cent sure, were sniffing at it like it was a carcass they could feed on. One of them pawed at it until it lolled onto its side, and the other, sensing it suddenly docile, started to bite into it, to tear at its hide so that its head raged from side to side until two things happened to make it stop: One, the fire-escape door opened and two men he recognised as diggers and yea-sayers, appeared in the dim, borrowed light, and two, the kitchen door boomed wide and a bucketful of slops was hurled in the direction of the dumpsters, some of which landed, but most of which showered over his foetal frame.

The kitchen door closed loudly. So too the fire-escape, the men gone. The two four-legged beasts left the mauled valise and ran. He waited a few minutes, and then stickily began to unfurl himself, this man of business, this man who, like his father before him, never spoke of failure. He went on hands and knees through the tack and slime, picked up his valise and, smelling of a goulash of wet vegetable skins, stood and walked away. From somewhere, out beyond the town, beyond the churn of the burial grounds, came the sound of a shotgun.

*

No-one asked her how she knew about Madeline. No-one asked her anything about how she'd watched her for weeks, or how she'd broken into her apartment one night and found enough to know that she was not who she or Vincent Clay said she was.

She folded up the mermaid dress and laid it flat on the belly of the case. She left some of her shoes, some of her objects and belongings. For Delilah Morris, there was no nostalgia, no ache of fondness for what she might be leaving behind. For Delilah, her memories were only ever those of an outsider, an orphan, a fish forever out of water. And, if that made her elusive and remote in others' eyes, if it made her prissy and cold, then so be it.

It wasn't to escape that she was going. It wasn't to get out of the town that'd shunned her most of her life. And it wasn't for love that she was taking the train out the next morning in her own winter coat and boots. It wasn't to follow the illusion of a better life somewhere else, nor to relinquish who she was to become someone else. She expected no jangled bells wherever they might go, no glow of light nor better air to breathe. She was not Lily Mallender, nor Rita, nor any of those women in the town who asked so little of life that they were granted only its scraps. No, it was to be with John Cassidy, the scoundrel, the peasant, the thief, who spoke to her very little, who, even on his return to the town, told her next to nothing as to why he was there, who would never once come home with a spray of flowers, but who, whenever he was with her, understood her like nobody else ever had. And for Delilah Morris that was enough.

She watched him at the small kitchen table, the crooked nose, the hands that twisted hatpins. She watched him as she pressed the clothes down into the case, the closing of the eyes, the tapping of the frontal lobe. She liked to lay her hands on his scalp as he slept, to hold onto the shape of his skull so that she could sense the thrum of his thoughts, the routes that no-one else in the world knew of. She liked to groove her thumbs into his shoulders, to prop his rib cage from behind to stop him falling. She liked it when he washed her feet, when he moulded the cream into the scars on her back, when he snipped her nails with scissors.

When she was done and the case was clasped shut, when the midnight bells struck across the town, he stood up from the table and put on his peacoat that shook with watch-chains and pins.

"I have to go out," he said. "I'll be a couple of hours." And with that he rested the tips of his fingers on her cheekbones, and she nodded.

*

"They're calling me a liar, Lester. That fucking clotheshorse walks in and tells me that. That leech, that pampered sponge stands there and tells me that's what those hicks are calling me. A liar, a cheat, and a trickster. Amongst others. Not a man of business anymore, not an investor, not the taker of risks or the man who gave them their hope in the first place. People have short memories, Lester. Yes, they do."

Vincent pulled another chunk of peel off himself and cast it onto the floor with the others. He sat next to the bed on a plastic sheet twice the size of the reclining chair it covered, and that squeaked out like a toy dog every time he moved.

"And show me anyone who hasn't fabricated something," he said. "Show me anyone who's never stolen anything, or told a lie of any kind. Show me anyone who's never cut a corner once in a while, who's never cooked the books, who doesn't always manage the figures, who'd rather give than take, who has a moral compass pointing north the whole time. Show me an accountant, a realtor, a finance man, show me any man of business anywhere who conducts his affairs one hundred per cent above board, for whom those things are not part of his modus fucking operandi, and I'll show you a failure and a liar. Hillbillies and hicks. That's what they are," he said, "and I'm running from these people, Lester. I'm standing in the hotel room, which has been sneaked into by the way, and I'm checking every car that goes past. I'm going through the hotel in my socks. And the desk clerk, can you believe this, the one with the deadpan look who, for fourteen whole months has his slack head inside of his puzzle book, chooses right then to lay it to one side and do his fucking job. I'm climbing down a fire-escape. I'm hiding between dumpsters while animals are ravaging my valise, and I'm getting covered in shit."

Lester twitched. He was part-upright, part-slumped, the drooped side of his face turned, the eye neither blinking nor closed. His forehead glistened with sweat, his hair was plastered down across his scalp in pale-gold strands and the cuticle neck of his pale-green gown had slipped down to his monitored sternum where a small, circular sticking-plaster rested like a third, erroneous nipple.

"I'm reduced to this, Lester. And there isn't a single silver lining anywhere. Nothing. There's no gold lying around. We are all but bust. The only money we can get to, and not yet, is the pittance from the ruined land. Ted won't help us out. And I have no fucking shoes."

Lester coughed. His lime-green heartbeat jumped a moment on the screen. His blood pressure rose in figures, and then fell again. One of the pillows behind him slipped so that his head dropped and leant out and a line of stringy saliva oozed from his slackened mouth. Vincent didn't notice.

"And I am something I have never been before. I am a beaten man, a fooled man. I am that thing that my father could never say. I am Rocky Marciano until right now, undefeated, afraid of no-one. What did he say? There will always be fall-out. If there's no fall-out you haven't done it right. And there will always be casualties. The world is full of them. They're everywhere, Lester. That's what makes it work. That's the whole reason why it works. Because the world is full of people dumb enough to fall for something. That's it. The world is full of people you can sell anything to, people you can step over easily, who don't string one thought to the next and don't know what you're doing to them even while you're doing it. People are clay, Lester. People are dough. There's no such thing as a fair fight. And then this," he said, his hair streaked with brine and sap, like he'd washed it in the juice of apricots, "Who is this? Who is it that's done this to me?" He paused. The sound of a buzzer somewhere. "You know, I asked myself the same thing over and over again. I tried to understand it. And I couldn't. I couldn't see it. I couldn't see where the gain was. I couldn't see what the point of the whole elaborate thing was if there was no gain anywhere. But now I know. The gain, Lester, is my failure, and my humiliation and pain. That's it. The gain is Vincent Clay as a beaten man, creeping through the streets of the town, despised, thought of as a trickster. The gain is Vincent Clay all but bust, covered in shit on a plastic sheet. That's what the gain is."

Lester flickered, his good arm flexed, the fingers moving in baby-shakes.

"So, I ask myself, who would want to do this to me? All the planning. All the extent of everything: The letters, the maps, the reassurances, the guidelines. To take us to that town, at that time, to make us do all those things that we did, to buy up the land, to get rid of the mill. All the fucking hearts and minds, Lester, week after week, month after month. All the not saying boo to those fuckwits. Who would do such a thing?"

Vincent closed his eyes. He slumped back, his arms out wide over the chair. A slice of peel stuck to the back of his neck like a leech, and his feet dangled out beyond the edge of the chair, damp and ripe.

He fell asleep, greatly troubled, in the heat and the quiet of the hospital side-room with Lester right beside him, his reliable man, part of a network of wires and tubes, staining his pillow with drool.

*

Everything was clear. As clouds as puffed as gunsmoke rolled over the prairies from the flatlands further east and, as the sunlight fell upon the town of Serpentine and the hospital to its north, set in grounds of poplar and pine and with driveways split by buzz-cut lawns, as it strained at the sand-coloured blinds of those rooms that ran the length of its second-floor, Vincent was in the bathroom, trying his damnedest to give himself a clean-up. And, as he twisted to get the juice from his scalp and bent to wash away the tack of the peel and lose that godforsaken stench by lavishing himself in a host of powders and sprays, so John Cassidy sat at the kitchen table, lacing up his winter boots.

And just as he drank his black, sweetened coffee and ate his apricot crescents by hand from the tin, as Delilah walked the half-empty spaces of her apartment for the last time and, despite the spring sunlight, draped the winter coat around her shoulders, so Vincent kicked his stinking clothes into a pile on the floor, dressed in his pale-grey suit and his shirt the colour of spruce and stood barefoot in the room, swathed in his incongruous scents. He looked down at Lester, studied the modest palsy of his face, and followed the routes of the wires and tubes to measured bags and machines. And, as he did so, as he sifted again through his clothes, he realised, with a spasm of his own heart, that he had neither shoes nor money, that, at some point, his billfold must've jumped ship.

He glanced at Lester, and then at the bedside table. He saw the right eye still unclosed and the mouth a pale-plum sag, and he looked at his billfold and shoes. Lester had small feet. The shoes were a good size too tight but he had no choice other than to squeeze his feet inside. He took out the notes from the billfold and picked up his valise. He took a last look at Lester, walked out of the hospital, left the rented car on the parking lot and headed down the driveway towards Serpentine station.

And, as he did so, John and Delilah closed the door on the apartment and went out into the sunlight and a town broken up; not only by all those hopes ground down to nothing, not just the pillaged land, or the transcendent deceit, or the skewered guts of every one of its people, including Ted Mallender, who stared at the blasted portrait of his headless ancestor and the hole in the wall behind him, but by the return of the beetle runs and the juju chains hung in doorways, by the assortments of stones, and by every beast in every herd of every field being so transfixed they couldn't move an inch.

As the two of them stood on the stone platform riddled with bugs and waited for the train to come up from the south, Vincent was twenty miles further on, in a waiting room the size of a prison cell, with Lester's shoes resting by his already bloodied feet. He closed his eyes. He was hungry and tired. Lester's money was enough to take him so far east and no further. He'd slept fitfully on the plastic sheet for no more than an hour and barely had any sense left in him. And what remained was shot through with one thing only: who the fuck would do such a thing?

The train was on time. Small crowds gathered in Mission, some to stand in loose, silent circles and look down at the stones and bugs, some to gaze at the static cattle, and some to go down to the woods by the rail-track and watch, slack and dumbstruck, as John Cassidy and Delilah Morris walked along the platform towards the very last carriage, and climbed in. None of them spoke. None of them could muster any words to explain how the young man with the crooked snout and the devil's ear had come into their town and spent his months out on the Cassidy land, how he'd lived the way he lived. They couldn't figure him. But then, none of them knew.

When it got to Serpentine, Vincent stood up. In spite of the businessman's suit and the shirt of a middle-aged golfer, he looked bedraggled and out of whack. His hair was half-wet, half-dry, his eyes bloodshot, and every time he put one foot in front of the other he squealed out like a piglet. He headed for the emptiest carriage he could find, laid the valise up on the rack and, as the train pulled out, sat facing east, staring out at the stretches of prairie land like a man who was running on empty, whose swagger had gone, and whose congruence and ease had been shredded into irreparable bits.

He peeled off the shoes and looked down at the blistered toes that smarted every time he moved. He took off the jacket and folded it down on the seat beside him, brushing away the last few remnants of dog-spit and only then noticing the slit in the navy lining, how clean and straight it was and how inside of it was a piece of paper, once-folded. He took it out and opened it, placed it down flat on the table in front of him. It was a letter; single-sided, type-written, double-spaced in plain sans serif font, addressed to no-one person in particular.

It was a letter that, on that bright, spring morning with the sunlight and the gunsmoke clouds, with the prairies and the blaze of rapeseed and corn, was found by a number of people; Dr Abraham Stone, for one, who came across it in the desk drawer of his office where the cheques used to pile up, Lee Shaw, for another, who saw it stuck onto a white supremacist poster right above his head. It was found in Steve's, pinned to one of the corner tables by a steak knife, on the counter in Harry's, weighed down by an opened bottle of whisky and a drunk-from glass. It was in Ike's and Sylvie's and old Mr Parker's, in the neighbourhood apartment of the gunshot man and his gunshot son, twisted like a corkscrew into the barrels of both. It was, somehow, found amongst the medications and creams of Ted Mallender's bathroom cabinet, and, strangest of all, it was in the bedside drawer next to where Lester Hoops lay half-propped in pulses and flickers. Nobody knew how they'd got there. But no matter where they were, how they got there and who found them, they all said the same thing:

To those it does concern,

My time in Mission is over, my deeds done. Everything is played out. The land is sold, the homestead and the mill, the river, the burial grounds either no more or not what they used to be. The taunting and the riling is finished, the ruses, the plans and reassurances, the false trails that led nowhere but down, and out, the manipulations and moves, the pulling of strings, the sleights of hand, the beetles, the cattle, the haystacks and stones, all gone.

You might ask yourselves why. You might sit in your abjection and wonder how and why and when it happened. You might then, having slowly and dimly figured it out and put it together, piece by shocking piece, baulk at the severity and the extent. You might consider the wholesale ransacking of your town, your land and your lives excessive and unreasonable. You might, Mr Clay, think the ruination of company, esteem, reputation and hairy-eared sidekick, to be disproportionate or heavy-handed. You might wonder, why so brutal, why so unforgiving and remorseless, why so lacking in mercy? But, let me ask you this. What did you expect? What did you think would happen?

You might ask, was it for revenge? No. It was more than that. You might ask, was it an eye for an eye, a tooth for a tooth? No. Too simple. An eye for an eye has little in the way of resonance. It doesn't stay in the system long enough. It's over too quickly. So, no. You had to be exposed. That was the whole point. You had to be revealed. You had to be shown back to yourselves as the people you are, to look at those reflections and not like what you see, to catch it in every surface; the greed, the deceits and delusions, the corruption, the hundred and more years of intolerance and presumption, and the maltreatment of a sick and dying man whose helplessness you spat back in his face.

Vincent let go of the letter. He knew, as if something had plumbed to the bottom of a lake, and boomed. And just as Vincent knew, so did everyone else. They pieced it together, wherever they were. Dr Stone knew as he looked down into his empty drawer. Lee Shaw knew even through his murk. Ted Mallender knew. All those in Steve's and Harry's knew, in Ike's and Sylvie's and old Mr Parker's. All the posses and the diggers and the panners knew. All those who'd let loose a door in the sick man's face, who'd watched his struggle with relish. All those who'd plunged a knife into his tyres. All the yea-sayers and the naysayers, all the women and the men in the town of Mission. They all knew. They all went back, to the moments of what they'd done, to the moments they'd weighed those actions up, or not. The only one who didn't was Lester Hoops, his letter read to him by a nurse in a pale-lilac uniform who frowned as she went to the end.

For every action there is an equal and opposite reaction. Every action has a consequence. Cause and effect. There will always be someone. Someone willing to wait and bide their time, to choose their own moment, to know just when that consequence peaks. But this is not justice for justice's sake, not a correction, a campaign or crusade. There are no angel's wings, no clarion call. I am not an apostle or a vigilant eye. I am not the righter of wrongs, not the merciful, nor the humble, nor the peace-maker. I put a spoke in my mother's life the day I came out. The first looks in my direction were those of disdain and regret. I was taught little in the way of guidance and nothing in the way of care. I don't always know what to do, what to say, how to be. I am an outsider. I am, so you say, a cut-throat and a savage. I am a housebreaker, a picklock, a cutpurse and a thief. I am, like my father before me, full of human frailties, and I am taking his redemption by proxy.

And you were played, lined up and aimed at, like fat-assed bowling pins staring dumbly down the lane. You were knocked and spun and dragged. And now none of you have any worth any more. You are crippled, no sticks to beat with, no carrots to lead by. You are no more than the cattle in the fields.

Yours

Epilogue

On a brighter than usual June morning three months later, Ruth Anderson walked out of her rented apartment in the southern neighbourhood in a cherry-red dress with matching nails and lipgloss and a pale-hide bag the size of a piglet. Her husband of fifteen years but not for much longer was out in the fields as he was every day, and her two milky ducklings, less roseate and rural as before, sat in a school classroom and tried to absorb the whys and wherefores of algebra.

She got to the sandstone building of the Land Management Agency just before mid-day. The inside had been refurbished since Ted had scrambled together his belongings and gone. The painting of old Edward astride of his stallion was no more. The Italianate cornicing had been replaced, along with the walnut angels and every other manifestation of pomp. The Mallender regime, rooted only in bloodlines and heirlooms, was done with, the dynasty dismantled, all evidence of its reign removed like stains.

Ruth paused at the glass partition, ran her fingers down the skin of the bag, and walked in. To her right, in their usual places, were the two white-shirted, but tie-less, ledger-men. Behind them, on the fresh-painted, magnolia walls the pins were still colour-coded but the maps of the land had been rearranged. The smaller, separate room, once the enclave of Ted, his neuroses, and his Lily in Oklahoma, was gone and, over by the window, in a room now as open plan as a cornfield, sat the new, fresh face of the LMA, Doug Sketchings, who looked up as Ruth stood in the centre of the room.

"I'd like to buy the land," she said.

The smell of rose-water settled like dew.

"Which land is that? Doug said, standing, a half-smile more than Ted would ever give.

"The land that Vincent Clay had. The rough terrain, the old Cassidy land, the land on which my home stood. It is for sale."

"Yes, it's for sale, but…"

"Then I'd like to buy it," she said.

Doug moved away from the window. He took a pause. "There are thousands of acres out there, Mrs Anderson."

"Yes."

"And the selling price is…"

"I know what the selling price is."

"The LMA bought up the land cheaply, but puts a high ransom on it, to avoid a similar mistake, you understand. Any company or concern or interested party will be vetted thoroughly, its intentions investigated and fully costed, its plans scrutinised to the very last detail."

"I have plans."

"We're looking at sizeable investments, above and beyond the actual purchase of the land. This is more than just buying your home back, Mrs Anderson. This is long term. This is infrastructure, consolidation. This is business."

Ruth fixed young Douglas straight. "A restoration of the burial grounds, with a plaque and a stone memorial," she said, "the detoxification and cleansing of the river and its banks. Full reparation of the damaged land. Considerable construction and reconstruction. Housing, public spaces, a library building, books to fill it, a new medical centre, a new physician to run it. There's more. I have the plans, and," she said, with a cherry-red smile, "I have the collateral."

She unzipped the leather bag, took out the cheque and held it up between thumb and forefinger like a prize.

"This," she said, "is the sizeable investment."

Doug watched as Ruth placed the cheque on the desk, put his snow-dome paperweight on top, and turned to go.

"Blessed are the meek," she said, "for they shall inherit the earth."

The day was cartoon-clear and bold, the few stray clouds nuzzling the crags of Rupture Hill like day-old lambs. She walked through the streets of the town, lighter in weight and look, the temperate air upon her face. She walked past an empty Sizzlin' Steve's with its half-price steaks and fries, past Ike's and Sylvie's, and past old Mr Parker's whose profit margins had taken a downward turn those past few months, checked only by the surge on bug-sprays and the book of incantations to defuzz the cattle. She walked past the chandlery and Smithson's loans, her head an inch or two more aloft, her faith in herself, if not her ability to devote, restored.

And, as she did so on that zingy summer's day, so Doug pushed the paperweight aside and picked up the cheque. He took it to the window to let the light fall on it, called over the ledger-men to look at the figures and the scrawl of the signature and watched as their realisation began to chime in with his own.

He felt the sunlight on his face, imagined a mid-iron to the heart of the green, the lush grass, the soft sand, and the eighteen delicious configurations of land. He imagined John Cassidy sitting down to write it, in his magician's suit, his old winter boots and a packed valise somewhere at his feet, his crooked nose sniffing out, adding his big zeros to the cheque, one after the other, like he was circling the words in his father's encyclopaedias.

"The Lord moves in mysterious ways," he said, aloud, walking to the wall and taking out the red border pins on the map of the Mission land.

Acknowledgements

My thanks to Sue, Olivia, Calum and Ellie Forrester-O'Neill for their unwavering and heartfelt support, and to anyone, anywhere, who has ever helped me along the way. Special mention to the MMU Writing School, peers and tutors alike, for being there while Mission grew.

About the author

Paul Forrester-O'Neill has been writing for forty years, while working in those early years as a bingo-caller, meals-on-wheels driver, care worker with the homeless and a quiz-setter in order to do so. He is currently employed in the more secure position of a Specialist Skills tutor at Keele and Staffordshire Universities. He has an MA in Creative Writing from Manchester Metropolitan University where he won the Michael Schmidt Prize for the novel of the year. Mission is his first published novel.